DATE DUE		
SEP 2 2 1983		
JUN 1 8 1984		
JUN 2 2		
APR 1 2 2008		
2 1 2012		

DISCARDED BY THE
URBANA FREE LIBRARY

EPSTEIN, Leslie

The Steinway quintet: plus four. Boston,
Little [c1976]
216p.
Contents: The Steinway quintet. - Lessons.
- Tell me my fortune. - The disciple of
bacon. - Memory.

I. tc.

S40630-10 CS

Also by Leslie Epstein

P. D. Kimerakov

The
Steinway
Quintet

Plus Four

The
Steinway
Quintet

Plus Four

by Leslie Epstein

Little, Brown and Company Boston – Toronto

Sic.

All of these stories have appeared in different form in _New American
Review #4, The Antioch Review, The Yale Review, The Atlantic Monthly,_
and _Antaeus._

FIRST EDITION
T 09/76

Library of Congress Cataloging in Publication Data

Epstein, Leslie.
  The Steinway quintet.

  CONTENTS: The Steinway quintet. — Lessons. — Tell me my
fortune. — The disciple of bacon. — Memory.
  I. Title.
PZ4.E6426St3 [PS3555.P655]   813'.5'4   76–15615
ISBN 0–316–24569–0

Designed by D. Christine Benders
_Published simultaneously in Canada
by Little, Brown & Company (Canada) Limited_

PRINTED IN THE UNITED STATES OF AMERICA

For Ilene

Contents

The Steinway Quintet   1

Lessons   67

Tell Me My Fortune   107

The Disciple of Bacon   137

Memory   161

The
Steinway
Quintet

Be not afeard; the isle is full of noises,
Sounds and sweet airs that give delight and hurt not.
—*The Tempest*

I

Good evening, my name is L. Goldkorn and my specialty is woodwind instruments, the oboe, the clarinet, the bassoon, and the flute. However, in 1963, on Amsterdam Avenue, my flute was stolen from me by a person I had not seen before, nor do I now own any other instrument of the woodwind classification. This is the reason I play at the Steinway Restaurant the piano and not clarinet, on which I am still proficient, or flute, with which my career began at the Orchester der Wiener Staatsoper. Examples of my work on the latter instrument may be found on recordings of the NBC Orchestra, A. Toscanini conducting, especially the last movement of the Mendelssohn-Bartholdy Fourth Symphony, in which exists, for the flute, a wonderful solo passage.

I wish to say that I am an American citizen since 1943. My wife is living, too. These days she spends most of her time in bed, or on the sofa, watching the television; it is rare that her health allows her to walk down the four flights of stairs that it takes to the street. In our lives we have not been blessed with children. Although the flute was in a case, and the case was securely under

3

my arm, a black man took it from me and at once ran away. It was a gift to me from the combined faculty of the Akademie für Musik und darstellende Kunst, when I was fourteen. Only a boy.

1963. That is what Americans call ancient history. Let us speak of more recent events.

It was at the Steinway Restaurant a quiet night, a Tuesday night, raining, only four tables, or five tables, occupied. The opinion of experts was that some time in the night the rain would turn into snow. Mosk, a waiter, came to the back of the room.

"I got a request," he told Salpeter, our first violinist.

"Yes?" Salpeter replied.

"From the lady. Purple dress. Pearls. A bowl of Schav."

This lady was a nice looking young person, a nice purple dress, her hair a mixture of red and brown. She smiled at the orchestra members.

"Yes?"

" 'Some Enchanted Evening.' "

Salpeter picked up his bow. Murmelstein, also a violinist, put his instrument under his chin. Also present were Tartakower, a flautist, and the old 'cellist, A. Baer. For an instant there was silence. I mean, not only from the Steinway Quintet, which had not yet started to play, but from the restaurant occupants, who ceased conversation, who stopped chewing food; silence also from Margolies, Mosk, Ellenbogen, still as statues, with napkins over their arms. You could not see in or out of the panes of the window, because the warmth had created a mist. Around each chandelier was a circle of electrical light. Outside, on Rivington Street, on Allen Street, wet tires of cars made a sound: *shhhh!* Salpeter dipped one shoulder forward and drew his bow over the strings. The sweet music of Hammerstein's partner filled the room.

It was during the performance of this selection that the door opened and two men, a tall Sephardic Jew, and a short Jew, also of Iberian background, came in. Their hats and the cloth of their shoulders were damp. They walked through the tables to the bar, which is located directly opposite the platform where the musicians are seated. It is possible for my colleagues and me to see ourselves in the mirror of this bar while we are playing. Without removing their hats, the two men ordered some beer to drink.

After a time a party of four, who had dined on roast duck and Roumanian broilings, stood up, then departed; as they did so snowflakes came in the door. The night in the crack looked very dark. Murmelstein, who had wonderful technique, received a specific request: "September Song." Of course from *Knickerbocker Holiday*. When this selection came to an end the lady in the purple dress put on her coat and, with a gentleman companion, went out to Rivington Street. Eleven o'clock. The members of the Steinway Quintet had then some tea. The figs and the cakes were removed from the window. At a side table Martinez, the cook, was eating a plate of potatoes. Tartakower smoked. The heat went off; the temperature dropped. It helped to warm clumsy fingers on the outside of a glass. At eleven-fifteen Salpeter nodded. We played selections from Mister Sigmund Romberg's *The Student Prince*.

At this moment the mouth of Ellenbogen's wife, who served liquors at the bar, dropped completely open and her hands rose into the air. The explanation for this was in the mirror behind her: both Sephardim were holding big guns. Out of the open mouth of Mrs. Ellenbogen came a loud scream. The music, except for the violoncello, ceased. The tall man stood up and put his hand over the barmaid's face. Ellenbogen himself allowed a tray of something, strudel perhaps, to tip slowly onto the floor. Tartakower leaned toward the old musician:

"Mister Baer, time to stop."

The short man climbed to the top of the bar. "We don't want no trouble and we don't want nobody hurt. But you gotta cooperate with us. Anybody who don't cooperate completely is gonna be hurt very bad." This man had still his hat low over his eyes. However, it was possible to see that he had a thin moustache on his lip and at the end of a long chin were a few added hairs, just wisps. A young man then. In profuse perspiration.

"The first thing is to cut out that music."

This was a reference to A. Baer, who had come to the end of the vigorous "Drinking Song," and was now beginning again.

"Psssst! Psssst! Mister Baer!" said Tartakower, pulling on the 'cellist's shoulder.

"Mister Baer!" Salpeter echoed. "I ask you to stop!"

"No! No! Reprise!" said A. Baer, and hunched further forward, peering at the music on the music stand.

The tall man — it was now possible to see that he had also a moustache; yet he was older, not so slight in his physique, with eyes that seemed almost sad, that is, they were close-set, drooping, filled with liquid: this man came quickly toward us, seized the bow from the aged musician and broke it over his knee.

"Er hat gebrochen de strunes fin mein fiedl!"

Murmelstein stood up. "That ain't right what you done. He don't hear."

"Er hat gebrochen mein boigenhaar!"

"I am the conductor here," Salpeter said. "What is it you want? Why have you done this? Why, please? Never has such a thing happened before! Do you know what Goethe said about music?"

"Raising the hands! Up! Up! Onto the wall!" The sad-eyed man held his pistol in front of the face of the first violinist. Salpeter turned, he joined Tartakower, who was already leaning against the famous murals, by Feiner, of classical Greece. And I? I stood up, I also turned about. From the corner of my eye I observed the first man, the young one, still standing on the bartop, motioning with his gun. He was making the others, the waiters and patrons, face the wall, too. "Oh! Oh!" a woman, the wife of Ellenbogen — "Oh! Oh!" she was saying. In front of my eyes was Socrates — Feiner was an artist who put real people into his paintings — with a group of young men beneath a tree. Murmelstein turned around. Behind our backs A. Baer was talking.

"Young man! You have broken my bowstring. *Mein boigenhaar!* Now how can I play? Do you know what it costs such a bowstring? The horsehairs? I paid for this thirteen dollars. I am

Rothschild? I have such a sum in the bank? *Ai! Ai! Er reist mein bord!*"

Without thinking Murmelstein, Salpeter, Tartakower and I, we all turned our heads. Terrible vision! The tall individual had taken our colleague by the hair of his beard. In only a moment he pulled the old man off his chair onto his knees. What happened next is almost too painful to speak of. The gunman released his hold upon A. Baer and leaped into the air and came down with both feet through the back of his violoncello.

"I am an American citizen since 1943!" some person cried. The voice was familiar. It was certainly that of Leib Goldkorn.

"This was no accident! No, no, it was a purposeful act!" Tartakower speaking.

Murmelstein, a young man, not even sixty, began to advance on the terrorist, who, still with sad eyes, was smiling with bright, white, shining teeth. "You done that to an old man. You got no idea how old this man happens to be. Ain't you ashamed? A venerable man? To pull his beard!"

Salpeter reached out his hand. "No, stay, Mister Murmelstein, what is the use? He does not appreciate music."

"There is a hole in it. A hole in it." A. Baer held his instrument in his lap as if it had been an injured child.

"What's so funny? What's the joke here? This is a tragedy. A tragedy!" The second violinist stepped in front of the man, who, under his hat, still smiled; then that villain raised his pistol so that it pointed straight at young Murmelstein's chest.

Suddenly from across the room his partner cried out in Ladino: "*¡Jesús! ¡El cocinero! ¡Está tratando de usar el teléfono!*"

The gunman whirled about to where his colleague was pointing. There, next to the door to the kitchen, Martinez was dropping nickels and dimes into the box of the pay telephone. The next thing we knew the hoodlum was flying in the air, Martinez was shouting, the weapon was raised and — in front of everyone's eyes — brought down upon the cook's head. More than once. Twice. And the victim fell to the floor. Is this not in many ways an act as terrible as the destruction of a violoncello? To attack a man's head, where great thoughts often are born? Everyone was still. No person dared to breathe. Then Tartakower spoke:

"Friends, these two are not Jews."

I felt a chill on my neck. Like a cold hand. Then Salpeter said what we dreaded to hear:

"Hispanics!"

From Murmelstein: "Puerto Ricans!"

The tall man's hat had fallen onto the floor. He put it back on his head, which was pomaded. Without difficulty, with a swipe of his hand, he tore the phone box off of the wall.

II

Greetings! L. Goldkorn once again. I have paused for some time. It was necessary to mix medicaments for my wife. Now she is sleeping, my life's companion, with no obstruction of nasal passages. Sweetly. Also, it is sometimes desirable to settle the nerves. I am too old to speak of such terrible things, the destruction of property, attacks to the head, without becoming myself upset. This is to explain the presence of Yugoslavian schnapps. Alcohol is good for you; it allows to breathe the hundreds of veins which surround the heart.

Now I will confess that this lengthy delay was not due to what I have already described; no, it is rather a hesitation over what remains to be said. Such abominations! There, out the window, over Columbus Avenue, the huge night sky is growing lighter. Like color returning to the cheeks of a patient. Yet at the Steinway Restaurant, where the temperature continued to fall, it was not yet even midnight. A storm of snow. I shall speak briefly of Tartakower, my successor in our orchestra. He is a cultured man, born in Bialystok, and like all Bialystokers he possesses a full, a

9

rich, an unwavering tone. But he has no breath. We do not permit him a single cadenza. The reason for this is cigarettes. It is a disgusting habit that has stained his fingers permanent yellow. Tartakower! Tartakower is not the point!

To understand what happened next you must know a detail of the Steinway Restaurant, which is that when you come through the door the men's water cabinet and the ladies' water cabinet are together down the stairs to the right. Many times Hispanic people, Colored people, Ukrainians even, would descend this stairway in order to move their bowels upon the toilets below. Such freedom is now and has always been the policy of this dining spot, since the day it was founded by M. P. Stutchkoff, the belletrist, in 1901. 1901, by a coincidence, is also the year of my birth. Of course Vienna then had many such Jews, young Zweig, young Schoenberg, and the head of the Hof-Operntheater was Mahler himself: thus no one looked twice when a fresh little flautist arrived in the city. Finished, Vienna. *Kaputt*. In America, too, on Rivington Street, have occurred similar changes. I have been told there was once throughout the neighborhood of this restaurant a lively Jewish culture: opera houses, concert stages, recital halls, an Academy of Musical Art. Now there is nothing but Pipe, a bedding merchant, and the fish store of Scheftelowitz. Even A. Baer, one year ago, moved away. Living here now are the Colored peoples I have already mentioned, poor as poor Jews, downtrodden, silent, without even plumbing.

Also downstairs, between the two water cabinets, is the room of the son of M. P. Stutchkoff, V. V. Stutchkoff, a room whose door is perpetually closed. From the time that I joined the Orchestra of the Steinway Restaurant in 1959 until the snow-filled night I have described, no more than ten greetings, or fifteen greetings, had been exchanged between myself and my employer. What I know of this man I have learned from others.

They say he was a pale child, a pious child, a non-eater, so thin that he would blow on Allen Street like a leaf, a feather, and not a person. When he was just seven years of age people would come from north of Fourteenth Street in order to sit with him, to

listen to him, to ask his advice. Stutchkoff's son! Only a boy! I
am the contemporary of O. Klemperer and Bruno Walter. We all
read the *Fackel* of Karl Kraus. I have attended a lecture by Otto
Rank. Impossible to believe in wonder-working rabbis, *zadikim*,
whiz-kids, and such. But the others believed whatever he told
them, and finally it was decided to send him to Europe to study.
The year, I think, was 1930. They sent him to Godiadz. A town
in Poland. Young Stutchkoff was then eighteen.

What occurred in the war years is not precisely clear. It is
certain that in spite of his American passport the young scholar
was put by the German invaders into a Jewish district, they say in
the Lubartowsky quarter of Lublin. After that everything is confused. According to Margolies, the waiter, a miracle happened.
One day storm troopers came to shoot him, only when they fired
they missed. He fell into a hole and other Jews fell on top. He
waited beneath those bodies until the night and then he got up
and walked away. Let us assume this account of events is a true
one. Is it a miracle? The gift of life to a scholarly child? In my
opinion it is a weakness of human nature to think such a thing.
Many died. A few escaped. That is all. If you want to know
more, ask Margolies. Ask Ellenbogen.

What is known for a fact is that after the war M. P. Stutchkoff
died and V. V. Stutchkoff returned, not quite so thin as he had
been before. Also, he took at this time a blond-headed wife. We
see the sensualist element here. Yes, he was eating, he put on
weight. Even in the sixteen years I have been at the Steinway
Restaurant he developed from a man of average size into a cor-
pulent figure. In the recent past I have seen him only rarely. He
remained in his room, and on occasion sent up a request for the
music of Meyerbeer, or potted meatballs. By his wish everything
here has remained the same, with the window divided in little
panes, the chandeliers each with one dozen bulbs, the bar-top
zinc, a chip on the leg of my Bechstein, and, in the mural of
Feiner, ladies in togas, the figure of Archimedes at rest in his
bath. The pay telephone, the register — these are new. Every
man has heard some story in which a wild and profligate youth

reformed himself and led in his manhood an exemplary life. It must be said of V. V. Stutchkoff, the pious boy, the man of flesh, that he had reversed the traditional tale.

I return to the events of Tuesday night. The door opened. Who then came in? The lady in purple! "I left my handbag" is what she said. Thus the many events that occurred — selections of Romberg, A. Baer's persecution, the blow to the head of Martinez — which seemed to take hours, had gone by in only five or six minutes, just long enough for this woman to walk away, to discover the loss of her handbag, to return.

"This it, lady?" The speaker was the young gangster. He had in his hand a leather purse, whose contents he then emptied onto the bar.

The woman did not reply. She looked quickly around, saw the patrons with their hands on the wall, saw the two Puerto Ricans holding guns, saw, on the floor, with red blood in his hair, Martinez: and she uttered a scream. *Eeeeee*, and then, *eeeeeee!*

Now others began also to shout. "Help! Help!" "They will kill us!" Such things as that. The young man with the wisps of hair on his chin jumped down from the bar; his older companion put his pistol into his belt. In my opinion they were on the point of taking flight. But at that instant we all heard, upon the stairs, a tremendous reverberation. It was a kind of snorting, snorting through the nose, and crashing against things, and the thud and bang of heavy feet from stair to stair. Everyone became motionless. There was the sound of whistling breath, a boom, a further snort, and then the rounded dome and then the fierce red face of V. V. Stutchkoff appeared on the stairs.

"WHAT THE FUCK IS GOING ON HERE?"

With one hand on a banister railing and another hand braced against the wall, Stutchkoff pulled himself higher. He was wearing a black bowtie and a white shirt. It was possible to see the pink skin through it. His mouth was open. Into it he sucked the air.

"I SAID WHAT THE FUCK IS GOING ON?"

The tall Puerto Rican, called Jesús by his colleague, fell to his knees with his arms held before him. In my confused condition of mind I believed he was beginning a Spanish prayer. But I soon saw the gun in his hands. It was pointed at the spot where Stutch-koff was pulling himself out of the stairwell. Higher and higher, the air rushing into and out of his mouth, he rose. It seemed as if there would be no end to him. With his white shirt he wore shiny black pants, in size large enough to cover the top of my Bechstein Grand.

The gun went off and a bullet emerged. One of the extreme left panes of the window suffered a hole. Stutchkoff brushed his right ear with the back of his plump hand. It was a bee, an annoyance, to him.

The second Hispanic crouched on the floor. He rested his gun arm on the seat of a chair, tilted his head, narrowed his eye. His weapon detonated with a terrific report. The ceiling above Stutch-koff's head splintered and pieces of plaster fell on his shoulders. But Stutchkoff himself continued climbing the last of the stairs. To the men on the floor he must have seemed like a figure in one of Feiner's murals, like some ancient deity rising out of the water, or the god of the sun appearing over the hills.

Both robbers shot once again. Unbelievable fulmination. Sal-peter with his hands over his ears. Screams. Screaming. Sulphuric smells. Yet the consequences were not of great moment. Addi-tional plaster dropped from the ceiling. A glass of tea on a table broke into two. Stutchkoff, however, who had emerged from the stairwell, and was moving rapidly in front of the window, had not been touched. When he reached the aisle between the tables he paused, he swung himself around; then he descended upon the assassins.

The shooting stopped. Both Puerto Ricans, the young man with the wisps of a beard, and his bright-toothed colleague, crawled backward, got to their feet and with wild eyes ran toward the rear kitchen door. Stutchkoff took two or three steps, and halted. His mouth fell. His hands went to his chest. He stood there a time, like a basso singing an aria, then his red face went white, and he hauled himself about in the other direction. He lurched toward the front of the room.

"HILDA! HILDA!" he shouted.

His wife ran from behind the cash register counter. She had a red mouth painted over thin lips, and wore a feather boa because of the cold.

"Vivian!" she cried. "Vivian!"

"HILDA!" said her husband and sought to take her in his arms. But he staggered, he missed her, he clutched only the air as he fell slowly and ponderously, the way a great tree falls, to the earth.

In that room, after that crash, there was silence. Slowly Salpeter lowered his hands. A. Baer looked up from his violoncello. One hatted figure, a second hatted figure, peered around the edge of the kitchen door. Then, into this stillness, this hush, came two extraordinary sounds. By this I do not mean they were in any way noises removed from the course of everyday life. On the contrary, what could be more common than this rip-rip-rip? This rattle-rattle? But after the bang and roar of the gunshots (in my lifetime the only pistols I have heard fired, even during the adventure of my journey from Vienna to Basel to Lisbon), no one was able to imagine the existence of such simple sounds. People were looking about. "What's that?" they whispered. "What could it be?" Then Margolies started to move.

"Hildegard," he said. "You shouldn't do it." He came up to where Mrs. Stutchkoff was standing alone, tearing the sleeve of her dress.

"Why not to do it? How come why not?"

"But this is only a fit. A spell. Something to do with the nerves. You see, there is no blood. I will revive him. Mister Stutchkoff! Mister Stutchkoff!"

At my side the flautist started to laugh, a thin, high, hysterical laugh. "Look, look," he gasped, pointing toward Margolies. "He still has his napkin over his arm!" It struck him as something amusing.

"Mister Tartakower, control your emotions." This was Salpeter.

"Not moving! I knew not moving! Not blinking his eyes! Is finish! Is the end!" Hildegard Stutchkoff resumed, in the orthodox manner, ripping her clothes.

But what was that noise like a rattle? At first I believed it came from the throat of our stricken employer. Then a movement above him drew my attention. The gold-colored doorknob was twisting around. The door itself shook back and forth inside of its frame. A person was attempting to enter; however, the body of Stutchkoff, with the belly upwards, was blocking the way. Now somebody actually pounded.

"Beverly! For Christ sake, Beverly! I'm double-parked!"

"Eeeeee! Eeeeee!"

In a windowpane of the Steinway Restaurant the face of a man appeared. The lady in purple saw him, screamed once again, and then the short Hispano-American, the one who had promised that no harm would befall us, snatched the napkincloth from the forearm of Mosk, and stuffed it into her mouth. The gentleman companion stared an instant, and then he vanished. Just disappeared.

"¡Ay, Dios! ¡Nos van a cojer! ¡Vámonos de aquí!"

"¡Un momento! ¡La registradora!"

The young man, in truth only a boy, the perspiration flying from him, leaped to the front counter. He opened the cash register and swept the money from the drawer into his own jacket pockets. No person attempted to stop him. Then he and his colleague ran through the restaurant into the kitchen.

"Are you well, Mister Baer? Mister Goldkorn, are you calm? They are gone. They will escape through the door in the rear."

"No they won't, Mister Salpeter. You forgot that door is locked."

"Mister Murmelstein, where is the key?"

The second violinist pointed to where Margolies was shaking the shoulder of the great black-and-white form. "In Stutchkoff's pocket."

"¡Oh, no! ¡Demonios! Locked! They got bars on it!"

"*¡Empuja! ¡Empujemos a la vez!*"

Mosk, meanwhile, climbed on a Steinway Restaurant chair. "We need a medical doctor! Doctor Fuchs! How about you?"

A bald man in a nice brown herringbone suit turned around, although he kept his hands on the wall. "Freudian analyst. Sorry." Mosk persisted. "You're a distinguished man. You could make an examination."

"Doctor Fuchs! I am asking, too!"

At the appeal of the grief-stricken woman the alienist dropped his arms and went towards the prostrate restaurateur.

Now the Ellenbogens, the man and wife, ran to each other. Mosk got down from his chair and began to mop up the pool of spilled tea. Salpeter and Tartakower sought to help A. Baer to his feet. He waved them away. "*Azah teire zach!*" The violoncello, a priceless item, was still rocked in his arms. "This was from Genoa, Italy. This was made by Italian hands."

Trotting fiercely, yes, like yellow-eyed wolves, the intruders burst out of the kitchen and went to the blockaded front door. The tall one started to take hold of Stutchkoff's feet, stopped, then said to his junior colleague:

"*¡Jala!*"

"*¿Yo? No. You* pull."

"*¡Ha! ¡Ha! ¡Cobarde! El muchachito es cobarde.*"

"*¿Yo? You* are the coward. *You!*"

"*¡Espera! Tengo una idea.*"

The last speaker turned toward the two elderly men. To Mosk, the Lithuanian. To Margolies, a Steinway Restaurant waiter fifty-five years. "Hey! You mothas! Legs! Legs! Pulling the legs!"

Just then Doctor Fuchs, who had been snapping his fingers by the ear of his patient, got up. "A moment, please," he said, and went to where Hildegard Stutchkoff was standing. He plucked a feather from her stole and turned back to V. V. Stutchkoff. With care he laid the fluff upon his lips. It was pink in color. A flamingo feather. It did not stir.

"Dead," the alienist declared.

From the waiters, an echo: "Dead."

"Blessed be the True Judge!"

From outside, from far off, came a sound of many sirens.

"¡Los policías!"

Each of the killers then jumped for the doorknob and pulled energetically at it; but the son of M. P. Stutchkoff still barred the way. The sirens, already louder, were approaching from several directions. The tall hoodlum, the one with the liquid-filled eyes, abandoned his effort to open the door, and began striking his own head, through his hat, with his hands. The other pulled with even more vigor, so that his whole body trembled. Then, on Rivington Street, the police forces arrived. Brake sounds and tire sounds, sirens so grudgingly fading. Now it was possible to see through the Steinway Restaurant window the fall of the snowflakes: red snow, blue snow, holiday snow, lit up by the flashing lights of the cars.

"Chino! Tell me! What to do?"

"Wait a minute! Give me a minute!"

"*Unschätzbar! Unschätzbar! Eine Antike!* What will I play on? I'm supposed to whistle? To hum? Next they will sew on a yellow star. *Zei hoben gebrochen meine boigenhaar! Zei hoben gerissen mein bord! Ich volt bedorfen zein a Rothschild? A J. P. Morgan?*"

At just this moment of tremendous tension — police outside, inside the guns — the widow Stutchkoff dropped to the floor and began to untie the laces on her late husband's shoes. As soon as she had completed this she crawled to his head and with her long fingers loosened the knot of his tie.

"What's going on, man? What's she doing?"

Doctor Fuchs answered: "She is undoing the knots that might hinder the release of her husband's soul. His *anima*. It's Jungian psychology."

"No, no," said Margolies in a hoarse whisper. "Not his soul. The Angel of Death! Otherwise it would be tempted to linger. You can look it up in Zev Wolf of Zbarazh."

"In that case," Ellenbogen added, "you must open the window as well. This is according to the Maggid of Mezritch himself!"

"Maggid, schmaggid!" Mosk, a skeptical man, declared.

The tall hooligan waved his gun as ex-Mrs. Stutchkoff got to her feet. "Crazy lady! Black magic! She got the eye! Jewish lady! Jewish! Viva Puerto Rico!"

But the cashieress ignored him. She began to walk — from her eyes tears were dropping — through the restaurant tables toward the back of the room.

"Stop, lady! Nobody moves! Stop! You gonna make me kill you!" Chino, the wispy-chinned lad, aimed his pistol at her back: the Steinway Quintet dropped to the floor.

There are those who maintain that this Hildegard Stutchkoff was not a Jew at all. I have already described how a red mouth was painted on top of her own. Yes, and her long fingers. In addition she curled her hair, her blond hair, until it looked like small sausages. Her eyes were plain Polish blue. It was necessary to look away from her bust, both parts of which were young, strong, and well-developed. I did not think she had a musical nature until one night, three years in the past, it was also a Tuesday, she sat beside me on the bench of the Bechstein and played the bass, while I played the melody, of "Stout-hearted Men." Perhaps I did not mention that the nails of her toes were painted, too? After the piety with which she mourned her husband, the rumors on the subject of her Polishness, her youthfulness, her fox-furs, have ceased at last.

The murderer did not, however, fire his gun. The fresh widow stopped and removed a tablecloth from a table. With this she began to cover the surface of the bar-area mirror.

"The Spola Grandfather!"

"No, Shmelke of Nikolsburg! The dead man must not see his own spirit depart!"

"Mister Ellenbogen, am I not correct in assuming that the purpose of this action is to prevent the Angel of Death from becoming entrapped in the glass?"

"That is a valid interpretation, Mister Margolies."

"Pfui!"

Doctor Fuchs spoke from the viewpoint of science: "I agree

with the negative opinion of our friend Mister Mosk. These are Jungian daydreams. A regression to primitive thinking. Even children —"

"Look, gentlemen! She has finished!" It was Salpeter, our first violinist, who was speaking. "Now dear V. V. Stutchkoff, patron of the arts, may depart!"

Every person's eyes swung back to the corpse. The pink feather remained attached to its lips. It did not stir. It did not tremble.

"THIS IS THE POLICE DEPARTMENT SPEAKING. YOU ARE SURROUNDED. COME OUT WITH YOUR HANDS IN THE AIR. YOU MUST SURRENDER."

That voice came from an amplified horn. One of the gangsters, an adolescent, a boy, shouted back:

"We ain't going nowhere! We got hostages! We're cold killers! You gonna find out, because we going to kill them one by one!" He threw a blue-colored pill into his mouth. His colleague smiled, and swallowed a red one.

"¡Mamá!" The cry came from the rear. "¡Mamá!" Martinez, the cook, raised his bloody head from the floor.

III

Hello? Hello? Leib Goldkorn here. What a poor memory! Have I mentioned my performance of the *Italienische Symphonie?* Or have I not? Only a short time ago I happened to hear this same recording on radio station WQXR. The difficult aspect of playing in the orchestra of A. Toscanini — of course there were also many joys — was tempi, tempi, always the tempi! An artist went as fast as he could and — "No, no, no, no: Allegro! Allegro *vivace!"* The key to the final movement, this thrilling passage, is breath control: whether I possessed it or whether I lacked it you will judge for yourself.

Now the radio is off; this is because of the television for the entertainment of my wife. She is watching from the sofa, with her medicaments on the table. A red cotton nightdress and a white lace cap: adorable, the little mouse! You will pardon me? I am sipping hot milk with hot coffee. No sugars. I am fond of sugars. However, Clara has diabetes. I think now we are having a spring morning. The tree on the street has birds in it and the buds of leaves. The clouds are not serious clouds. I have suffered since

February from a disturbance in sleeping. A result of the events in the Steinway Restaurant? A sign of advancing age? Brandy from plums is good for this condition. Yes, but the bottle is nearly empty. An inch at the bottom is all that remains.

I remember from the night not so much fear, but the cold instead. No heat, and outside a sudden wind: snowflakes went from the left hand to the right. The tall Puerto Rican took Salpeter's waterproof, his silk muffler, his fur-lined gloves. Salpeter is two years older than I: precisely seventy-six. Chino, the young man, took the coat of a middle-aged patron, an eggplant eater, who then rolled himself into a tablecloth and fell asleep. This others did too, lying so that they touched, it did not matter about men and women. But Mosk, Margolies, and Ellenbogen walked up the aisle and down the aisle, wearing black coats. Their breath came out in clouds. Tartakower suffered. He is a thin man, with a thin face, on which there are prominent bones. He wore an orange-and-black-colored muffler and a topcoat which had, in the place of buttons, clips, paper clips, and pins. Widower. He sat in his orchestra chair with his knees together and a lit cigarette in his mouth. The whole platform shook when he trembled.

I too sat at my place and my toes were burning. That is the sensation of extreme cold, a fire in parts of the body, in kneecaps and earlobes and nose, and the wish to sleep was the same as the wish to put it out. I then had a dream of Hildegard Stutchkoff. I must say that in this dream she was on the seat of a toilet, and I must say she was not wearing clothes. The feeling that accompanied this sight was one of familiarity, and friendliness. My life has been such that I have never seen in this way any woman, not even Clara, my wife. I looked down of course and felt great pity for her uncovered feet. I removed my greatcoat and laid it upon them. "You are getting warm," she said, and at once things returned to normal: I heard china piled upon china, and the clink of waiters carrying plates. I woke. It was still night. From the four corners of the Steinway Restaurant came the fierce sound of chattering teeth.

The chandeliers were no longer shining. But the light was on at the bar, and so were the illuminations for types of beer. Both villains sat there, facing the room, with their hats pulled to the level of their eyes. They were laughing together, and slapping each other's cheeks. I rose from my Bechstein. I left my colleagues, who now were sleeping. Tartakower's face was white as dishes. I walked alone to the counter of the bar. A row of red pills and blue pills were lined up on the zinc top. There was scotch whiskey in glasses, and both the grey guns.

"A French cognac, please." This was L. Goldkorn speaking, but the voice itself belonged to a young piping child.

The hooligans looked at each other. They blinked their eyes.

"Courvoisier. VSOP."

"What you want, you little man?"

"*Un brandy,* Chino. *Un cognac,* ha, ha!"

"Oh, sure, you wanna have a little drink!" The youth opened the *fine champagne* and filled to the brim a tall highball glass. "So, Mister Weinberg, Steinberg, Feinberg! You wanna drink to one hundred thousand dollars?"

"Ha! Ha! Ha! Weinstein, Feinstein, Steinstein! Ha! Ha! Ha!" The tall man, the man with the successful moustache, slapped the face of his younger colleague. "Names of Jews!"

"Ha! Ha! Listen, Mister Greenberg —"

"Mister Goldberg!"

"Ha, ha! Drink it down!"

Only once before in my life, thirty-two years in the past, have I tasted a liquor of this class. The Hispano-Americans continued to slap one another. They each swallowed a pill. They put more of the cognac into my glass.

"My name is L. Goldkorn, specialist in —"

"Ha! Ha! Ha! We gonna get a hundred thousand American dollars!"

"No. No. ¡Un cuarto de millión! Y después aceptamos cien mil. ¿Verdad?"

"Ha! Ha! Jesús is smart! We gonna demand a quarter million! Or more! Maybe a million! Then they gonna say, we don't got that kinda money and then we gonna say, okay, two hundred thousand, and then they gonna say we don't got that either, and then we say, okay, okay, one hundred and fifty, and when they say, no, no, that's too much too, we gonna say one hundred thousand in tens and twenties and fifties or we gonna shoot every dude in the room! Ha! Ha! Goldkorn! It's gonna be a negotiation!"

"*¡El avión! ¡El avión!* Goldkorns! In the air! In the sky! Like a bird! Tell him! *¡El avión!*"

"Yeah, we gonna have a plane, a big silver plane. No other passengers. Just me and Jesús. And maybe we gonna go to Cuba, and maybe we gonna go to Egypt, to China —"

"*¡La China!* Ha! Ha!"

"We gonna look down from the window and see the ocean, you know, Goldkorn, with ships on it, a blue ocean, and I heard that from a jet you can tell the world is round, like a ball, and the millions of people on it are just like a bunch of ants."

"*Pantalones de* silk! In China I am *un héroe! ¡Un revolucionario! ¡Sí!* Is true! *Pantalones de* silk!"

"What's that?" The adolescent hurled his body forward and picked up his pistol. The whiskey spilled from the glass. The weapon was aimed at the front of the room, where something black moved before the window glass.

"*¡Espíritus malos!*" shouted Jesús, and he also leaped for his gun.

"No! Please! This is Margolies!"

It was in truth the aged waiter. He walked slowly to where the corpse of V. V. Stutchkoff was lying and sat down beside it. He put his head on his ex-employer's chest.

"Goldkorn, man! What's the mothafucka doing? Is he talking to that fat-ass's ghost?"

"Ha-ha! Is only a jokes! The mirror! Untying the tie! Is stunts, no? No is *espíritus malos!* Listen, little Jewish man. *Un hombre es solamente un hombre. No tiene alma. No tiene nada. No es nada. El resto es superstición.* Chino, tell it to him!"

"He said a man don't have no soul."

"Right? Right, Goldkorns? Right?"

I did not at that moment answer. In faint light, which came

through the window as well as from the bar, I saw Margolies listening for his master's heart. Nearby was Hildegard Stutchkoff, with open eyes. Among the patrons one person cried out, as if some terrible vision oppressed him. A woman whimpered: had she seen it, too? A. Baer lay upon his back on the floor of the platform. There was his beard, his brow, the curled end of his violoncello. It looked like the head of a sleeping bird. The widow Stutchkoff wore shoes. I wished to ask her if she were comfortable, if there was something I, Leib Goldkorn, might do. Instead that same Goldkorn, a Viennese of some culture, an atheist during his youth, spoke exactly as follows:

"Well, gentlemen, but what if he does have a soul?"

Margolies rose to his feet and passed once again, in his black coat, in front of the window. The snow was now blowing in the opposite direction, from the right hand to the left, although after a time it seemed to drop down in the normal way, and still later it stopped. Then that night, in some respects no different from any other, came to an end.

IV

Rivington Street in the morning was covered with snow. It was on top of everything, sweet-looking, like *Schlagsahne* in a cup of coffee. From the window of the Steinway Restaurant it was possible to see a crowd standing behind the barriers that had been erected at either end of the block. But the street before us was smooth, without even a footprint.

"Pam!" said the kidnapper with the perpetual smile. "Ha! Ha!"

He was simulating a gunshot at a tan-colored spaniel that ran down the street, stopping at one sugary curb, then the other.

"Pam! Pam! Pam!"

The dog disappeared. Across the street a window opened. A person shook out a duster. The window closed. The gangsters drank each Ballantine Beer.

The small group of patrons, the musicians, and the wife of Ellenbogen sat at the tables. The waiters put plates of hot kasha before them. Nobody ate. Tartakower had something wrong with his neck. A. Baer was flushed with a fever. Hildegard Stutchkoff, her gown in tatters, did not leave her chair. The heat, which

25

worked automatically, by some kind of clock, came on, and the window panes filled up with steam. The two Hispanics rubbed constantly a clear place on the glass. Vivian Stutchkoff, looking alive, started to thaw.

"Goldkorns! ¡Atención! ¿Qué pasa?"

"A gypsy! A Checker cab! Okay, Goldkorn, you stand in front of the window. You wave."

The automobile which came slowly across the snow was a Checker brand, but no longer a taxi. Taxis are yellow. This car was black, with black tires, a black grill, and black curtains over all of the windows. At a speed of perhaps one mile in an hour it approached the front of the restaurant, then stopped. Nothing happened. No person got out. The engine appeared to be off. It was not possible to see any movement inside.

"I don't like it," Chino said. "I don't like the looks of it. Why's it sitting there, huh? What's it want? How come you can't see inside?"

"Pam! Pam!"

Margolies came up with a tray and three bowls of kasha. He peered through the misted glass. "A hearse," he said.

The tall man, Jesús, vigorously rubbed the window. "Where? ¿Una carroza fúnebre? ¡Sí! Curtains on windows! Same like the covered mirror! Ghosts! Ha! Ha! Ha!" He took a bowl from the waiter's tray.

The plumpish widow rose from her seat to look. She wore a Polish perfume and the back of her shoulders was rounded. "Mister Margolies, we must to make preparations."

"Nobody moves, got it? Nobody touches him!"

"But he must be buried by sundown," said the old man, and bent over Stutchkoff's unlaced shoes. The woman kneeled by his head.

Jesús spit varnishkas upon the Steinway Restaurant floor. "In China! Mu-shoo pork!"

"I like the smooth feeling of killing. Old man, to me you're just a fly." Chino pointed his gun at the head of the waiter. At that instant, with astounding volume, the black hearse broke into "La Cucaracha," and followed this with a medley of Latin American tunes.

"Ay! Ay! Ay! Ay!" Martinez, with a soup-cabbage and of course in need of a shave, was singing in the door of the kitchen. "Come to your window!"

The two killers swayed slightly and made their fingers snap. They too sang the words of the songs: the hardly-haired man did so poorly; but the tall man, what a surprise, was a light and elegant tenor. Then the music stopped. The black Checker-brand car, which had been trembling, as though from its exertions, was now silent, was now perfectly still.

"More! More!" cried the desperados, and as a matter of fact the auto, or rather some person in it, a woman with a low, soft, flavorful voice, began to speak:

"¡Oigan, muchachos! Is it lonely in there? No one to talk to? No one who understands? Sí, I know you have troubles, such big, sad troubles. You can tell them to me. I am listening. Come on, yankee-boys, put your head in my lap and tell me all about it. My big, brave soldier-boys!"

"Womans! Real womans! Quiero llevarla a la cama. Tengo que mamarle las tetas. Tell him, Chino. About the tits. Tell this to Goldkorns."

But the adolescent's eyes had rolled up in his head. "Ooooo, I feel like she was blowing those words in my ear."

"¡Mamá!" This from the cook, still in the kitchen-door.

"Cold, boys? And hungry? Guess what I am going to cook for you? Hot honey plantains! Vegetable soup! ¡Especialidades cubanas! Ay! My hero-boys! What about a nice hot bath? Would you like that? That's for me, muchachos! Lots of hot steam! Then you can sleep. How tired you are, how much you want to sleep. Sí. Sí. I know. I understand. You don't want to hurt anybody. You want a lullaby. Who wants to die because of some Jews? Come on, yankee-boys! Come over to my side! Put your heads here, on my warm breasts!"

The older villain had climbed onto the belly of V. V. Stutch-koff and was in an insane manner pulling the handle off of the door.

"Surrender! Okay! Surrender!"

"No, man, listen, man, I think the whole gig's a trap. You cats — start playing! Play long! Play loud!"

This was an instruction to the membership of the Steinway Quintet, who, with a lively selection from Offenbach, tried to obey. But it must be remembered, first, that our orchestra possessed no means of amplification and, second, that A. Baer, although he sat in his place and moved his arms, had no instrument inside them. Thus, even in the passages of the "Can-Can," the voice of the Siren was all too clearly heard:

Duerma, duerma, mi niñito
Duerma, duerma, mi amor
Su mami lo está cuidando
Y lo besa con amor.

Ladies and gentlemen, we are adults here. There is not a great deal left in this modern world to cause us surprise. Yet even those with the most experience among us might wish, from the present scene, to turn aside their eyes. The tall man, his name was actually Jesús, took by the arm the lady with the pearls, the lady with the reddish-brown hair, and rubbed his body against her. Then he put his hand inside her nice purple dress and pushed a part of her bosom. I cannot tell you how strenuously our orchestra played the "Barcarolle," even Tartakower with his twisted neck produced a full-bodied tone. But we, and all our art, did not prevail.

For there then began the process which each one of us had held, perhaps, in fearful suspension at a dark spot in his mind. By this I mean that here after all were men with great power, but lacking the voice of conscience: and such men were in a room with desirable women. Otto Rank once remarked that — no, no, it is not necessary to recall his statement. We know, do we not, what men are? From my position at the Bechstein I saw the crazed man lower his victim — she did not resist, perhaps she had fainted? — to the Steinway Restaurant floor. *Here the poorest boy may rise to the highest position in the nation. Many have done so: many more will do so in the years to come.* From what source, and from what distant time, had this thought come to my mind? At once I knew. These were the words of Judge Solomon Gitlitz, spoken to me, as they have been spoken to thousands of others, upon the occasion of my American naturalization. I stopped playing Offenbach then. I stood up on my feet. Murmelstein, near by, pulled my clothing:

"Don't make trouble. Sit. Sit down."

I thought of myself as I had once been, young, proud, with the thick lips of a woodwind player. 1943. Dark days for the United Nations, and for International Jewry. But the spectacles of Solomon Gitlitz were shining, shining like coins, and so, too, were each of his words: *For you, policemen walk the streets, firemen are always ready to save you, doctors are trying to make the land healthful, brave soldiers and sailors are guarding the coasts.* The song of the temptress had ended. The black automobile drove away. One by one the other members of the Steinway Quintet put their instruments down. A. Baer alone continued silently bowing. Everything was still. The only sound to be heard came from the lips of the despoiler. Panting. He had his hat on. And therefore Leib Goldkorn, a citizen you see, a person who had for thirty years every benefit, every blessing, he stepped off the platform and went up to the Puerto Rican.

"Listen, young man, you must not do this. You have a fine tenor voice."

But it was as if I were addressing a figure of stone. No person spoke a word. The eyes of the woman in purple stared up into mine. Two small lines, signs of anguish, appeared on her brow. What were the possibilities in such a situation? I tapped the shoulder of her attacker, who slowly turned towards me his head.

"You are dragging the flag of your country in the dust."

Still, he did not respond. A film was over his eyes. His trousers dropped by themselves to his knees. Little time to lose. The younger assassin was staring out of the Steinway Restaurant window, with his hand up, extending the brim of his hat. In a few steps I stood before him, this child, with the wisps of hair for a beard, with his nearly pupil-less eyes, with his dreams of an airship, of stars, clouds, and sky. "Young man, I believe I understand you and your companion. I was young once, like you. I, too, wore a moustache over my lip. Nor was I always a city-dweller, a cultured man, no, I once spoke a language that no one about me could understand. It is an error to think I was actually born in Vienna. The truth is I first saw the light in Gloggnitz, which is over two hundred kilometers away. There was in our town only a single paved street, although it was a part of the Austrian-Hungarian Empire. Is there not a similarity in our destiny? Both of us colonial peoples? I came to the Imperial capital when I was six years of age, holding my sisters' hands. The sun at that time was setting. People were sitting in cafes. Drinking drinks of a raspberry color. The glass of the shop windows reflected the evening lights. Everyone was speaking the German tongue. I saw a man in a turban."

I confess that my own words had carried me away. I heard gasping. Behind my back Jesús had risen on all fours. The foot of the woman had lost a shoe. It was at this point not possible to look longer. "Young man, one thing more. My dream on that day was to ride on a tramcar. These went through the streets of Vienna, throwing out sparks, and each was equipped with a musical bell. If you work hard, if you learn to speak American English, you will be able to ride in a silver airship. I guarantee this to you! We have a land of opportunity! Do not commit this terrible crime. Stop your colleague! It is nearly too late!"

"Oh! Oh! Oh!"

The second shoe of the lady was gone. Each of her legs was now forced into the air. What happened next was that Leib Goldkorn, I myself, had knocked the hat of the tall Puerto Rican off of his head onto the floor. Not only that, violently I was pulling his hair. Success! The man rolled aside, and the lady —

she was missing her collar of pearls — began to adjust her purple dress. The degenerate then clutched my throat with his hand and narrowed his wolf's yellow eyes. "¡*Vas a morir! ¡Judío sucio! ¡Judío cabrón!* Chino, tell him. Say what I say!"

But it was not his colleague, it was A. Baer who translated: "The Jew is going to die."

"*Sí! Sí!* Going to die! All Jews! ¡*Judíos sucios!*"

This Puerto Rican, the one with the pomaded hair, then put the end of his pistol underneath Leib Goldkorn's chin. At precisely that moment, upon the point of my death, the telephone, with its wires every which way, rang. No? Not possible? But it rang.

Mosk got up — a plate of groats was before him — and picked up the receiver:

"Hello, Steinway. You don't need no reservation. He ain't here. *Kaputt.* Some kinda heart attack. Yeah, they're here. You wanna speak to them? Yeah. Hang on a minute." The old Lithuanian shuffled over to where the killer was pressing the trigger. "It's for you."

Jesús took the pay telephone and began to shout in an insane manner directly into the mouthpiece: "Kill! Ha! Ha! Ha! Kill all! Sundown time! I kill them myself!"

"Look, Goldkorn. There." The other youth was pointing outside, toward the intersection of Rivington Street and Allen Street. There was a phone box there, with a dome of snow upon it. Inside were two men, crowded together, wearing brown hats and brown coats.

"It's them. Yeah. The Hostage Squad."

The tall one, still hatless, continued screaming: "*Pantalones! Pantalones de* silk! You bring it! Ha! Ha! By sundown The *pantalones!*"

"Goldkorn, you gotta make the negotiation. You know what we want, the plane, the money. I got six clips, Goldkorn, six shots to a clip, Jesús got the same. It ain't just you. It's enough to shoot everyone here through the eyes, man, and the ears and the mouth. I see anyone move on that snow, anywhere from Eldridge to Allen, I open fire. You say anything wrong, like mentioning names, like giving descriptions, I fire, too. That's square business. Tell them tonight we got to be out of the city. Tell them we got to be high in the sky."

The boy raised his weapon to a spot near my heart. I looked again through the Steinway Restaurant window. The officers of the Hostage Squad were speaking earnestly into the public phone. I walked then to the back of the room, and took the other end of the line.

"Hello? Hello? This is Leib Goldkorn speaking, former graduate of the Akademie für Musik und darstellende Kunst."

"Hello? This is Officer Tim of the Hostage Squad. I'm awfully sorry but we don't speak Spanish."

In the background, a different voice: "What are you apologizing for? Ain't this America? Ain't English the common tongue?"

"Ha, ha, Officer Tim again. Are you a hostage, actually? Or an armed bandito? Don't be ashamed to admit the latter. We are going to meet every reasonable demand. You'll be calm, won't you? You won't be rash?"

"Give me that. Hello! This is Officer Mike of the Hostage Squad. You won't get away with this. You're surrounded. If you don't come out we'll come in and get you. And it won't be with kid gloves! We're going to smoke your black butts!"

"Hello! I am the artist on pianoforte for the Steinway Quintet. A Bechstein grand. I am not —"

"Goldkorns! ¿Qué pasa? ¿Qué dice?"

"Goldkorn, what do they say?"

"One officer asks for calm. He has promised to meet all demands. But I believe the second officer intends soon to attack."

"Aha," said Doctor Fuchs. "That's psychology! The gentleman and the bully. Carrot and stick. Superego and Id. Very clever, very sophisticated."

"Hello? Hello? Señor? Are you there? This is Officer Tim. We have gifts to offer you. First of all, there's actual cash, up to fifty dollars, and surely your wife would appreciate a toaster or a new electric broom. How about a loan for that new car? For your bedroom here's a pair of matching lamps."

"I will say what is needed. A medical doctor. There is a sick man here, a man aged in his nineties. It is a case of brain fever. Also warm blankets because of the cold of the night. For the same reason a bottle of cognac. Of French manu —"

Through the receiver of the telephone the second man, Officer Mike, was screaming: "Outrageous! Do you hear me, Bechstein? Those are outrageous demands!"

Chino took the instrument from my hand.

"Listen good. I am a stone-cold killer. You don't do what I say just like I say it a lot of Jews are going to die. We got to have a plane to go to China. We got to have a copter to get to the plane. We want one million dollars. You two cats got to personally bring it right up to this door. In tens. In twenties. In fifties. Anybody else comes near this building we open fire. Get here by sundown. That's a non-negotiable demand. What do you say? Huh? Yes? Yes or no? Hello! Hello!"

Through the Steinway Restaurant window I saw the two officers, like men who had lost their senses, first pull inside out each one of their pockets, and then begin to crawl about in the snow.

"*Chino! ¿Qué pasa? Dígame.*"

"*¡El teléfono! ¡La operadora!* She cut us off!"

"Ay! Yids will die!"

A patron — pitchai appetizer, and grilled kidneys after — came up to Jesús. He was a short fat man, with a rumpled shirt. "I think I shall now intend to be going. This is not after all a Greek restaurant. I made a simple mistake as I was passing by. Anybody could make it. I am not a Jew. I am a Greek and speak in a dignified manner. Well, farewell!"

The fat man went through the tables to the front of the room. Mosk, the waiter, walked toward him at an angle.

"Hey, Printzmettel, you forgot your coat."

"Yes, yes, foolish, of course." The patron, with one arm through a Chesterfield jacket, reached the door. His way was blocked by the corpse. He stopped there a moment. V. V. Stutchkoff was warm and somewhat maroon. There was a slight odor, too. The shoulders of Printzmettel dropped. His nice jacket dragged. He went and sat by the wall.

Pop! I believe everyone jumped. Then the sound, *pop!* again. The two desperate men had opened each a can of Ballantine Beer.

V

Greetings, friends! Leib Goldkorn returns! Look, ha-ha, my hands are shaking! The reason for this is not cold weather. It is still warm in the house. No, not for twelve years have my fingers trembled like this, not since a man in green trousers took from me my flute, a Rudall & Rose, made a century before in London. Here is a bottle of Mission Bell, a wine of California manufacture. For this half of a pint the price is forty-nine cents. I have been, not more than a few moments ago, on the premises of the same liquor store from which it is my practice to purchase plum brandy. For the first time they would not allow me a bottle on credit. "Boss's orders." And where was this boss, a Jewish man named Herman I have known for thirteen or fourteen years? "Lunch." Returning when? Not returning. I pointed out there had been a mistake. "Look, young man, I am a citizen. I am a musical artist, until recently employed. Just a bottle of slivovitz. A small one. Herman does not have to know."

My friends, from the border of Spain until shortly before sailing from Lisbon I had to wear the most startling disguise: a

35

striped shirt, a felt hat, and around my neck strings of garlic. Never, in the depths of these indignities, not even when I had to hop on one foot and hum folkish tunes, was I — a former member of the Orchester der Wiener Staatsoper — so humiliated as when I had to beg a favor from this youth in his Eisenhower jacket. From my pocket I took one quarter and change. It was just at this moment, when I put down each of four pennies, that my hands, by themselves, began to shake.

There is in this wine a strong taste of sulfur. *Mein Gott!* It is nearly opaque against the light of the sun! I would not drink it if I had not suffered, only one hour ago, a particular shock to the nerves. What was this shock? It was a fright brought on by Clara, my wife. I do not know what it was that indicated to me that something was wrong. When you live for many years with another person there develops intuition. I am speaking to you from a chair next to the kitchen window. From this position I am able to see through an open doorway the back of the television, and the end of the sofa. Everything seemed normal, except that in the heat of noontime Clara had kicked her coverlet to the floor. Somehow the sight of her bare feet disturbed me. I stood up and went through the door. The cap and the nightdress had been thrown off, too, and the bedclothes bound her body like ropes. Her mouth was open. Her eyes were open. A coma? Death? Actually death? For some reason — no, without a reason, it was simply madness — I turned around to see what was on the TV. It was some sort of film: men and women driving in an automobile, while speaking to one another. However, the horizontal and the vertical controls were poorly set on the appliance, and this caused the deformed heads of the actors to rise to the top of the screen and appear again at the bottom. With a terrible sound Clara took a breath. It was like a person drowning in air. With this rattle she breathed again. Croup! A case of croup! I am not a weak man. I carried my wife to the bathroom and turned the hot water tap of the tub. In a moment the room was filled with steam, and the crisis, which is caused by a kind of dryness in the membranes, had ended.

On Columbus Avenue the trucks are following one after the
other and I cannot easily hear my own words. The wine is burning my larynx, too. Of the events of three months ago I shall
speak no longer. Why should I continue? What more do you want
to know? There are not any surprises. How could there be surprises when I am here, alive, a survivor, speaking to you? The
suspense element is gone. To listen to more is simply *Sensations-
lust*. At the Steinway Restaurant bar there is a beer illumination
in the shape of a windmill-clock. This we often consulted. *We* did
not know the end of the story; for *us* suspense existed, and in our
ignorance we thought that each passing hour brought us nearer to
our doom. Terrible! During the night we prayed for the morning
but when the morning came, with its threats, its insults, its fierce
demands, we prayed again for the night.

At the middle of the day A. Baer took a turn for the worse. He
spat on the floor. Dark spots appeared on the surface of his
clothes. "*Naronim! Idiotin! Zei vellen tsushterin yiddishe geshef-
tin. Reissen yiddishe bord. Farnichten yiddishe Kultur. Loifts!
Behaltzich! Doss iz a toit lager!*" By the time of my teens I had
forgotten all of my Yiddish — instead we had Schnitzler, we had
Karl Kraus — and this has remained a gap in my knowledge I
have not rectified. However, if you are familiar with the German
tongue, you have certainly grasped that the aged gentleman had
confused these Hispanic intruders with members of the National-
sozialistische deutsche Arbeiterpartei. Now defunct.

The condition of others had deteriorated also. Do you remember that Salpeter had been forced to spend the night without his
waterproof cloak? He now periodically sneezed, and there was a
clear drop of liquid near the end of his nose. Catarrh. The neck
of Tartakower, moreover, had locked in the position of a violinist
supporting with his chin his violin. Patrons, even Doctor Fuchs,
were forced to visit regularly the water cabinet for men or the
water cabinet for women. Yet in my eyes the saddest situation
was that of the woman in the purple dress, the same person who
had that morning come so close to being the victim of an unmen-
tionable act. Now she sat for long periods upon the zinc of the

bar, with her hands touching, or seeming to touch, the pearls that were no longer around her neck. One leg was crossed over the other, and moved up and down; a shoe hung by only a strap from her foot. She smiled, she giggled, and — does this not wrench the heart? — made inviting moues in the direction of Jesús, whom, under the stress of circumstances, she took to be her former gentleman companion.

"All things get worse," remarked once Sigmund Freud, who lived at Berggasse 19, only a few blocks from my boyhood home; "they don't get better." Of course the famous alienist was referring to the condition of living persons, but at the Steinway Restaurant, on Wednesday afternoon, it applied to dead people, too. By this I mean the corpse of Vivian Stutchkoff, which now unmistakably smelled. It was not hot in the room, although it had grown uncomfortably warm. The problem was the airlessness. Not a fresh breath came to us from the world outside. The smoke of Tartakower's, and others', cigarettes hung in layers over our heads. And with every inhalation, even when done through the mouth, came the smell of — it is difficult to put the experience of one sense into the language of another: it was a thick, sweet smell, and a tangy smell, too. Like boots, partly, and partly like caraway seeds.

"He stinks!" said Mosk, the Lithuanian waiter. "P.U."

Also, he was for some reason swelling. Large already, an impressive man, Stutchkoff had begun to bulge even further — not dramatically, not all at once, but steadily, like bread that is rising. By two o'clock his buttons were straining, and several had burst. But perhaps the most painful of these transformations was the way in which his skin altered its color. It had been, that morning, pink and rosy, as if through some miracle he had been frozen alive. Think of the pain for Hildegard Stutchkoff, seated nearby at the window, as that complexion deepened to purple and then turned an absinthe green. He had become like a statue of V. V. Stutchkoff, with a statue's patina; and on this green figure the only tone that resembled life was that of the little feather that still clung to the lips of the restaurateur.

And what of this Hildegard Stutchkoff? Alas, the Polish beauty was also subject to the process of disrepair. Her blond hair was no longer curled on top of her head. The red lips on her mouth had entirely vanished. Her gown was torn in many places and on her shoulder was the white strap of an undergarment. She kept her eyelids lowered over her eyes, underneath which were blue semicircles. Slowly, not according to any plan, the staff of the Steinway Restaurant gathered around her. Although the clock said only two-thirty, her face was already in shadow. Moment by moment — how quickly this happens in winter — the light was leaving the visible part of the sky.

"And after?" This was Ellenbogen, a waiter, speaking first. "Hildegard, what about after?"

The cashieress lifted then her lids from her eyes. "Mister Margolies, what is 'after'? Is already 'after.' Is the finish already." She raised an arm toward the body of her former husband, and dropped it again in her lap.

"But the Steinway Restaurant, Mrs. Stutchkoff. Next year is seventy-five years at a single location. Leon Trotsky ate here, what about that? And the Attorney General of the State of New York."

"Also champion boxers. B. Leonard. B. Ross."

Hildegard blew for a moment cool air down the front of her bosom. "Steinway Restaurant is finished, too."

"Wait a minute!" cried waiter Mosk. "This is a moneymaker! A goldmine!"

"Is losing eighty dollars, in cold weather ninety dollars, Mister Mosk, each day, this goldmine. Is five hundred each week, such American dollars, is each month two thousand —"

"That's all right, lady! Don't worry! Please you don't worry! Everything is all right! I make mamaliga!" There were real tears on Martinez's cheeks.

In a soft voice Margolies said. "We are old men here. It is not a good time in our lives to go on the street."

"I wish to remind everyone that music is an aid to digestion.

Schiller writes that harmony is a feast for the ears. A feast for the ears!"

"My good, dear friends! Mister Martinez! Mister Salpeter, please! What am I to be doing about modern times? About American peoples? Mamaliga? Pitchai? Who comes in such an expensive taxi so far for pitchai? They want Gershwin? Gershwin is on the radio, the TV, the movies — is not necessary to make a request from the Steinway Quintet."

"Look, I am going over here. Attention everyone, please." Margolies called to us from a table by the wall. "Who sat in this chair? This very chair? Here is where her elbows were on the table, and she put her chin on the back of her hands. Do you remember who sat in this pose, Mister Mosk?"

"Yeah. Sarah Bernhardt."

"Yes! It was Sarah Bernhardt who sat in this chair! And smoked a cigarette in a holder! Never mind if I am crying. It is nothing. Never mind."

"Is to pay Mister Margolies no money. Is no more time. Is no more Jews."

"*Zei vellen arois reissen unzere tzeine! Zei vellen arois nemen de gold!*" A. Baer was spitting onto the floor. "Yes, and lamps out of our skins!"

All at once Ellenbogen, a married man, sank to his knees and grasped his ex-employer by his black suspenders: "What will become of us now, Mister Stutchkoff? What are we to do?"

Everyone gasped and looked around at our captors. The tall one, Jesús, was seated at the bench of the Bechstein, where he played one note, two maddening B-flats over high C, a shrill note, over and over again. Chino, the youth with the immature beard, stood at the window, with his hand on his hatbrim, shading his eyes. Outside there was a black crust, soot, shadows, on top of the white of the snow. The sun was falling like a stone out of the sky. Across Rivington Street the bars of the fire escapes were lighting up one by one, like filaments in a lamp. How long until the end of the day?

All the others now joined Ellenbogen next to the corpse.

"What to do, Mister Ellenbogen? Once I saw a grown man ask Mister Stutchkoff the very same question, and Stutchkoff — this was 1923, he was only a boy — he said, 'Floor coverings,' and this man went on to invent some kind of linoleum that made him rich. In those days he told everyone what to do."

"A coincidence," said Mosk.

"Once is a coincidence," Margolies replied, "but not twice, not three times. A woman came, this was even earlier, 1921, and she had a definite cancer. The doctor wrote a prescription which she brought to Stutchkoff. It had two items on it. Stutchkoff said, 'Take this but don't take that.' A month or two later the cancer was gone. Another time when a certain man was sick Stutchkoff told him to buy medicine, fill up a teaspoon with it and pour it into the sink. This man also got well."

"It's a lotta hooey," said the Lithuanian waiter. "What about when they dropped dead?"

Salpeter was shaking his head. "No, Mister Mosk, what Margolies says is true. I will tell you a thing that occurred in 1928, when I was in the position of Murmelstein, that is to say, when I was second violinist in the Steinway Orchestra. I was not then the leader. Perhaps for that reason I would often arrive early at the Steinway Restaurant in order to practice. Even before you would arrive, my dear Mister Margolies."

"I remember. Ragstatt was the first violin."

"One afternoon — I recall the bright sunshine—I was playing the Concerto Grosso of Ernst Bloch, when a man walked by in front of the window. 'Quick! Stop him! Bring him to me!' Rarely had I seen young Stutchkoff so exercised. I put down my instrument and ran into the street. It is not necessary to describe each detail. I brought him inside and Stutchkoff, who was then barely sixteen, asked him where he was going; but the man would not say. Stutchkoff then refused him permission to leave. O'Brien, our cook, and I restrained him by force. At last the man began to weep and said, 'Rabbi, I want to confess. I had the intention of committing a sin. I was about to be baptized. But you held me back and now the evil hour has passed.' This same person went on to become a very pious man and a lover of music."

Tartakower said, "But that is a miracle!"

"Unbelievable! Amazing!"

From an inside pocket the Litvak took out a cigar, and lit it. His face seemed perplexed. It was difficult indeed to reconcile the tales we had heard with the sight of the green giant that lay before us. Even I, from Vienna, a free-thinker, found myself, in the mounting excitement, somewhat disturbed.

"Baloney," Mosk said.

Margolies then spoke:

"I came to the Steinway Restaurant in the summer, 1920. This Stutchkoff was then aged seven or so. Just a boy. Mister Mosk, I advise you to listen and not blow disrespectful rings in the air. One day M. P. Stutchkoff, Stutchkoff himself, and I sat down to a meal of Roumanian broilings. He was then a thin child, with a thin face, a long face, and he had black eyes and black lashes. It's true, he never ate much; but on this particular occasion he would not even touch the food. In addition, he said we must not eat either. Everything was getting cold. A delicious platter of broilings. But Stutchkoff, with that thin face, insisted: he would not budge. On the other hand, he would not give a reason. Nothing. So M. P. Stutchkoff and I decided, all right, we'll eat by ourselves. Attention, please, everyone: you have not heard a thing like this before. The meat was on my fork, not an inch from my mouth, when Premisher, the butcher, rushes in screaming and waving his arms: 'Stop! Stop! It's not kosher!' It turns out there was a mix-up with a side of a cow. An inch, Mister Mosk! An inch!"

"Ooooo," said Tartakower.

"A Rabbi! A Prince!"

"Blessed be His name!"

The staff of the Steinway Restaurant began to rock back and forth. Suddenly I was knocked rudely to the side and someone rushed by and fell on top of V. V. Stutchkoff. It was Murmelstein, the second violinist.

"Boss! Boss!" he cried. "I'm asking a favor! I got a kid in school! In college! University of Wisconsin! Boss! You hear me? Boss!"

What could one think, except that young Murmelstein, in the course of this night and day of terror, had lost control of his senses? An act of a madman. We cried out, of course. We took hold of our colleague's shoes. But Murmelstein only wrapped his arms more tightly around the mound of the corpse and clung there, as if to the top of a wave.

"¡Ay! ¡Ay!" The Hispanics cried. "No talking! No talking! ¡No hablen! ¡No hablen!"

The tall Puerto Rican grasped the back of Murmelstein's jacket and pulled upon it. The second violinist, with the strength of his mania, held on to Stutchkoff's waist.

"No talking! Talking not allowed! This is dead individual! Talking to ghost? Ghost? Ha-ha-ha! No such thing! Ain't spirits! Jew! Listen! Ain't anything! Ain't anything! Ain't anything!" With the gun in his hand, Jesús was striking Murmelstein, a parent, on the back of his head.

"Hey, cut it out!"

"You are striking a trained musician!"

"No! No blows on the head!"

The staff of the Steinway Restaurant had become agitated. Someone restrained the hoodlum's arm. Someone else — this is true, I am an eyewitness — began to strike him upon the hip. Let people say what they wish; let them even deny it. We acted, friends! At that hour we fought them back!

There was then a gunshot and a cry of pain. A second shot; but no cry came after. Murmelstein rose from the body of Vivian Stutchkoff. He had a smile, an unusual smile, on his face. "Hee, hee, hee," he said, and walked away.

"I warned them, the mothafuckas! I told the mothafuckas I'd shoot if I saw anything move." Chino was standing by the window, from which two panes were now missing. He rubbed the mist from the rest of the glass. In the snow, between the two curbs, was the tan-colored spaniel. There was enough light from the low sun to see the blood on its fur. From this sight I turned away. I went to the rear of the room.

"Psst! Look, Mister Goldkorn." Murmelstein was waiting there. He had a thing in the palm of his hand. "Hee, hee, hee. I got it out of his pocket. The key! The back door key! Hee, hee, hee. It was all a plan!"

VI

Yass! Yass! Goldkorns here! At the kitchen table. And the window is right over there. A moment, just a moment, while I breathe in some air. I am a vigorous man but the flights of stairs are now a problem. Breathlessness? No, no it is fatigue. *A flight of stairs* — is not this a strange way to say it? For three months I have been unable truly to sleep. However, pills are not acceptable to me. Goloshes, M.D., gave me tablets in March of this year. With these tablets it was like falling down a long staircase with something dark, a black thing, at the bottom. In English you say *falling asleep*. Ha, ha! What a language!

The reason I have mentioned Doctor Goloshes is that a short time ago I was speaking with him directly on the telephone. That is why I have gone down and up once again so many stairs. He told me he would come by for a visit after his dinner. Clara is not well, after all. I thought it was the croup but she is making a sound as though she meant to bring up her phlegm. There is also incontinence of the bowels. We treat this as a little joke between us, but if I dared, if it were not undistinguished, I would request

45

that she wear rubber pants. Am I not speaking of a disgraceful human condition? What a scandal! And what is the point? Tell me! She does not even know that she is alive! "Am I living or dying?" she said. A better way to treat old people would be to kill them. Kill them off would be better! There is no mind in her. No mind left! And when does Doctor Goloshes eat his dinner? Already it is growing quite dark. But where was I? Yes, I remember. I would accept any employment in the woodwind area, if necessary even the saxophone. In the percussion group I have at times played the piano. Is that something you already know?

Four flights. Four. Tartakower, with his yellow fingers, would be unable to do it. Have you ever attempted to make a call from a phone box in this city? The kind where you insert a dime? We have not here the spotlessness of Vienna. Remember this was an emergency situation. A call to a doctor. I went to three kiosks, first one then another, and each time the earpiece hung down, yes, like the neck of a butchered goose. And then, while speaking with Goloshes, M.D., a respectable man, my feet were in a person's urine! There was for me a moment of fear in that place. The darkening sky. A wind springing up. All phonebooks torn. I then saw myself as if I were outside of the transparent glass, as if I were a second caller impatiently waiting: fearful to see the light bulb exposing my hands, my shoulders, my large ears, my hairless head. *Hello, hello, Doctor Goloshes? Clara is ill!* What is that telephone ringing? We have here no telephone. I see that already there is a full moon. What a joke! And stars! Do you know what I think? These are simply holes, just pinpricks, in a black cloth. Do not tell me they are proof of a vast universe. In the American language: do not make me laugh. But what is that ringing? A month ago the Bell Telephone Company came and removed from our flat the telephone. Ringing. Still ringing. Yass! If I remember correctly, Doctor Fuchs, the Freudian, picked up the Steinway Restaurant receiver.

It was the friendly Officer Tim. I was at that time examining the mural of Feiner and listened with only slight interest to the conversation. Of course there was a shout of joy, an outburst, when it was announced that both officers would soon arrive with the money, that all demands would be met. Before my eyes was a skillful depiction of the death of Aeschylus: an eagle, they say, dropped a tortoise upon his head. Thinking the latter was stone. The telephone rang once again. Naturally — this was their plan — it was Officer Mike. An attack was about to be launched. All hostages must at once lie on the floor. Here was the philosopher Anaxagoras, whom Feiner portrayed as middle-aged, explaining the theory of atoms to a boy with a squint in his eyes. Socrates?

You would like to ask, perhaps, why I showed such little interest? Such small concern? It was my belief that the specialists of the Hostage Squad, even if they were serious men, and sincere in what they said, canceled each the position of the other. I mean by this that the ransom funds would not be paid and there would be no airship to the People's Republic of China. Equally, there would be that night, or the next day, upon the Steinway Restaurant, no armed attack. The windmill had turned to quarter to four. The deadline was now approaching. The only question was, what would, at sundown, our captors do?

The tall kidnapper, the one who had stepped through the back of A. Baer's violoncello, was at that moment throwing a pill into his mouth. Somehow he missed; it flew over his shoulder.

"Benny! My last benny!"

He fell to his hands and his knees and began inspecting the floor. The room full of Jews watched without a word as he threw down chairs, upended a Steinway Restaurant table, and knocked a cart of desserts onto its side. But the little red capsule had rolled into a crevice, a crack. Not to be found. Jesús was weeping. He was uttering curses and cries. He pounded with his fists, his forehead, his shoetips upon the floor. It was surely a dangerous moment. All at once he sat up, with his back straight and his legs crossed underneath him. His eyelids came down. His chin struck his chest. His hat fell into his lap. Sleeping? No soul dared move. Then he said, "Ah! Ah-ha! ¡El jefe Mao!"

Chino, the youth, was no longer at the Steinway Restaurant window, whose panes were now partly rose-colored and partly

grey. He was instead behind me, with a cognac glass in his hand.
"For you, Goldkorn."
"This is a very good cognac. Imported."
"Turn on the lights, man. It's dark in here."
"Dark? On the contrary, young man. It is quite light in this
room. The overhead chandeliers do not go on until five o'clock. It
is so early."
"Don't be punk-hearted, man. It ain't personal. We ain't going
to do this because of you. It's just the way the thing broke down.
Hit the lights."
"Please. Take this. I am finished. Not thirsty."
I myself put the cognac glass, which was mostly full, back into
his hand. I turned from him to the wall. Why? I do not know
why.
"What are you looking at, man? What's this painting called?
The one all over the wall."
"This is a mural by Feiner. Perhaps it is his finest work. I
think the title is 'The Golden Age.' "
"Yeah. Uh-huh. Which is when a country is at the top, right?
At the peak of its glory."
"Yes, at the peak of its culture and influence. You have, for
example, Vienna at the turn of this century. It was then that the
young Schoenberg composed his *Verklärte Nacht*."
"What place is this? Is this a country? Is it Greece?" The
youth with the ridiculous moustache pointed to a spot on the wall
where workmen, it appeared, were laboring upon the Parthenon.
"Yes. Correct. I believe that the man sitting there is Pericles,
the leading citizen of Athens. He encouraged art, literature, and
philosophy, in addition to music."
"And what's that building? The one they're working on?"
"The Parthenon. It is where the Greeks worshipped Athena."
"Magnificent. Right, Goldkorn? Magnificent."
The temple rose above the mass of men. Its columns were
fluted and gleaming. The bright marble shone.
"Feiner was a well-known artist."

"You know something funny? I needed two hundred dollars. I owed a couple of dudes."

At that moment, as if it had plunged into a pot of water, the light from the sun went completely out.

Before I, or the youth, or any other person could locate the switch for the chandeliers, the shadow of Salpeter appeared on the musical platform. With a pencil he rapped sharply the lid of the Bechstein.

"I shall ask the members of the Steinway Quintet to take their places. Quickly, please! Gentlemen, quickly!"

From different parts of the room the musicians emerged. A. Baer could not by himself climb onto the platform. We gave him assistance by holding his arms. Through the cloth of his coat his skin was hot to the touch. Salpeter, with a handkerchief under his nose, continued speaking:

"Ladies and gentlemen, as you are certainly aware, our concert last evening was unfortunately interrupted before it had reached its conclusion. How long ago that seems, and not merely a matter of hours! However, in spite of the vicissitudes that have crowded upon us, we are still alive, and still here together. Therefore, I am pleased to announce that the Steinway Quintet will present at this time a special program. Our selection is dedicated to the memory of our colleague and co-religionist, V. V. Stutchkoff, a true friend of the arts."

"Play anything by Irving Berlin!"

"Thank you, Mister Mosk, for your suggestion. But I am sure you agree that tonight is not an ordinary occasion, and for that reason we shall not entertain the usual requests. The fact is, throughout the long years of its existence, the Steinway Orchestra has numbered among its members many distinguished composers, some of whom, like S. Romberg himself, or Maximilian Steiner, the winner of three Academy Awards, are known and loved all over the world. Yes, Romberg played at the Steinway Restaurant the double bass for nearly one year. Other members of our orchestra are appreciated more often by connoisseurs. I

am thinking, as I am sure you have guessed, of Rubin Goldmark,
K. Goldmark's nephew, whose difficult *Samson* was composed
between these walls; and also of our dear friend Joseph Rumshinsky, our pianist until his untimely death in 1963. It is the
work of these men that we shall play tonight, beginning, for
artistic reasons, and for morale also, precisely at that point at
which our concert was suspended. Ladies and gentlemen, *The
Student Prince,* followed by 'The Indian Love Call'!"

Murmelstein took his seat. Tartakower took his seat. A. Baer
had his damaged instrument propped between his knees. And I,
Leib Goldkorn, Rumshinsky's successor, slid onto the bench of
the Bechstein. Salpeter sat, too. Then everyone noticed that there
was a bare music stand among us, and one extra chair.

"Oh, yes," said Salpeter, and rose to his feet again. "I have
placed here the chair of the late Albert Einstein, the recreational
violinist, who once, in the year 1949, joined our little orchestra
for a musical evening. In the entire history of our organization,
he was the only guest soloist allowed such a privilege. However,
he brought his own instrument, and of course to such a world
figure it was not possible to say no. And the truth is he played
quite well. We were not embarrassed at all."

Salpeter sat down a second time, and picked up his bow. But
for some reason Tartakower was standing. Because of the sprain
to his neck he had to walk sideways. He came over to me.

"I'll sit here, Mister Goldkorn, and you take, please, my chair."

"What are you suggesting? What can you mean?"

Tartakower held out his instrument. Yes, he was holding it out
to me.

"Here, take it. I want you to play it tonight. I shall attempt the
piano. For the *Phantasie* by Rumshinsky I shall play only
chords."

His silver flute was in my hands. It was a Powell model, only
thirty years old, of American manufacture. But it was light, was
balanced correctly, and seemed to float up, to spring up, toward
my lips.

"Short of breath, Mister Tartakower?"

"No, no, please. You are the older man, a woodwind specialist. I beg you not to argue."

The first violinist rapped with his pencil the edge of a music stand. Tartakower abruptly sat down and I, I stood up, I walked to his place, I eased myself onto his chair.

"What's this? What's this?" Salpeter wanted to know.

"He — it is his neck, his neck, you know."

Salpeter looked at me closely. He wiped, with a white handkerchief, his nose. Then he dipped his shoulder and we started to play.

I have remarked that it was dark in the room. The music on the music stand was obscure and difficult to read. The instrument, after so many years, felt strange to my hands, my lips. It was as if I were again speaking German, a dear but in part a forgotten tongue. I made many mistakes. My breath seemed to whistle. And soon it became necessary, for a moment, to stop. I looked about me. The revival of the Romberg selection seemed to have brought A. Baer to his senses. He had no bow, but he hummed his part softly, and the violoncello produced a pizzicato in spite of its broken back. The Bialystoker, meanwhile, with his chin on his clavicle, had mastered the pianoforte. I could not rest longer. The melody of the 'Indian Love Call' is played exclusively by the flute. The Powell model felt heavy. It nearly fell from my hands. Salpeter nodded. I believe that Murmelstein encouragingly smiled. I played a wrong note. A second wrong note. Something was smarting my eyes.

"Stop! Stop!" Salpeter cried. "We shall begin once more."

This we did. From my instrument there came at last — as had happened on one other occasion, the Graduation Day Recital of the Akademie für Musik, at which my grandparents, and parents, and my two sisters were present — a series of perfect and lucid and golden-throated tones.

I cannot say how long our concert lasted. Less than one hour perhaps. The light in the room soon faded completely. Between selections there was no applause. Yet in the seventy-four years of the Steinway Orchestra there had not been such music as this. I am struggling to find words to describe it and I fear I shall fail in this task. Not, however, because music is, as some critics say, an abstract art. I have never believed such fantastic statements. Each note corresponds to a nuance of feeling, just as every word of a poem does, or the brushstrokes of a painting. Very well. I must then simply describe what these feelings were. This is taxing. Difficult. Yet my emotion that Wednesday night was not in essence different from that which I regularly experience upon hearing a broadcast — perhaps Bizet — on station WNYC. Only sharper. It was what we used to call *Zusammengehörigkeit*, a feeling of connectedness. Connectedness, in the first place, to the man whose music I was at that moment hearing or playing. In that final hour at the Steinway Restaurant I felt nearest, I think, during his Concert Suite and the score from *The Life of Émile Zola,* to Maximilian Steiner. The reason for this is perhaps that he was Viennese. And a former pupil of Gustave Mahler. Indeed, I soon felt this connection not only to the film composer, but, behind him, so to speak, the whole world of the Imperial city, its streets, its river, the Kaiserliche und königliche Hof-Operntheater, and even at light moments, when I, myself, was executing a difficult trill, the Wienerwald, with its trees and its birds.

As our program continued, this feeling of closeness — better to say an absence of division, of divisiveness — grew to include those with whom I was playing: Murmelstein, Tartakower, A. Baer, Salpeter. It was as if the Steinway Quintet were a single person, giving a solo performance, as if invisible threads bound us one to another, so that when Salpeter moved his arm upward I felt myself pulled so slightly in his direction. And at last there grew to be a similar bond with those who were listening below. We could at that time hardly see them — only the shine from a pair of eyeglasses, a white shirt collar, the napkin on Margolies' arm. Like heads bobbing in an ocean of darkness. Then I felt myself to be not this Leib Goldkorn, no longer the separate citizen, but also a part of that ocean, like a grain of salt, no different from those other grains, Mosk, or Ellenbogen, or the woman, Hildegard Stutchkoff, or the lifeless corpse of her husband, yes, even — do not be alarmed by what I now say — even the two murderers, for they were a part of that ocean, too. That ocean. That darkness, friends. We know what it is, do we not? And this is my feeling concerning the nature of music: that it connects those who have died, Stutchkoff and Steiner, and before Steiner, Mahler, with those who are merely waiting to do so. All in the same boat, as Americans say.

The last notes of our concert sounded. The violoncellist plucked three times — C-sharp, E, A — his violoncello; Tartakower removed his foot from the foot pedal; both violinists drew simultaneously their bows across their strings. The flautist sealed his lips. There was a pause of a single moment. Then the lights came on and the world went to pieces.

The elder Puerto Rican, still crosslegged, cried out in a voice of despair, "Oh, Chino! Such dreams! *Un sueño. ¡Estuve en China, con dragones y el jefe Mao!*"

The youth helped him to rise. "I know. Come on. The time is up."

"In China! Eating lemons! Only a dream!"

The men stood under the light from the chandeliers and put bullets into their pistols. Several of the patrons began to whimper. A woman was weeping. Then Chino told us what we should do:

"All right! Okay! Everybody! The deadline is over. The stars are already out. They ain't coming. Understand? They ain't going to come. I want everybody down here. Everybody in the middle of the room. Quick! Quick! Move quick!"

"Mister," said Mosk, "I ain't electric."

With his arm Chino motioned to the members of the Steinway Quintet. We climbed down — A. Baer had now practically fainted — and stood with the others, in the center of the restaurant.

"Okay. Now, don't argue, don't think, just do it: you people take off your clothes."

Immediately Printzmettel went to the sad-eyed tall killer. "I am Greek. Greek! Bazouki! Metaxa! You must let me go!"

Jesús, with his free hand, ripped the patron's shirtfront, from top to bottom. Each button was gone. "Off! Shoes! The socks! Everything! Off!"

"Put your stuff in a pile. Pile it all up in the middle."

Printzmettel did this. We all did this. There were for some moments only the sounds that persons make when they are removing their clothes. Not then even weeping. Not even sighs. I, myself, felt embarrassment at the great amount of hair upon my shoulders, which showed so clearly under the twelve bulbs of the chandelier. Murmelstein, in his boxer shorts, was helping A. Baer take off his shirt.

"Is it you, Mister Murmelstein? *Lust mir iber mein bord.*"

Slowly there grew a mound of coats, trousers, and, shame to say, ladies' blouses, stockings of nylon, a feather boa. Shoes of all types stuck out everywhere. We were not at that time, however, entirely naked; before this could be demanded of us a shout went up, I believe from Margolies, who was standing nearest the window.

"Here they come! They are bringing the money! I can see them!"

"We are saved!" Everybody started to shout this out. "We are saved, hurrah!"

In an instant the taller of the two gangsters was at the window, rubbing away the mist from the glass. "Goldkorns! Goldkorns! *¡Ven acá!*"

I came to where I was called, and looked out. It was dark on Rivington Street. Light fell through the panes of the Steinway Restaurant window onto the snow. On Allen Street the lamps were already burning. From the other direction, still in the shadows, two figures approached. They were of the same height. Both wore brown trenchcoats, and, it seemed, brown-colored hats.

"*¡Sí, sí! Son ellos. Tienen todo el dinero.* The money. Ha! ha!"

As they came nearer the rectangle of light we could see that one of these men carried, upon his shoulder, a large sack of some kind, and the other man had a pail in each of his hands. They walked steadily toward us, lifting their feet high out of the inches of snow.

Chino shouted from the center of the room. "Tell them that's close enough, Goldkorn! Tell them to leave the money and go!"

But before I could respond the two men walked directly into the light and stopped in front of our window. They stood restlessly, shifting the weight of their bodies from one foot to the other. I crouched low in order to call to them through the panes of broken glass. In that position I looked up under the brims of their hats: I knew them at once from their faces. These were not the officers of the Hostage Squad. One was Sheftelowitz. The other was Pipe.

"Fools! *Idioten!*" I hissed these words. "What are you doing here?"

The two men simply stood there, swaying a bit from side to side. I cried out once more: "What is it you want?"

Sheftelowitz answered: "What else? Pee-pee."

"We been waiting a long time," said Pipe.

I put my hands to my mouth: "Run! Run for your lives!"

"Run! Ha! Ha! Run, you policemans!" Jesús waved his gun in the window.

Both Jews dropped their burdens. They looked at each other. Then they fled into the shadows on the left and the right. Chino, with no more beard on his face than on the previous evening, came quickly over.

"Where's the money? How much is it?"

We three looked out the window. Both pails had turned over and spilled their contents onto the snow. Fish: for the most part perch. The bag had split open. Feathers.

"Ay! Ay! Ain't dollars!"

"A mockery! An insult to us! Now everybody will die!"

One of these villains grasped the waistband of my shorts and pulled them, what awful tomfoolery, down to my knees. To my ankles. I was then a naked person.

"Get your clothes off! Yids, move your asses!"

Our antagonists then stepped into the crowd of Jews and began to rip from their bodies the last shreds of their clothes. Now there were plentiful screams, wailing, and exclamations. But the two men went about their work grimly, and pushed us, bare, trembling, and sick with sudden fear, toward the open staircase that led to the floor below. Then they stepped back ten, or perhaps fifteen, paces. All of us, musicians, waiters, patrons, were huddled together, as if on the lip of some common grave. Our bodies in the light of so many bulbs were extremely white. Ghosts of ourselves when clothed. Above the prayers, the groaning, the heart-wrenching cries, the voice of Doctor Fuchs — even without his herringbone suit an imposing man — was calm and clear:

"What is the cause of this fear of death? Let us think of it in a rational manner. Is it not in reality the childish fear of losing the penis? Of being cut off from this source of guilty pleasure? Notice how when we recognize the source of our anxiety it at once disappears. Now we feel truly joyful."

The alienist went on in this manner a moment longer, but in truth I no longer heard his words. For, as chance had arranged it, I found myself standing next to and in fact pressing against the body of Hildegard Stutchkoff. There was a wrist of mine against the small of her rounded back. She turned about. There were two breasts that depended. It was impossible not to feel how life stirred in my member; at the same instant I felt come over me a red wave of shame. The reason for this was not my sexual excitement, for how could one not respond to the proximity of such a sportive figure? No, it was just that at that very moment, for the first time in all these hours of terror, I happened to think of Clara, my wife.

Like a child in a classroom I raised my free hand. "Please! I must call on the telephone! My wife! She needs injections!"

Chino, who had previously offered me cognac to drink, now pointed his gun toward my head:

"Goldkorn, you gonna be first to die!"

I closed my eyes. I shut from my ears the sound of screaming. I prepared for what lay at the foot of the stairs.

However, there was no gunshot. Instead I heard Ellenbogen declare, "Look! Stutchkoff!"

I opened my eyes and turned toward the base of the door. At first I could make out nothing; then I saw, by the head of the corpse, a small pink blurr. The fluff of the flamingo had lifted off Stutchkoff's lips, and was rising slowly into the air.

"Ooooo!"

From the open mouth of the restaurateur there now issued a thin grey-colored shadow, a mist, a kind of a cloud — impossible to know what precisely to call it. Steam perhaps. Perhaps smoke. Everyone saw it slowly rising, more and more of it, growing taller, spreading outward, almost the size of a person.

"Ghost!" Chino exclaimed, although in a whisper.

"¡Un diablo!"

The two assassins were of course standing nearest the dead man; the sight of them was, even to my eyes, to the eyes of their enemies, pathetic to see. They had dropped their weapons and thrown their arms around each other. Their mouths were open, their eyes rolled about, and, strangest of all, their legs kept moving, in the manner of dream figures who wish to run but cannot. The cloud, now as large as the man had been himself, detached itself from Vivian Stutchkoff and floated toward the two terrified Puerto Ricans.

"Ah! Ah!" they cried, and disappeared inside the mist. Even their hats were gone. Then the cloud passed away: the men were the same, clinging each to the other, except that tears in sheets flowed from their eyes.

Ellenbogen, who had socks on, ran down the center of the restaurant turning all of the chairs upside down.

"The Maggid of Mezritch!" the waiter cried. "So his soul won't be tempted to stay!"

And in truth the cloud followed behind him, moving from table to table, like an eager proprietor. At the end of the room, it covered the zinc top of the bar, and obscured the rows of glasses and bottles. It rose to the first chandelier, then to the second. It enveloped the Bechstein. It touched all the walls. I was not able to resist the thought that it was in some fashion saying to the Steinway Restaurant farewell. Then it descended onto my head. And onto the heads of the others. When it lifted we were all weeping.

"You see?" said Margolies, as he wiped his eyes. "What did I tell you? It's just like Zev Wolf says!"

Mosk, to whom this was addressed, replied in a gasping voice, "Zev Wolf, my eye! It's what you call tear gas. Look there!" The Lithuanian pointed with a thin white arm to Stutchkoff, or rather to just behind Stutchkoff, where a second cloud was now materializing from under the crack in the door.

The Hispanics saw this as well. They let go of each other, and retrieved their guns.

"Pssst! This way! Follow me! Hee, hee, I have the key!" It was Murmelstein, beckoning us toward the rear of the room.

"Nobody move! Freeze!" The cruel youth shouted those words.

However, the gas had already grown thick in the air. It was difficult to see one another. We joined hands and, in this chain, moved slowly between the platform and the bar, toward the door to the kitchen. The second violinist had already gone through and was fumbling with the lock on the back exit. "I got it!" he cried. "Eureka!"

We all moved as fast as possible — Doctor Fuchs had A. Baer over his back — through the small kitchen to where the barred door was just swinging open. But before we went through a mysterious sound made us stop wherever we stood. It seemed to be everywhere about us, a kind of a hum, a drone, growing steadily louder. Then the floor under our feet began to shake, the stacked dishes and pans rattled, and the whole building trembled through its foundations. We looked back through the gloom of the Steinway Restaurant proper. Strange lights were descending in beams from the sky. The snow had risen from the ground and was swirling in the air. The noise was now like fists beating upon a rooftop.

"Ay! Ay! Angel of death!" the pair of doomed men were screaming. "*¡Espíritus malos!*"

"Ladies and gentlemen! Do not hesitate! Go quickly outside!" Salpeter was urging everyone through the open door. I, myself, the flautist of the Steinway Quintet, glanced one final time over my shoulder — the shafts of strange light, the thick clouds of gas, our tormentors crying out with their hands stretched high above them — and plunged with bare feet into the alley of snow.

VII

This is Leib Goldkorn. You do not want Goldkorn. You want
to know what happened next. Am I not able to convince you that
it is over? Finished? *Kaputt?* Listen: I never, from that moment
in the snow until this moment — and it is now nearly midnight,
Doctor Goloshes has been here already an hour, more than an
hour — set foot inside the Steinway Restaurant again. Not even
to retrieve my shoes, my clothing. These Hildegard Stutchkoff
sent some time later in the public mail. For such a warm day,
almost like spring, it has become a cold night. Wind blowing. We
possess a small electrical heater, and the electric current is still
being supplied; but it is plugged into the socket by Clara's bed.
What is he doing there? Why is he taking so long?

I cannot describe adequately our journey — slipping on ice
patches, feeling blindly the person before us, unable to hear our
own anguished cries — through that narrow alley. Worst was
the noise. It struck at one. It blew one's thoughts away. It was
like the dum-dum-dum of waves on the outside of a ship's metal
plates. Inside which you are sleeping. The shock of such sounds

on my American voyage made me fear my own mind was splitting. I have always thought of myself as a rational man. Once, in a cafe, I met L. Wittgenstein, and after we had spoken for a few moments he made a remark about the quickness of my brain. Not one of the violent, even bizarre actions in the twenty-four-hour period I have been describing caused me to doubt for a moment the nature of reality, or the stability of my mind. Everything could be explained. However, as our group of former hostages emerged from the passageway onto Rivington Street, I felt that the familiar world, one of cause and effect, of physical laws, had been left behind. It was like a new planet.

What we saw was that between us and the Steinway Restaurant the snow was actually rising. It was a whirlwind. At the top of this swirling storm, a black shape hung in the air. It neither rose nor descended, but simply remained, roaring, in defiance of gravity, of physics, of reason itself. From the belly of this form columns of light shot downward and played over the surfaces of the snow. In the tremendous thunder it was difficult to hear what people were saying; but Salpeter pointed toward the Steinway Restaurant door. This had swung open. Standing inside it was Vivian Stutchkoff. He appeared to be stuck. He backed up, into the light of the chandeliers, then came forward and once again caught in the doorframe. It was at this point, naturally, that my own sanity came into question. I was not able to suppress an inappropriate desire to laugh. *Dum-dum-dum* came the sound from the sky. The dead spaniel was, I noticed, only a few feet away. On the third attempt, by turning a few degrees sideways, Stutchkoff got through the door. He came then bobbing toward us. Our party retreated to the opposite curb. "Golem!" some person cried. Margolies and Ellenbogen were rocking in prayer. Still Stutchkoff came, enormous in size, rising and falling, skimming the snow, like a gas-filled balloon. I barked with laughter again.

From a spot nearby four figures, all clothed, in brown trenchcoats and hats, rushed forward toward the abandoned door of the Steinway Restaurant. Two local merchants. And the two members, no doubt, of the Hostage Squad. They all went inside. Stutchkoff, meanwhile, had glided to the center of Rivington Street. There he paused, bouncing about, turning left and right; then he fell face down into the snow. A tall and a short Puerto Rican stood in his place. It had been some kind of trick! Yes! The restaurateur had been their shield!

Some person was pulling my arm. Mosk, the Lithuanian waiter: "Whirlybird," he said.

Everything, for me, now fell into place. I had been guilty of an error in logic, and my confusion followed from that. You must remember that I had thought that the promises of the Hostage Squad, so contrary in nature, would in the course of things cancel each other out, that nothing at all would be done. False assumption. In truth both plans had been put simultaneously into action. The tear gas belonged to the adamant Officer Mike. What hovered above us was the rescue ship provided by Officer Tim. Indeed, I now saw that hanging from the bottom of this aircraft, nearly invisible in the snowdust around it, was a kind of ladder, perhaps made from rope. Chino had started to climb it, was in fact halfway to the top. Jesús was just getting on.

Then, from the direction of Eldridge Street, a man wearing clothes came running toward us. "Beverly! Beverly!" he cried. It was the gentleman companion of the lady in purple. He was staring wildly about him. "Has anyone seen Miss Bibelnieks?"

I, myself, pointed her out. She was standing alone, near to the curb. Her hands were clasped under her chin and she was peering into the center of the whirling storm, where Jesús had climbed to the top of the ladder. He paused there. His hat blew away. With one hand he held the ladder and with the other he waved. Then he disappeared inside the airship. The gentleman friend of the lady put his wrap over her bare, wet shoulders. She seemed not to notice, only stared, and moved her lips. "Don't hurt him, don't hurt him," she said.

Suddenly the black shape, with an even greater volume of sound, began to rise straight up in the air. I resisted the impulse, an unusually strong one, also to wave farewell. A light came on in the bottom of the aircraft, and winked on and off. In only a moment this was all that we could see. The sound soon faded completely. The air became clear. There was only the single, silent, red jewel in the sky; and then this vanished, too. We remained, not speaking. Not sobbing either. The yellow light poured from the Steinway Restaurant window and door; but it did not quite reach the street center, where V. V. Stutchkoff lay buried under a mountain of snow.

VIII

Goldkorn. Did you know there was a well-known composer named Korngold? An artist, like Steiner, for films? These are the tricks that life plays. I could not, that Wednesday, return directly home. The police officers insisted that we follow certain procedures, and afterwards there was a frostbite treatment in the emergency room. It was the middle of the night by the time I pulled myself up these four flights of stairs. My wife was, as I feared, on the floor, in a serious coma. Blood sugar too high. I gave her, as prescribed, injections of insulin; and when she regained consciousness she did not know it was Wednesday instead of Tuesday, that a whole day had gone. It was on this occasion that she remarked, "Am I living, or dying?" She is in a bad way, Clara. The day for her is the same as the night. What is the point of life under these conditions? And I must pay Goloshes, too! How? With what money? Let him obtain it from the government, since it is the government, with all its laws, which insists that such a creature, no spark in her, remain alive!

I shall tell you about the waiters of the Steinway Restaurant, which of course has been closed. Ellenbogen's wife has found part-time work, although Ellenbogen himself has not. Still, they manage to live on her salary alone. Margolies was for many weeks quite ill, with fever and a coating of phlegm. Inflammation. But I have recently learned that he has left the hospital and is living with his young son and his daughter-in-law. They say that Mosk has a small sum of money, in addition to a house of his own in Brooklyn. I believe this is true. Martinez I do not know about. I thought one month ago that I saw, on Broadway, Hildegard Stutchkoff, the cashieress. The same springy curls, and she had a handbag that swung by her side. I called out, but she did not hear me; before I could reach her she had gone into the express stop of the subway. It is possible that I saw somebody else. It might not have been she.

What of our tormentors? In China? Possibly. But it is more likely that the pilot of the airship simply maneuvered it to the roof of a nearby prison. In my opinion they are at this moment in jail.

I am sorry to announce the death of A. Baer. I saw this in the newspaper only one week after our adventure had been concluded. It was a complimentary obituary and contained an interesting description of his student days in Hannover and Paris, his Red Cross concerts, and of how his two little pieces, a sonata for pianoforte and violoncello, and a partita for violoncello alone, were once played by masters all over the world. Salpeter is in Florida. I have lost contact entirely with Murmelstein, as one does at times with younger people. He is in many respects a resourceful and original artist, wrongfully overlooked, and there of course remains the possibility he will yet find a place worthy of his talent. Tartakower. Tartakower has now a position with the celebrated Epstein Brothers Orchestra, and may be heard at weddings, Bar Mitzvahs, and special occasions, in addition to that organization's regular concerts. It is an amazing thing, really. Of course he is a nice man, a generous spirit, I rejoice he has obtained such prestigious work. But does he have the breath-control for that type of music? The truth is, when you own your own instrument that kind of question becomes merely academic. It is beside the point.

I hear noises now, footsteps, from my wife's room. Yes. Goloshes is coming soon. "Well, and how is she, Doctor?" That is what I shall say. I shall smile, too. This is my address: 134 West 80th Street. By Columbus Avenue. I would appreciate knowing of even the smallest position, on any type of musical instrument. Oboe. Cornet. English horn. No matter which. I have not in this account attempted to hide any shortcomings, but, on the contrary, to present myself as I am. You know that I drink sometimes schnapps, for example, and that I do not possess a religious temperament. Yet I am speaking truthfully when I tell you I feel myself to be now the same person who received the gift of a Rudall & Rose many years in the past; and like that young boy I am still filled with amazement that merely by blowing upon such an instrument, and moving one's fingers, a trained person may produce such melodious, such lyrical sounds. You are no doubt aware that with the flute the breath passes over the opening, and not into a mouthpiece, as with other woodwinds. Its music is, therefore, the sound of breathing, of life. It is the most ancient of instruments, and the most basic, too. A boy can make one with a knife and a hollow twig. This is what shepherds did, playing to sheep.

Lessons

I

In a dream that Errol was having he flew a little Cessna in the clear Chinese sky. Sunlight glistened on his wings, his struts, and the cockpit glass. He dropped through the clouds, which closed around him, suffocating him, squeezing him like a policeman's white glove; then they released him surprisingly low over enemy territory.

He took in the situation at a glance. Northward, on the horizon, was the Yalu River, largely hidden by the columns of dust that marked the limits of the Communist advance. Similar columns stretched away to the south: the Turks in disarray, Americans in headlong retreat. Immediately below he saw the stragglers of the fourth platoon emerge from the forest and head for the bank of the tributary. The northern shore was densely timbered, except for a wedge-shaped staging area that funneled down to a narrow pontoon bridge. There, hundreds of tree trunks lay blasted and frayed, like a field of trick cigars. Two stretcher-bearers picked their way across the stumps and slid down the shallow bluff to the water's edge. Across the river an armored

69

vehicle waited, its motor running. A line of jeeps, each pulling a piece of artillery, had already moved out. *Hurry, you mothas,* Errol thought. *Hurry!*

One more soldier trotted over the bridge. On the south bank he paused, turned, and waved his arms at the circling plane. It was the signal that the last American had crossed the river. Errol's job was to relay it. He swept over the field and waggled his wings. At once there was a flash of light, the Cessna was punched skyward, and a cloud of splinters rose to where it had been flying. In the river the bridge, cut in the middle, writhed like halves of a worm. Errol licked his moustache and checked his fuel. He figured they beat the Reds by twenty minutes.

Then a lost squadron tumbled into the clearing. Errol put the Cessna into a steep dive, directly at the abandoned figures, who were waving and yelling and holding up fists. He leveled out over them and banked to see. They were black! Every one of them! Twelve black brothers! Little lights blinked in the forest and zoomed up and shredded his rudder. Pit pat went the bullets as they struck the armor plate beneath his seat. He veered across the river, fighting for control. Again the points of light appeared in the foliage. The plane spun steadily down. The river turned, the clearing turned, and the forest. Errol told himself that people don't die in dreams, they wake up before hitting the ground.

But he didn't wake. The plane had disappeared. He was peering over the bluff of the river. Someone lay exposed in the clearing, a black man, and Errol feared that it was he, himself, who was dead.

"You don't watch out," Butler said, "they gonna take off your head."

Errol pressed closer to the protective embankment and focused the glasses on the green leaves of the trees. He saw the Chinese, like monkeys. An officer lay along a branch, hardly separable from it, talking into a telephone. In the crotch of two limbs a young soldier folded a handkerchief and put it between his cheek and the stock of his gun. Like a violin player. Errol lowered the binoculars to the stumps in the field. There was a soldier behind every one. He saw a man open his mouth, he heard him scream, *eeeeeee*, and then he ran into the open, right at them, and hurled a bomb overhand through the air. It fell short of the embankment and exploded harmlessly. But the Chinaman fell over, with his face in the dirt. "I laid out that dude," said Butler, blowing on his knuckles. "I got a sharpshooter medal."

Broom, a fat private with glasses, placed his forearm casually atop the bluff and fired three satisfying rounds into the body of the Chinese soldier.

Vernon pulled his T-shirt over his head. "Now we got a flag of surrender."

"A white flag," said Mullings, who had already stretched his shirt over his bayonet.

Pfc. Clark, the youngest man in the squadron, ripped off his combat jacket to get at his undershirt. The corporal ordered him to stop. "The sergeant is dead," Clark said. "Who are you, man, telling me to be a fool?"

"I got the authority here. Put on your clothes and face the enemy."

"What enemy, man? We been deserted! They blew up that bridge and left us to die!"

Errol, hearing this, felt as if he were once again falling. *I did it!* he wanted to cry. *It was me!*

A man named Putnam said, "We'll cover you until you're gone."

Vernon eased his rifle over the edge of the bluff; the wind billowed his improvised flag. On both sides the shooting stopped. Clark tossed his rifle to Errol, climbed up the side of the embankment, and held his shirt up over his head. Mullings joined him, waving his bayonet. Vernon paused on the lip of the rise. "Who else wants to go?" Nobody moved. Vernon, half-naked, shrugged.

The three men started forward, and in a moment they, and their flags, disappeared. It was perfectly quiet. Then from the line of standing trees a high-pitched voice said, "Good afternoon, friends! All tarbabies!" A hundred shots rang out at once. The squad ran to the cliff. Vernon and Mullings were down, crisscrossed upon each other. Clark fell in two pieces on top of the others. From the midst of the men someone heaved a deep sigh. A slight soldier, Sampson, dropped his rifle and fell backward from the embankment. He had been shot through the neck. A hole gaped there, like a second mouth. His breath rushed out of the gash, still sighing.

A gangling private, Holland, with a pointed jaw, held up his boot. "This is our doom," he said, and began to cry.

Another man, Loone was the name on his shirt, began unstrapping his boots as well. "Shit," he said, his own voice breaking, "I figured on more mercy than that." The two men walked quickly down to the river.

"Listen, now," the sharpshooter called to his comrades. "You got no play in water like that."

Loone went in to his ankles. "It ain't all that bad. It's surprising. I been in streams a lot colder'n this." Beyond him, Holland's head, glistening with tears, bobbed on the water. Then it went under. Loone swam out to the same spot and simply vanished. Broom half-whistled through his teeth.

"I like that. I like anything clean."

Something flew over the embankment and rolled off Sampson's chest into the group of five survivors. "Grenade!" Putnam shouted, just before it burst. Errol was knocked backward, toward the river, by the blast. The front of his jacket was covered with blood: not his own, he saw immediately, but the corporal's, who had been thrown halfway into the water and lay there now, bleeding into the current. A Chinese stood shrieking on top of the bank. Broom, uninjured, killed him with one shot. Putnam's foot had been splintered by the explosion. Butler took him by the belt and dragged him to the cliff, where he propped himself up on his sound leg and his elbow. Errol and Broom joined them. Three of the enemy lay completely exposed twenty-five yards away. A fourth sat upright, working the pin on a defective grenade. They took their time picking them off. Errol kept the man with the jammed grenade in his sights and the instant the pin came clear he shot him in the belly. The weapon went off in their midst.

"Man," said Butler, slapping his hand, "You squashed that!"

Broom looked up from the stock of his gun. His glasses were shattered.

"I'm blind as a bat and black as a cat, but, man, I adore this killing!"

"I'll devour them," Putnam yelled. "Give them to me, serve them up, I'll gobble them alive!"

"Hooray!" Errol heard himself scream. "Isn't this a great day!"

There was a muffled explosion deep in the woods, followed at once by another; then, in the air, they heard the sound of someone expertly shuffling cards.

"Mortars, mortars, mortars!" Broom howled, and the embankment lifted beneath Errol and then crumbled under his fingers. An instant later the entire cliff gave way, pitching him down. Again the double explosion, the sound of the riffled deck. Both shells fell behind them: the first wounded every man, the second dismembered Broom, whose single-armed torso flew against Errol and pinned him to the earth. *Grrrrrr*, went Putnam, faceless. Butler alone pumped shells into the enemy. There was a wild scream, and all the Chinese, those on the ground and those left in the trees, came into the open and ran forward. Dozens of grenades knocked crazily about, and Butler turned to Errol as if he were going to kiss him. "Brother!" he started to say as all the bombs went off. The shreds of his body fell across Errol's chest. A half-severed leg, Putnam's, knocked hard against his head. Sampson's corpse was thrown upward, spinning like a projectile, and landed beside him, with one cold arm on his belly.

Eyes sealed with gore, suffocated by the weight of his own kind, Errol saw something shine at him from the upper air. He blinked away the blood. It was an airplane, circling. He looked intently. The light winked off it, cheerfully. At that instant, from beneath those bodies, he realized that he was the pilot of that plane, was the plane itself, each gleaming wire, both shining wings, and that he was the cloud as well, the knuckles that squeezed him before, their whiteness, just as he was the blackness that crushed him now, each of his brothers, sergeant and sharpshooter, thin Sampson, poor Loone; and, too, he was the square of handkerchief folded under the Chinaman's chin, and the tree that he hid in, its branches, its leaves, as well as the rising dust and the river and both of its banks and especially the broken bridge between them, *everything,* he thought, as his ribs gave way and his body expired, *I'm everything:* and waking, the dawn in his windowpane, it was this he tried to remember, but in a matter of moments forgot.

Someone was banging on the pipes for steam. The puppy yipped on the floor below. Joy's nightgown rustled by the stove, and the heels of her slippers slapped the linoleum. Errol peered through his eyelashes. His breath came out like cigarette smoke. The banging increased. He thought of Mr. Williams, the super, in the basement, with dishes of liver and kidneys fanned out around him on the floor. He sat, hands on knees, in a straight-backed chair. *You're one of them militants. You want to burn down the world.* Cats prowled over the old man's legs. The pipes implored. Joy lit the gas on the stove, and the flame illuminated her breasts and her belly through the gown.

Errol's body ached as if he had been pummeled. He looked out the window, which was blank and grey. An avocado plant drooped on the sill. Joy put on a heavier, quilted robe, out of which her slender neck and close-cropped head stuck like a turtle's. When he first knew her she slept with long, almost Polynesian hair pulled back and fastened with ribbon. When they made love he always untied the bow and brought her hair forward, over one shoulder. They sat lotus-legged opposite each other. "My turn," she would say, undoing the buttons of his pajamas and pushing the material back. Her eyes widened and shone beneath her broad, smooth, unusually convex brow. "Oh," she cried, seeing the pattern of tightly curled hair on his chest, "a bird!" Now, with her elbow up, she was pouring coffee.

"Joy, come back here."

He held the blankets open to her. She walked across the room

— pigeon-toed to save her slippers — and stood, while he sat, at
the edge of the bed.

"Just *feel* how cold my hands are." Her fingers moved icily
across his cheek. He caught her hand in his own and blew on her
palm. Behind her, above the glowing burner, the panes of window glass broke into a sweat. "Now the other." He took the pink
palm and kissed it, put his cheek against it, kissed it again. He
uncurled his tongue and licked the sea-green veins at her wrist.
Then he drew her downward, until, once, the two of them would
have been enclosed in her tumbling hair. "What I like, Errol, is
you are so slick."

He took her entire forearm in his jaws, gentle as an Alsatian
with the pencil of a child's wrist. Imprisoned by the great square
head, she leaned into his uncombed hair. He put his hands beneath her robe and began to move them up the back of her
calves, behind her knees, and into the looser flesh of her thighs.
She stood on his feet and let a breast swing forward. He clamped
her buttocks, and touched finger to finger in the folds of her
crotch, which at once liquified. Awkwardly, like tumblers, they
fell onto the bed.

Without a word he mouthed her neck, rolled with her, came
out on top. He penetrated blindly, and got a breast in either
hand. She craned up to him and her tongue made it into his
throat. Slowly, deliberately, he began his first move; her face fell
away and her eyes rolled up, showing white. Tortured, she looked,
hair shorn away, left for dead. Immediately he came, and with-
ered on the sheets. He slid down to rest his head on her stomach.
Her knees opened and closed above him. Her breath hissed between her teeth. What was happening to him, he couldn't get a
leg up on his wife?

Errol pulled himself out of bed. "Why's it so dark in here? We
have to pinch pennies, pinch pennies, all our lives?" He strode
about the room turning on lights — the overhead, the lamp,
bathroom, kitchen, closet. Joy retrieved her robe, put on her
slippers, and went into the bathroom. It still wasn't bright enough.

He threw open the window: a startled pigeon lifted off the sill, wings flapping like — like what? The bird rose to the opposite roof and settled on an antenna. Like linen, he thought, like sheets and towels in a breeze, and he smiled remembering the clothesline his mother hung between two trees, the graveyard he always called it, full of billowing ghosts that clutched at him as he ran screaming by, *eeeeeeee*, until they caught him in a wet, white embrace. He poured himself a cup of coffee. He got into his pants. Joy came out of the bathroom.

"I'm going to need some money," she said, her head and arms disappearing into her dress. "For clothes." Clumsily, she did up her zipper. "How do you want your eggs?"

"Fried."

"You want bacon?"

"Yeah, bacon."

"Get your own juice from the icebox."

"Listen, Joy, I got my eye on you. I didn't feel anything in there. I didn't feel no rubber protection." The bacon was in the pan. Joy cracked in the eggs. The whites spread and snarled in the hot grease. "I don't want you trying to put a kid over on me!"

"That's funny, coming from you, Errol, you got so little spunk."

"I'm forty-four, man! Forty-four!"

Joy looked at him over her shoulder. He was handsome as ever, a square face, square jaw, a thin moustache, the laugh lines at his eyes. Long, soft, black white man's hair. He looked like that old movie star, Errol Flynn. Her heart hurt to see his broad chest covered with hair that was going grey. She wished she could kiss him again. She wished he would say, *Joy, come back here.* "So what?" she said.

"Forty-four, there ain't no more."

"What's that supposed to mean?"

"Do you know what the man is doing?" he exclaimed. "Do you know he is killing people in their beds? It's a whole new level of *appetite!* He's not satisfied to hound us and jail us and beat us to our knees. It's not enough we've got to be his economic slaves. We're coming to the finish, Joy, where they hunt you to your home and shoot you in your bed." He jumped back, as the toast burst black and smoking from the automatic machine. He watched his wife pluck it out and scrape it over the sink. It made him mad. "You're very placid, it seems to me. Is that how you walk around, so super-calm, the brothers shooting and nodding in the street? Is that what you do, pick your way around our people, our poor folk in their busted shoes, with *distaste?* Is that your attitude?"

"Here's your eggs," she replied. She set his plate down across from him on the round white Formica.

" 'Here's your eggs,' " he mocked. "Yass! You'll be a fine sight with those eggs in your hand when this room is full of pigs. You don't see what's coming. You think for a brother to die he's got to first stick his hand through Greenberg's, Goldberg's, Greenstein's window to get him a pair of nylon stockings. I tell you they are on their way up the stairs! It's all-out war!" It had grown still in the apartment building. No spaniel barking. No banging pipes. Freezing air blew through the rustling avocado onto the untouched food. "You ain't going to bring a black child into a world where a black man can't even sleep."

"You make me out a fool for believing in anything," Joy said, going to the closet for her coat.

"Hear me, Joy. You get yourself pregnant we going to cut it out!"

"No, Errol. I've been through it in my head. I'll leave you before I let that happen again."

"What are you talking about, man? Leave me?"

"I thought you wanted black children. I thought you said those abortions were the white devil's trick."

"I got to pour lead in my mouth! I got to unlearn what I used to know!"

Joy snapped her handbag shut. She came out of the closet. "Take care of the dishes, will you? I'm going to be late for my classes."

He did not hear her. "I won't be sleeping! There won't be no spike in my arm to make me dream. I'm wide awake, I'm stone cool. All right, you killers, blow down the door. Hurray! I'll say. Come in, America! Here's my great day."

"So long, Errol," she called from the door. He sprang after her.

"Where are you going? I'm talking to you."

"I got my children waiting on me."

"I'm trying to tell you something. I'm telling you that I can't go on restraining myself, that I can't help myself, I got to bring whitey down. You hear me, I got to cling in the subway, actually *cling* to the knobs of the candy machine or I'm gonna push some cracker in front of the train." He broke into a little shuffle and a smile, "Forty-four, there ain't no more."

Oh Jesus, Joy thought, do you think I don't know what you mean? Immediately he fell before her and clasped her legs. She let herself go a moment, swayed, while he pressed the side of his head against her belly. Then she pulled back with, what was the word? with *distaste*, and opened the door — "Joy! Joy!" she heard him cry, "I hate too much to live!" — and closed it, on the rumpled bed, the dishes crusted with egg, and the man still on his knees.

He made the bed and scraped the plates, washed and dressed. It took him an hour altogether, and by then he was late for work. There was no hurry, Billy would take his class, and he'd teach the lab in the afternoon. The kids preferred Billy anyway: "Me!" they cried, thrusting their arms in front of each other's faces, "Call on me!" *Dig it,* Raymond would say, forgetting in his excitement to take his hand out of the air, *the Ashanti are royal, they got the golden throne!* His arm was like a salute. Errol crossed to his desk — a horizontal door flush against the wall — and sat down. The tests he had given yesterday were neatly piled atop layers of graph paper, which were themselves pinned down by a trilobite fossil he had once chipped from the side of his uncle's well. It was a shiny, black, primitive thing.

He picked up the first test booklet — blank. The student had
not dared to sign his name. He flipped open the second and
squinted to make out the scrawl. "Aps is hair animul get food
from tree — no hair animul get food from ground." The name on
the front, beautifully written, with a flourish on the B and M, was
Beatrice Merrywether, a shy, silent girl who had just come up
from the South. The next booklet printed the question — "How
Do We Tell The Difference Between An Ape and A Man?" —
clearly enough at the top of the page, but underneath, on a blue
ruled sea of white, floundered the sole word "The." He picked up
his red marking pencil and pulled two tests from the center of the
pile. The first said that "Apes is not so smart, man is real smart,
but Crutis T. James, Jr. has got to be the smartest of them all!"
and the second consisted of a comical drawing of himself, easily
recognizable by the moustache, on his hands and knees, with a
question mark for a tail.

It was not a dumb class. He knew they did not like — or
believe — the material, and that they grimly, sullenly resisted it.
Yet when he had written the question on the board, they immediately fell silent and started to write. Facing them, pretending to
read, he watched the rhythms of the exam: the girls' black legs
swinging back and forth beneath their desks, white socks collapsed at their ankles, the rapid jiggle of a boy's knee, eyes cast
up to the ceiling or dipped behind fluttering lids to a neighbor's
paper — jealously guarded by a moat of arms; quick glances in
his direction, or at the clock; Alexander's hot breath in his ear
whispering about the bathroom; pencils slanting in formation to
the left; a red tongue stuck to a wet lip, the child's cheek almost
touching the paper; sunlight melting like butter over a shoulder,
an arm; a page ripped, crumpled, thrown, the desperate *whirrrrr*
of the sharpener, taxi horns in the street below, a sneeze, a giggle,
silence, a sigh. He was always touched that so many heads should
be bent for him.

He flipped through the remaining exams, looking for Kenny's
booklet, Kenny Kiss Ass, Kenny the Suck, a smart, bespectacled,
fat black boy who wore the same red tie to class each day and

always got everything right. Errol snorted at the sight of the cover: Kenneth Moulton, The Frederick Douglass School, January 15, 1970, Life Science, Instructor: Mister Washington.

There are many ways you can tell a man from the Ape. As Mr. Washington told us, the Ape is covered with hair and lives in trees and when he walks he is bent over. However, man has hair mostly only on his head, he lives on the ground and his means of locomotion is to stand up when he walks. Man has the Gift of Speech but no one has ever heard a monkey or an Ape talk, except for basic sounds. Man uses many tools and is known as the tool-making animal. Australopithecus, the first man, lived one million years ago. The Piltdown man was a hoax. In conclusion, the single most important way to tell a man from an Ape is by the size of the brain. This is what makes the former so intelligent. The brain of the average Negro man is only a little smaller than the average white man but three times as large as any kind of Ape!

Errol dropped the booklet. He felt sick. When he stressed black hairlessness, the everted lips — progressive, unsimian traits — the class looked blank. But when they stumbled across statistics on skull capacity they all nodded their heads. Hopeless to explain that intelligence had to do with complexity, not size, senseless to point to the Neanderthal with the biggest brain of all. They *knew*. Dumb niggers! They would not learn. Mindlessly Errol reached for another booklet and noticed it was signed Avery Talbot, the Young Knights: "Man is the only animal," it said inside, "that kills its own kind."

There was a rustling sound at the window. The pigeon had returned to the other side of the glass. It wore an iridescent collar around its grey neck and looked at him with a red eye. Quickly Errol dropped the stack of exams into the wastepaper basket, threw his books and notes in his briefcase. He reached for the trilobite and rubbed it a little for luck. It was a habit he'd had since he was a boy. He held it up to the electric light. What fierce pincers! What wicked spines! His fingers burned, as if they were in touch with the force that had made, and unmade, his one-inch arthropod. Four hundred million years ago the trilobite had been the dominant form of life. It spread through every sea, in tens of thousands of species, hundreds of genera, crawled right through Georgia, a world-beater. Find one now! Yass! Yass! Utterly extinct!

He slammed and locked the apartment door, slipped the fossil in his pocket, and took the stairs at a run. Halfway down he remembered he'd left the lights on, paused, then continued downward. But carefully now, holding the banister, edging onto the landing, staring fixedly at his feet. When he reached the ground floor he shielded his eyes and attempted to rush out of the building. Yet for all his efforts, he could not help seeing the sign that Williams, that Tom, had stuck above the door: a picture of the assassinated preacher, the words, *our King will never die.*

II

Billy taught in a dashiki of yellow, magenta, and brown, and always wore sandals, even in snow. He was darker than anyone in Errol's class, except for Cyril Forbes.

"You tell me, Cyril, how old you got to be to know you're a man." Cyril pushed the eraser off his pencil with his thumb. Billy raised his hands to his head, as if he could not believe it. "All right — anybody." He waited. "Now that proves my point. Here is a room of fifteen young black people, ten brothers and five sisters, not one of which can raise his hand, can raise his *head* — ashamed as you are you got to stare into your books or tie up your shoes — and say I am a black *man,* a black *woman.* No wonder the white man calls you boy. How long you going to stay a bunch of little pissers?"

Avery shot up from his chair. "I'm a Young Knight, man."

"And what's the meaning of that?"

"That I been through a lot. I proved I ain't nobody's boy."

"I'm looking, I can't see no proof from here."

"I got me a piece — a piece is all the proof you need."

"How many here agree with that?"

Raymond's hand went up. Billy called on him and he rolled up his sleeve. "Look here," he exclaimed, "I got this bad tattoo!"

Now several hands were waving. Billy nodded toward Viola, who immediately lowered her arm. He shushed the others so she could speak. "I was going to say it might have something to do with sexual maturity."

"All right!"

"Right on!"

"Viola, you're a boss woman!"

"You know it!" Crutis cried. "When I got my alpaca vest, when I'm real fly, the chicks know who's a man and who ain't!"

"I got to laugh at you, Crutis. You ever get *out* of them threads, you'll find what's a man."

Felix looked up from his picture book, snorting.

"What I meant," Viola went on, "was that when I started to bleed I felt I was a woman for sure."

"Oooooh," Lelia sighed. "Lucky!"

"That Viola is mature," Gertrude said.

"I had a babies once," Beatrice murmured. "I had him before I came up North."

"You *got* to be old to do that," Arthur declared.

"It don't take heart to make a baby. Can you kill a dude, that's the thing." Avery remained standing, glancing toward the front of the room. Billy sat on his desk, arms folded, hands thrust up the sleeves of his robe.

"But I feel dumb," Beatrice said.

"My brother was a victim of tragedy," Cyril said. "He jumped off the building roof and knocked out his life. The women in all the apartments stuck out their heads and yelled *don't do it Roger boy* and I stuck out my head and yelled too, not to do it, but I wished he would, because, because the sun was kind of on his shoulder, and he did, he went right by me with his white teeth and his arms back like a bird. He went smooth, too, until he hit the far wall, and after that he fell crazy. So I say you can be ten years old, like he was, and be a man.'

Kenny raised his hand. "The Jewish people have a ceremony. When they're thirteen." Everybody groaned. Kenny stopped.

After a while Alexander, the youngest student, said dreamily, "When my father goes to pick me up he calls me *little man*."

Billy began to lecture. "I listened to what you had to say and it was like what I thought it would be. You are lost. You are so lost you can't be found. You think if you take off some ofay pretzel lady for one dollar and thirty-five cents, uh-huh, *one thirty-five*, that makes you big. Or if you wipe a cat out it makes you someone in his place. And what's the rest of this jive? You made it with some chick, huh? You hit some spike in your veins. What you got, Raymond, some half-ass tattoo? *Mother*, maybe, or a *heart*? Or your period comes or you have a child — all you left out was a stack of green, you *said* fine threads. Hey, you kids are messed up, you know, turned around bad. The word is brainwashed. I mean your heads have been washed, ironed, and set out to dry." He paced silently in front of them, then whirled about. "I like that Roger, Roger's my man, oh yes I think Roger had a clue. At least he was hip you got to check out the ancestors."

"But he split his head," Cyril said.

"You got to split your head. You got to die."

"He fell right by me. He never said a word. He never rapped to no ancestor."

"What's a ancestor?" Russell asked.

"It's like your father's father," Viola replied.

"It's *all* your fathers," said Maurice.

"I ain't got no father," Arthur declared.

"You still got ancestors," Viola said, then turned, with the others, toward the echo of the ivory spheres that Billy had tied to his ankle; *tack tack, tack-tack-tack,* it made the sound of bone striking bone.

"This rattle is worn by a *nganga,* a holy man, a shaman, in the African Congo. Groove to the beat." Imperceptibly, Billy moved his foot and the rattle responded, *tack-tack, tack-tack,* as if it were being violently shaken. "Evil spirits can't stand that noise; it drives demons wild." He moved about the front of the room, causing the rattle to whirr.

"I think Roger, my man, was flying because his ancestor was a bird. That's right! Only he didn't know how to find him. He was looking but he failed. And you are going to fail too! You don't know that's the first thing to do! Dig it, now, 'cause I'm going to teach you. You need a *nganga!*" He held perfectly still. The students didn't breathe. Far off, in some river, a ship sounded its horn. He began to pace again.

"The priest is the only one who can protect the boys during the initiation. They come up to him, in a group you understand, and he says, are you ready for the *nkumbi?* Have you provided for the voyage? Then he just turns his back on them and walks away; and the boys follow — out of the village, off the trails, into the forest. Their mommas wail, man! They cry for days! No, don't take my Raymond! Leave my Felix here! He is too young, too young! But they better cut their nails and cut their hair, on account of their sons are gone, gone to the *nkumbi,* to the ceremony, which is nothing to do with punks and Young Knights.

"In the forest the boys get twigs and leaves and make mats. They lie down on them, on their backs, with their hands by their sides, in the burial position, because they will never get up anymore. And weeks go by, and they don't move, not when snakes hang close by their faces and ants got used to using their stomachs for trails, or even when an animal comes curious to push them with his nose. Cool! But the *nganga* is there, see, with his fire and his songs, and he squeezes berries across their lips; and they get weaker, all the time weaker, until their bones start to show through like the ribs of an ark. That's when the priest walks between the boys and wounds each one with a knife. They bleed, and they go on bleeding, and the priest don't do a thing, because now the trip is ready, the voyage is here — they're going to sail to their ancestors, yeah! In a ship of their bones, on a sea of their own red blood! It's a dangerous journey, winds howl, demons and spirits try to scratch you and snatch up your soul. Turn around," he ordered. "Face the wall!" Instantly the class obeyed.

Cyril and Gertrude were visibly trembling. Lelia's mouth was open wide. Billy took a bull-roarer from an army duffel bag that lay on the floor. It was an oblong wooden slat, highly carved, attached to a leather thong. He whirled it over his head. Inez screamed and put her hands to her ears. Kenny hunched his shoulders and rested his head on his knees. Billy shouted above the roar. "Sail on! Sail on! Don't stop! Stop now and you won't return!"

"Stop! Stop!" Crutis yelled, as Beatrice slipped off her chair to her knees. Kenny had rolled into a ball, moaning. Billy let the instrument drop and the sound died away. In the silence he took a necklace of fierce-looking teeth from the bag, and then a leopard costume, the pelt, the claws, the gaping mouth, and put it on.

"Come on. Don't be afraid. You're in the land of the ancestors. You can look now. See? The priest is gone, the Leopard Man is here, spirit of the fathers. Sit up, Kenny. Smile now, Lelia. It's pleasant to talk to the Leopard. It's real sweet. It's fine. He tells you all the secrets of the tribe, that's right, where to hunt for the rumbling bear, the 'possum and the porcupine, and where the streams run clear. How to temper the stave of a bow, the steps of the sacred dance. He tells you who makes thunder and how the world began. There's nothing he don't know, from the way to paint a warrior's face to the words of a stone-dead curse. He's the all-time Mr. Bad! Fish leap for him, the clouds drop rain! And now you're in on all of that! *Tell me more,* you want to cry, but you're too weak, weak as a baby, and you can't do nothing but listen, yeah, and hold your breath 'cause right now, look! Mister Leopard's smiling and that means, yes! so fine! he's gonna tell you your sweet new name! Then he's gone, see —" Billy plucked off the leopard skin and dropped it casually behind him into the bag. "So you sail back to where you were in the forest and the *nganga,* he's all business, he just turns his back and walks straight home. The women rush up to the strangers: Who are you? What have you done with — Raymond, Arthur, Felix, Maurice? No answer. Stand aside! 'Cause Raymond, yeah, and

Arthur, Felix, and Maurice are lying dead in the forest, under the thickest trees, and proud in their place are four black men!" Billy finished with his fist in the air. Then he wheeled about and marched toward the door, where — over the heads of the spellbound children — he saw Errol, his eyes wild, grinding his teeth.

The school was in an old brownstone on 109th Street, east of Columbus. The building had been abandoned, taken over by the City, and then leased to the Frederick Douglass School under the terms of a grant that had not been renewed. No one came round to board up the windows, but Joy was soon forced to return to her third grade class in Spanish Harlem, and within a year only Errol and Billy were left, often on their knees, repairing the stairs, whitewashing the walls. The school withdrew to the third floor. The first reverted to the junkies, who swarmed into the building in the early evening and who cooked their heroin over candles and matches in twisted spoons. An old white lady lived on the second floor and demanded each day to be helped to her room. They had hoped to make a gymnasium of the basement, and got as far as three tin lockers and a basketball hoop before the funds ran out. No one knew what was on the fourth floor; the staircase was impossibly jammed.

Down the flights of the building Errol ran, pursued by Billy's cry — "Man, I didn't mean to blow you up," and the sound of the bull-roarer, simple wood and string, *eeeee,* a thousand memories — both of which echoed in the stairwell until he shut the cellar door. He cupped his hands beneath the wall tap and splashed the icy water onto his head. Damn that Billy! Man used to deal in the street with a black scarf on his conk, and alligator shoes. Now he was into Africa. Going to overthrow the power structure with bows and arrows! Blast the pig with warpaint and a deadly curse! Mumbo jumbo!

He shook off the water like a Labrador. The basement was a large empty room lit by a single bulb that hurt his eyes. The basketball net hung like a chrysalis. He was glad they'd run out of money. Yass! Glad about that Vietnam war. He didn't give a damn about the Frederick Douglass School as long as each day they trained black men to kill. Crush a man's spine with the flat of your hand. Twist a bayonet. The black army was coming home! With an unthinking movement he boxed out the electric light and plunged the room into semidarkness. Immediately he recalled what he had prepared to say to the class, "Children, all life began in the sea," but he kept seeing Billy whirling the oblong slat, making the terrible sound.

He sat down in the center of the concrete floor and stared up at the dim light which passed through the transoms. Errol thought of his father. There was always dry spittle in the corners of his mouth. Once, when he was playing his game, running among his momma's linens, dodging the wet slap of the sheets, he had plunged all of a sudden into the grip of the old man's arms. His father clasped both his wrists in one hand. With the other he forced a piece of wood, it was a stiff wooden clothespin, over his nose. Errol squirmed, shrieked, afraid he would smother. His father's gold spectacles glittered. His jaw stuck out. *Hold still, boy! We got to pinch your nose to make you look white!*

They didn't find Errol that night. He heard them calling, whistling for him as though he were a dog. But he was halfway down his uncle's well, clinging to the familiar holds among shoots and vines, the sandstone and shale. When they got closer, when he heard the lanterns swinging on their handles, he dropped even lower, past the place where he had chipped away the hidden trilobite, deeper than he had ever gone before. If he could have seen, if the sun had been, as it sometimes was, directly overhead, he might have detected the flattened leaves of conifers and ferns, the impression of the dragonfly and the dragonfly's wing, and lower still, in the Devonian soil, the ammonites in spirals, mussel, clam, and scallop shells, starfish and pink coral, and at the very bottom, in the Georgia of a billion years ago, the vaselike shapes of sponge. But he plunged down blindly, knowing nothing, and when he reached the water he thrust his head beneath it. His face was burning with shame.

Someone was vomiting into the iron sink.

"Who's there?" he demanded.

"Mister Washington!" Kenny exclaimed, looking up. His red tie was twisted. "Excuse me," he gasped and leaned again over the edge of the sink. He retched miserably, his whole body going up on tiptoe and shaking repeatedly. When at last he faced about, tears ran from his eyes, over his lips.

"You done?" Errol asked.

Kenny nodded. Errol took out a handkerchief and — too roughly, he knew — wiped his student's mouth. He let some water run in the sink. "I didn't know you were here, Mister Washington. I wouldn't have if I would have known. Really, I'm sorry."

"What for? For being sick? When you're sick, go home, don't apologize."

"I don't think I *was* sick, I mean, medically." He felt his own forehead. "I was scared."

"Scared of what?"

"There was a noise, a ceremony."

"It's wood, man, and Billy moved it around on a string."

"Oh, I *thought* it was something like that. Boy! The whole thing was phoney, wasn't it? I don't believe in the supernatural anyway. I'm going to be a paleontologist."

"You're going to be *what?*"

Kenny twisted his hands. "That was a great exam you gave. I really liked it. Did you read them yet? I hope I didn't leave anything out."

"I read them."

"What did I get?" the boy blurted.

"You got a F, understand? F for failure, F for fear. You said the black man was dumber than the white man. You're dumb, man, you don't know better than that."

"I didn't mean it!" Kenny shouted. "It was only a comparison!" He retreated across the basement and crouched in a corner, as far from Errol as he could get. Errol took a step toward him. "Don't! I'll tell you everything I know. The *Ichthyosaurus* is very interesting. It was a reptile that lived entirely in the sea. The

Tyrannosaurus was ferocious and ate meat. The *Brontosaurus* was the largest land animal that ever lived. The *Stegosaurus* had another brain in the back to work the tail."

From five feet away Errol smelled the boy's fear. He held his fist in front of the student. "I'm not going to hit you. I'm giving you something."

"I deserve an A," Kenny said.

Errol thrust out his hand. "Here," he said. "Take it. It's a real fossil. It belongs to you." From his crouching position, tentatively, the boy reached out his hand and took the stone. He looked at it and put it in his pocket. Then he seized Errol's wrist and buried his face in the palm. A moment went by before he looked up.

"You're my idol," he said.

The Lions and Tigers tramped on the stairs. "Yay-y-y-y-y!" they screamed. "Kill them! Smash them! Eat them alive!"

The boys ran downtown, in their helmets and pads. "On the double," Errol yelled. "There's not much time."

"Yay-y-y-y!"

They timed the light at Columbus so that everyone got across. One hundred and ninth ran uphill as far as Amsterdam where, not stopping, they ducked the traffic coming from their left and continued west, seeing nothing of the streets or walls, the shops and signs that flashed and buzzed, aware only that the white men and white women, into whose territory they jogged, scattered before them without a word. One after the other they began to throw out their arms as they ran, then brought their hands to their chests and threw out their arms again. It cleared a path. Errol hurled fists, fiercely, and muttered through clenched teeth, as if through the regular motion and repeated words he could fling from him and keep at bay those sudden memories — clothespin, clothesline, father, well — and that recent tide of dreams which rose together, day and night, and represented that part of him, now despised, which meant to cling to life.

The field in Riverside Park was frozen hard. Errol, the captain

of the Lions, drew crisscrossed arrows in a patch of snow. Billy
lined up the Tigers, Felix, Maurice, Cyril, Alexander, little Arthur, and kicked off the ball himself. Avery took it and gave it to
Crutis, who at once shot ahead — "a dazzling burst of speed!" he
cried — into the open field.

"Go, baby! Breeze!"

"First play! All the way!"

"Tear 'em up! Tear 'em to pieces!"

The hand-off fooled everyone. Crutis outran the Tiger de-
fenders. He slipped beyond Cyril's clumsy grasp. He was screaming: "A streak of lightning! A hundred pounds of dynamite!
What an amazing display!" As he neared the two bare trees that
marked the enemy goal he slowed up and began to do a little
Indian dance. It was a mistake. Maurice came up from nowhere
and knocked him off his feet.

The Lions made a circle about their man; they held out their
palms.

"Hit me, man!"

"Yeah, Crutis! Lay it on!"

Wearily the runner gave them his skin.

That promising start, just five yards from the end zone, was as
close as the Lions could get to the goal. The Tigers dug in along a
line of defense. Errol stood with his back to them and diagramed
a play on his chest. At center the blood rushed to Kenny's head
and the world turned upside down between his legs. What was the
signal? He forgot!

"Sssss," hissed Felix, practically into Kenny's ear. "Hike that
ball, you fat suck. Come on, jive mothafucka, snap the damn
ball!"

"One, one, two-hup, two-hup," Avery started the count. Sweat
ran into Kenny's eyes. He smelled Felix's sweet pomade.

"You so smart, punk, I'm gonna lay you out!"

"Three-hup! *Three*, hup-hup-hup!" That was the signal, *on
three*, he remembered, but trees grew out of the quarterback's
shoulders and buildings grew out of the trees. "Wake up, nigger!"
Avery yelled, and leaped frantically as the football sailed six feet

over his head. Kenny fell down and was hit on the side of his head. Up the field he saw the ball bounce crazily, like a dog on a scent, and thought he would faint.

"Fumble!" everyone cried, and ran over him.

"Loose ball!"

"Out of my way!"

Felix was on the bottom of the pile, grinning, blood smeared over his teeth. He had the ball.

"Unnecessary roughness," Kenny cried.

Billy walked up to Errol. "Dig it," he said. "A reversal of fortune."

But the Tigers could not score, either. They moved the ball halfway up the field, and then had to kick. The game settled down. It was a defensive battle. Billy and Errol threw themselves at each other on the line. Felix hissed threats into Kenny's ear. Maurice kept bumping Crutis on pass plays, and the two boys began to knock each other down. Now and then a player took himself out and lay exhausted on the sidelines. Cyril bent down with painful cramps. Suddenly, after hours, Arthur had the ball and followed his blocking for a twenty-yard gain. On the next play, a quick jump pass to Felix over the middle, the Tigers scored. When the Lions got the ball back there were only seconds left in the game.

"Time out!" Avery called.

Someone called from the other side: "Hey, you going down to defeat, man!"

Errol walked off the field and squatted by a mound of snow. The wind had died out beneath the low, yellow sky. Thousands of cars crept along the West Side Highway, shimmering in their own exhaust. He was choking. It hurt his chest to breathe. Then the Lions were around him, bent over, their hands on their knees. He drew a play for them on the ice; he rubbed out the enemy players. As he spoke he glanced up at the members of his team: Raymond, flat face, flat nose, the strange sleepy curve of his eyes; Crutis, who always smiled, smiling even wider at the prospect of defeat; Avery, concentrating, with wrinkles on his old-looking face; skinny Russell, raccoon-eyed, gashes of white scalp showing through his close-cut hair; Kenny, half-blind without his glasses, an egg-sized lump above his ear. All at once they dazzled him; his heart broke at the thought of their possibilities. He carved an arrow across the goal. "You can forget that jive you heard this morning," he said. "Because right this minute you better be men."

"Last chance," said Raymond. "We got to do or we got to die."

The Lions broke from their huddle and lined up over the ball. Avery extended his arms. "Ready! Set! Two, hup-hup!" The play went like clockwork. Kenny snapped the ball and, snarling, growling, hurled himself at Felix's vulnerable knees. The Puerto Rican went down with a cry of pain. Avery took the ball and gave it to Crutis, who hid it behind his leg. The defensive line, missing the hand-off, ran after the quarterback: much too late they realized their mistake. They turned about, helpless, abashed, and watched Crutis, who stood still as a statue holding the ball.

I got all the time in the world, Crutis told himself, and watched calmly as, far down the field, Errol bore down on Billy, faked to the middle, and then whipped past him on the outside and broke into the clear. Crutis led his captain fifteen yards and released the ball. Errol saw it spinning over all their heads and ran flat out, lungs flaming, to get beneath it. On the goal line he stretched out the full length of his frame; at that moment, off balance and vulnerable, something struck him with terrific force from the side and the ball bounced off his fingertips. He tried to recover it but again he was hit and this time his antagonist leaped on his body, grappling him about the knees, scratching, kicking, clawing upward, and the ball dropped to the ground. Errol tried to shake himself free but the little black thing clung like a monkey and began to pummel him and bite. The two of them went over together and through the arms Errol flung up to protect his head he saw the boy, Alexander, his face contorted with hate and rage, tears spurting from his eyes, tiny Alexander, who had a penny-colored head of hair and always whispered *I got to pee* through a cupped hand at his ear. Alexander now sat on his chest — "You said I came from an Ape!" he cried — and beat at him with fists of steel.

III

Errol walked directly back to the school. In the cellar he un-chained his locker door and changed back into coat and tie. He took the books out of his briefcase and replaced them with a first aid kit and the sawed-off stock of an M1 Garand. The rest of the rifle was wrapped in towels at the back of the locker. He un-wound the barrel and wiped it down. He put on his topcoat and slipped the rifle beneath it, holding it like a splint against his leg. The briefcase he tucked between his arm and body. Awkwardly he pulled himself up the cellar steps to the first floor, and from there went into the street.

The Columbus Avenue bus dropped him at 94th Street and he walked toward Broadway on his own, a quarter of an hour a block. The old hotel on the corner, plain brown brick and stone, except for a cornice of Ionian scrolls, dominated the immediate neighborhood. Errol managed to pull open the heavy glass door and limp into the lobby. Old ladies sat among green plants. He caught himself in many mirrors.

Calvin, his back turned, flicked letters into pigeonholes.

95

"I want a room, 1210, the same room I had before."

Calvin turned around, wide-eyed. He had sideburns down to his jaw. "So soon?" he whispered. "Just like that?"

"Now."

"It's not ready. I didn't know. You didn't put out no line."

Errol shoved his briefcase onto the counter. His arm was numb, his hip rubbed raw, and his face, he knew, was bruised. "All right. What about the room underneath, what is it?" 1110, 1010, any of those?"

"They're *taken*, man. People live in those rooms all year round. Right down the line."

"You eat *shit*, Calvin, man! Give me a key to any room high up facing Broadway."

"The shack is full, brother! It's the truth!"

"What is it you want, Mister?" A small, elderly white man came up behind Calvin and touched him on the shoulder. The clerk backed away and returned to the mailboxes. Errol looked down at the man, bald, bespectacled, wearing an open-necked shirt over humped shoulders. A rubber-lipped Jew.

"I want a room, a bright, sunny room, you understand, up high."

"We don't have such a room. Maybe Monday."

"What you got now?"

"Only in the back. On the third floor a double. A single on the eighth, but not nice, dark, without sunshine."

"I'll take it."

"Thirty-five dollars for the week, you got to share the bath." Left-handed, Errol plucked two twenties from his wallet and slid them on the counter. "Number 858," said the man. "Sign here."

Errol leaned carefully against the desk and pulled his hand from his pocket. His fingers were cramped from the strain of the gun. The old man looked up at him. He forced his hand around the pen and started to write his own name — then stopped himself in time. His head spun. The pen began to slip. Behind the staring Jew, Calvin reached up, tapped a letter in the topmost box, and turned his hand into a fist. *Vernon Butler,* Errol wrote, not knowing where he had got such a name.

Room 858 was narrow, dark, and dry as a desert. The only furnishings were a bed, a dresser, a chair. Feeble lines of light squeezed through the slats of the venetian blinds. A painting of sailboats hung on the wall. Errol locked the door behind him, pulled down his pants, and let the gun fall sideways onto the bed. The mechanism had rubbed his flesh raw. He buckled his trousers and cracked the window blinds; they opened onto an unrelieved brick wall. The briefcase had fallen on the carpet; he picked it up and emptied it on the bed. The first aid kit contained a set of wing bolts and clamps, a telescopic sight, and a dozen clips of .30-caliber ammunition, eight cartridges to a clip — a minute's worth, going good — which he arranged into two even rows on the pale pink spread. He strode about the room, turning off the hissing radiator, throwing the bolt on the bathroom door, switching on the overhead light. He ran a bowl of lukewarm water and plunged his arm into it, up to the elbow. His skin tingled, his hand relaxed. He continued to soak until the blood ran in his fingers, quick, steady, a beat and a half a second.

It took only a moment to reassemble the gun, load it, and adjust the sight. He wrapped it in his topcoat as best he could, leaned it by the door, and filled his pockets with the extra clips. Then he sat on the bed, his head in his hands, listening to the last of the water drain from the sink, the hiss of the radiator, the muffled sounds from the street. He took, finally, a pen and a fresh sheet of paper and spread it on his knees. It was Joy he wanted to write to. He tried to think of her as she was that moment, as he had sometimes seen her, through the window of her classroom, obscured by purple animals and backwards flowers, the white chalk snapping in her hand. The thought that he would not see her again made him moan aloud. *Forgive me,* he wished to say, but wrote only the name of his wife, over and over, and then crossed even these words from the page.

Across the room twin sailboats heeled toward the surface of

the sea. In one quick motion Errol leaped from the bed and hurled the painting to the floor. A nail stuck out of the wall. He returned to the bed and rummaged through the papers that had spilled from the briefcase. The chart he wanted was on the bottom of the pile. *Early Man,* it was called, supplied by *Life* and *Time.* It unfolded into a long, narrow, battered strip, with a multicolored time scale across the top. He rammed it over the nail at one and a half million years, the age of *Australopithecus,* drawn below in profile, brutish skull and jutting jaw, hair-covered, a club in his huge hand: the first to stand erect, the inventor of the tool. There were fifteen specimens in all, each walking behind the other, left to right, right foot forward to cover the monkey genitals. And as they marched, from the little *Pliopithecus,* who danced with limp-wristed arms in the air, a gibbon, a fairy, through twenty-five million years to the end of the line, Rhodesian, Neanderthal, Cro-Magnon men, the backs straightened, height increased, hair fell away and the great toe gradually ceased to diverge. Stones and clubs showed up in their hands as the jaw began to recede and the ridge of bone over the eyes disappeared. The Modern Man strode confidently off the page, straight-backed, smooth-skinned, toward the future. He seemed to shine in highlights. Errol left him on the wall when he abandoned the room, a red circle around his classical head, red crosshairs meeting behind his eyes.

The hallway was deserted, the light gone out behind the exit sign. Errol took the five flights of steps in leaps of two and three. A blow from his rifle shattered the lock at the top. The door opened. He sprang onto the rooftop. Keeping low, Errol trotted to the northwest corner of the roof and looked over. Broadway was wide open below, the winter trees shriveled, providing no cover. He picked out the areas of fire: the green-roofed comfort station, completely isolated between opposing lines of traffic; the subway stop south of 96th Street, into which, out of which, faces descended, the backs of heads emerged; the jumble of shops and stores on the far side of Broadway, before whose lettering and glass the people passed, shadowless, downcast, exposed.

In the center of the roof, toward the back, two huge water tanks rested side by side on a steel trestle. Errol crouched lower and half-ran, half-crawled until he was beneath them, staring up at the hooped and banded wood that soared a hundred feet in the air. He circled the structure twice before he found the iron ladder bolted to one of the girders. At once he climbed the rungs and squirmed down the length of the steel support until he was directly beneath the immense tower. In the twenty inches that separated the bottom of the tank from its supports, he lay, invisible. Suddenly his heart shook him. He gasped at the stagnant air, overcome by a terrible thirst. The column of water hung above him in countless fathoms. He turned on his back and raised his mouth to the icicles and moss.

The edge of the roof cut off the street opposite the hotel, forcing him to aim uptown, at longer range. He piled the ammunition beside him, fitted the stock of the gun to his shoulder and cheek, and closed one eye. Foreshortened taxis flashed by a lumbering bus. Flattened figures disappeared into perspectiveless walls. The whole undulated in vapors and gas, blinked, blurred, trembled. He steadied his arms and focused on the streaming signs: *Riverside Theater, Burton Taylor, Lester's Hair Stylist, Forward Discount Clothing, No Parking No Parking No Parking, The Eat Shoppe Bus Stop Ping Pong Telephone, Paragon Fuel,* two old ladies talking, one, in a collar of fur, wrinkled her face and put her hand to her chest as if she felt the bullet he put through her heart. *Thom McAn, Mid-City Drugs, Food Stop n' Save N.Y. Casino, Broadway Self Service Dept. Store No Parking Adler Shoes Wergenburg Massagic,* a short man in a leather jacket bit a cigar as he lifted boxes from a double-parked truck to the sidewalk. Errol shot him through the crown of his head. *Europa Coffee Shop Peter Pan Cleaners Joyeria Payrite Jewelers Cigars Symphony Wines & Liquors SymphonySal'sPizzaNellieshoplingerie,* a couple walked arm in arm behind a bulldog on a leash; he pumped the dude twice and dropped the girl with a shot and the dog ran in a circle, wrapping them up, papers swirled on the windless street, a mist of traffic, a shoeshine stand, the newsdealer's tent hard against the subway: he shot a man through the neck descending and riddled the back of a cop going up, fired twice into a group of schoolgirls, aimed for the head of a bearded cat, missed, watched the shoestore plate glass split and crash. He got a motherfucker through the belly. Pots and pans through the unfocused branch of a tree, dancing musical notes in ballroom yellow lights, a blue diamond with a figurative sparkle in bright blue lines, the back of the bootblack, bent over a middle-aged cracker getting a shine. He blew his face off for him, and raked the intersection, attacking the cars like people, shooting for windshields, tires, gas tanks, hoping for flames.

On the far side of 96th the movie theater made a blank white wall, down which a metal staircase ran in graduated levels. Three boys, Jew kids in caps, threw a rubber ball against it and caught the rebound in the street. They ran awkwardly, jumping out of range and focus, then padding up between the crosshairs with goofy smiles. He fired at opportunity, a soft, pale face, a flabby arm, a sneakered foot, to bring them down. One boy, hit in the hip, struggled around the corner past manikins and wigs and fell before the poster of great stars embracing. Errol swept his sight back and forth over the scene of slaughter. He spotted an old man fumbling with the comfort station door and killed him. Another man, trapped in the telephone booth, was shivered by exploding glass. Fifteen seconds had elapsed. It was finished.

Slowly Errol swung the rifle down the block, through the intersection, past the subway stop, over the tarpaulin of the newsstand. The shoeshine boy was a man of sixty, in a herringbone coat. Deliberately, he put down his brush and rag and looked over his shoulder toward the distant hotel. His face was black, black even as Cyril's, with sunken cheeks and a flattened nose. Why was he looking up here? Why did he furrow his brow? Errol curled his finger on the trigger and chose a spot on his throat. A bus drove up between them, bearing civic messages. *That's a brother!* Errol told himself. *A brother!* But when the bus pulled away, the gun, for the first time, went off and the recoil struck his face like a fist. A hundred pigeons rose into the air. The shot went wild. No one bothered to look up. Errol hung from the trestle and dropped to the tar. He picked out the shoeshine man with his own eyes, a small busy figure on the avenue, a dot, no more, among the many dying.

Beatrice sat on her desk and tried to remember the event that made her a Queen. She pulled on her lower lip, exposing a gold tooth that Inez thought very womanly.

"It didn't hurt? Not at all?" Gertrude asked.

"Not hardly," Beatrice replied. "After I had him I had to rest a little."

Lelia blushed to ask her question: "Didn't you have to, you know, lie down with a man?"

Viola snorted. "Shoot, Lelia, I thought you were somebody smart."

"I only wanted to know who he was, was all."

Beatrice leaned over on the pretext of pulling up her crumpled white sock. She wished she had a photograph to help her memory. "Oh," she said, "just a boy."

Inez saw the clock move past three. Maybe Mister Washington wasn't going to come. She touched the hem of Beatrice's dress.

Felix sat with his feet on the windowsill, looking through the pictures in his text. Alexander stood in the back, his hands in his pockets. Cyril dozed. Russell held the microscope upright to Crutis's mouth. "That certainly was a tough break, Crutis, losing the game like that on the last play."

"Yes, Russ, you certainly got to hand it to those Tigers. They were fired up for this one and they played real well." The boys slapped palms and smothered their laughter.

"What about these rumors of your retirement? Our viewers sure want to know if you're going to be suited up next year."

"Well, Russ, I'm going to go down to Florida and sit in the sun and see how I feel. I'm not getting any younger, you know."

"You didn't look too old on that opening kickoff return."

"Yes, Russ, I was pretty quick on that one. Yes sir! The fantastic flash! Ever see a run to match it? Not since the days of the great Jim Brown! And you should see me with chicks! Dynamite!"

Maurice walked up and took the microscope from Russell's hand. "Ladies and gentlemen, what you just seen was a escaped madman that got away from the zoo. And now, back to our regular programming. Here he is, girls, the one and only and just for you — Maurice Westerman! *I've been loving you too long to stop now, wawawawawa!*"

Viola left the other girls and performed a swoon. "Ooooooooh," she said.

"Ooooooh!" Maurice sang. "*I love you, I love you with all my soul, going to give you, uh-huh, what I got, ooooooh!*"

"This is the man in the street." Avery thrust his head over the microscope and spoke quickly. "I got a piece. Nothing going to stop me. I want a million dollars and a closet of clothes. I want a chauffeur to drive my Fleetwood sedan."

In the front of the room Raymond put a finger to Kenny's chest. "All right. Human beings devolved from Apes and animals like that. But what I want to know is where did *they* come from?"

"From a lemur or a tree shrew," said Kenny, backing into, stepping over the duffle bag that Billy had left behind.

"A *what?*"

"A sort of a squirrel."

"Haw!" Felix said, not looking up.

"So where did the squirrel come from?"

"I think a kangaroo."

"Who gave birth to the first kangaroo?"

"Reptiles."

"Like rats?"

"No, man," Arthur cut in, "snakes is reptiles. Lizards and snakes."

"Yeah, but what I'm trying to find out is who started *them* off."

Arthur answered. "Amphibians. You know, frogs. What lives half in water and half on the land."

"And they came from fish," said Kenny.

"All right. All right. Cool. But what was before the fish?"

"Insects."

Maurice slammed down the microscope. "Man, you're crazy. Dig my size. You say I come from a bug?"

"A cockroach!" Lelia cried.

"Bullshit!"

Raymond did not join the laughter. He narrowed his eyes. "Listen here, now. Tell me who's the father of these insects."

"Worms."

"Those the first things to come out of the ground?"

"No," Kenny replied. "Jellyfish came before, and before that, sponges."

"What the man is getting at," Avery interrupted, "was what came first, without all these jive fishes in between."

"Right on," Raymond declared.

"One-cell animals."

"That's the first?"

"Yes."

"Now here's my point. Where did *they* come from? Answer me that."

"I — I don't know."

"What do you mean you don't know?" said Russell. "That's a lie."

"They have to come from *some* place," Lelia said.

Kenny backed away from the class. In his pocket he rubbed the trilobite's belly, felt its spines. "I didn't learn that yet."

Crutis cut off his line of retreat. "We gonna get an answer from you."

"Yeah!"

"Where did the first animal come from?"

"How come you don't know?"

"Because I never saw a one-celled animal," Kenny wailed. "It's too small. It's just a lot of chemicals and stuff and pretty soon it starts to move."

"What are you trying to stuff on us?"

"This is one of the fat boy's tricks!"

"Where did the *chemicals* come from?"

"What makes it move?"

"Answer, you motha, you *got* to know!"

"Hee! Hee! Hee!" Beatrice laughed, covering her mouth. "Look at *Cyril!*" They all swung around. Asleep, Cyril bared his teeth grotesquely and put his arms straight behind, as if in flight: *rrrrrrrr*, he went. The class fell hushed. Cyril swayed and groaned.

"Oh, Crutis," Viola said, inexplicably moved, "it must be an awful dream."

Alexander, listening by the door, was the first to hear the step in the hall. He raced to his desk and slid into his seat. The class scrambled to their places. Someone woke Cyril with a tap on the head. Crutis walked cool. "Shhhh," everyone said.

Alexander watched silently as his teacher came into the room. He knew that something was wrong. Mister Washington kept his arms crossed and his hands shoved into his armpits. Like a straightjacket patient. He came around the front desk and faced the class.

"Life began in the sea," he said. "And we still got the sea inside us." For a second he leaned on the top of the desk, but instantly withdrew his hands. "All right. Alphabetical order. You first, Alexander. Look through the microscope. Examine the drop of blood. Tell the class what you see."

The boy started to answer, but Mister Washington left the desk and started toward the back of the room. "Go on, man," Russell said. "He said you first."

"I'm next," Arthur shouted.

"Hurry up."

"Quit draggin'."

Alexander went to the front of the room. The microscope was set up on the table above him. "I can't reach," he said.

"Here, man, take a chair," said Avery, who had already gotten up to take his place in line.

Alexander put his eye to the instrument. Neat little cushions, doughnut-shaped, floated by. He adjusted the focus. Shapeless things, blobs, mostly white, sometimes blue, appeared and disappeared. His heart pounded to see them. "What's the story?" Raymond asked.

"Yeah. What'd you see?"

"Little things. Animals."

"Cells!" Kenny announced. "The building blocks of life." He looked around to catch Mister Washington's eye, but the teacher was sitting down, his back against the rear wall.

"Let me in on that," Arthur said, pushing Alexander off the chair.

Cyril stood up and beckoned Gertrude to follow. "Uh-uh," she said, "Forget it."

"This ain't my shot," said Felix, but he got up to look.

"They look like inner tubes!" Arthur exclaimed.

"They're like one-celled animals. The ones that lived in the ocean."

"What are you saying, man?" Raymond asked Kenny. "Are we down to it? Are these the first things?"

"Clear out, man." Avery took over the microscope.

"That ain't real blood," Cyril said.

"Yes it is!" Felix exclaimed. "It's all over the top of the table!" Raymond, Russell, and Maurice rushed to the front. *Let me see! Get off me, man. You looked long enough!*

Raymond swiped up the sticky stuff on his finger and put it in his mouth.

"What's it taste like?"

"Salty! Like the sea!"

Errol struggled to speak. Not a word came out. "Eeeeee," he heard a scream. Avery was chasing Gertrude with a finger of blood.

"Eeeeeee, eeeeeeee." Inez was cornered against the table. One of the boys was chewing at her neck. He closed his eyes. There was no pain where he had cut his wrists. The microscope went over with a faint, almost musical tinkle of glass. There were more screams and a shout. Someone sang. Someone chanted. There was a clatter of chairs. When he opened his eyes the light was failing. He saw dim shapes milling across the room. Maurice danced shirtless on the tabletop. Felix had painted red lines symmetrically on his cheeks. Again his eyes fluttered shut. Everything was in a foreign language. A female laughed and the sound turned into the click of bone. Far away he heard a familiar buzz, which grew to a deafening roar. He gathered the last of his strength and pulled open his eyes. His cupped hands held pools of blood. The room was grey and full of ghosts. One of them, larger than the rest, detached itself and floated near. He saw the teeth around its neck, the upraised claws, the spotted skin. Closer the spirit drifted. The Leopard was whispering to him, a sound like sheets in the wind.

Tell
Me
My
Fortune

I

Phyllis woke up, shivering, and heard the Angelic Choir singing on the radio. "He has banished, banished, banished all my fears." Across the hall Mary was coughing into her pillow, and in the bedroom something sucked the thin white curtains against the open slats of the venetian blinds. It took Phyllis a moment to realize she had been asleep. The covers were down around her feet; her pajamas had gotten as far as her knees. It was not hard to see: the full moon was reflected off the surface of the swimming pool and into her room. A witch's moon, thought Phyllis, watching the silver light alternately dart upon the ceiling and walls and then hold tremblingly still.

She could not have been sleeping long, because her parents hadn't returned. Her bedroom was above the garage, in one wing of the house, and she never failed to wake when the cream-colored Buick drove into it and her father gave the motor a final hard burst before switching off the key. It had become a game to lie awake and count the doors: the car door on his side and her side made two; the garage door rumbling down — three; the screen door before the spring was fixed — a slam, four; and the fifth door was the one that let them inside. After that, it was important for her to know the movements of these people through the enormous house. She imagined the sounds she could not, or could barely, hear: footsteps on the kitchen linoleum, the murmur of voices, the click of a light, stairs creaking, the rustling of her mother's dress as it moved down the narrow hallway and then became real in the shaft of light that fell through the opened door. If she lost track of them, she immediately jumped out of bed and put her ear to the floor, to the wall, even to the grill in front of the heating duct. No one was going to take her by surprise!

And no one did, not since the time that her teeth began to fall out one by one and she would wail inconsolably for a gold tooth like Mary's that could never be lost. Mary had a shining smile! Her mother told her that if she didn't cry a fairy would give her something better than gold, something to make her happy. What fairy? Phyllis wanted to know. Her mother said it was the same fairy that brought babies into the world and kissed them when they were hurt, and loved them with all of her heart. Phyllis had gone to bed certain that loss is balanced by recovery, and unhappiness by inevitable good fortune. That morning she woke to find a dollar bill beneath her pillow; raging, she pulled out the goose-feathers and hurled them about until they covered everything in the room like a blanket of snow. After that night her parents always found her awake. No matter what time they came to her room her eyes were open, fixed on both their faces.

Phyllis shivered violently. "You're a cold-blooded animal, that's for sure," Mary had told her when she was only six, and she never forgot it. When she saw a picture in her Life Science text of a snake, caught in a desert frost, tears of sympathy came to her eyes. "It doesn't freeze in Los Angeles," her mother had said. But why was she always cold? She had to wear sweaters half the year. A new chill shook the bed. Phyllis drew her feet up and clutched them. It was a pun. Cold feet. Chicken. Yellow. The trembling went on. All mammals were warm-blooded. She was a mammal. Ergo — she rolled the word like a sour ball on her tongue, ergo, ergo, ergo — she was warm-blooded, too! She didn't want to be Madame Lola! She didn't know about Gypsies! Why did they have to choose her?

"What about Phyllis Marx, Miss Kirsh?" asked Marjorie Tenner. "*I* can't do it. I've got to sell kisses."

Phyllis pretended that she had not heard. She hid behind the long dark hair that fell across her olive face, and continued to draw with her colored pencils. She balanced a perfect blue circle upon the point of an isosceles triangle, which she began to shade in. "Heaven and Earth," she thought she'd call it.

"*Thank* you, Phyllis, for your attention," Miss Kirsh remarked. She said it sarcastically, and the chalk in her hand snapped in two. Phyllis began a new design, which she entitled, "Song of Love." All of her drawings had similar names, "Song of Nature," for instance, or "The Universal Force," and all of them were simple designs in which geometrical shapes, parallelograms and cubes and see-through boxes, were balanced on top of each other. The colors ran toward blue and purple and aquamarine. She felt calm when she was drawing. She hated that blond Marjorie Tenner!

"Does anyone remember *The Man in the Iron Mask?*" Miss Kirsch was saying.

"I do!" piped Harold Sverdlove, in his funny accent. "He was the man in jail who wouldn't let anybody see his face."

"I think we've a man in the iron mask in this class," said Miss Kirsch, "except the iron mask is made out of hair." Phyllis remembered the story only vaguely. There was a nobleman who had a disfiguring disease. She raised her head and with her fingers parted her hair.

"*Wel*come among us, Miss Marx! Marjorie has suggested that you be Madame Lola at the Charity Fair. I think that is a fine idea. Don't you?"

Phyllis pressed her semitransparent pink eyeglasses against her nose. "I'd rather not do it, Miss Kirsch," she said.

There was a snort of laughter from around the room. Her heart raced terrifically. She saw Howard Sverdlove and Stanford Kramer whisper and laugh behind her, saw Howard's moist lower lip.

"I could paint something and sell it," she said.

"David Olds is the artist of the class," replied Miss Kirsch. "We can't have more than one. I don't see why you object to being the fortune-teller, Phyllis. I'm sure you would do very well."

"But I don't know how to do it," Phyllis cried. "I don't know anything about it."

"All you have to do is tell whoever comes in that they are going on a long journey, or to save their money for an important event, or that they are going to meet a tall, dark handsome man. You tell the ladies that, or something else that's pleasant and nice. Then you ask for twenty-five cents. Is that so difficult?"

"Don't forget your broomstick," Stanford blurted out.

"Wait for the full moon," Joel Berman shouted, cupping his hands superfluously around his mouth.

"Phyllis the witch, Phyllis the witch!" Stanford yelled, getting to his feet. He was the tallest boy in the class. "Phyllis isn't a witch any more. She's a Gypsy!"

"Yeah!" they yelled. "A Gypsy! A Gypsy!"

"I am not a Gypsy," Phyllis cried. "Don't call me that, Stanford."

"You are so a Gypsy," Geraldine Stallings shouted. "Look how dark your skin is."

"She's a black Hungarian Gypsy," Stanford said solemnly, as if resolving the issue for good.

Someone was plucking at Phyllis's arm, and when she turned around, Terry Pinter said, in a thick stage accent, "Madame Lola, tell me my fortune!"

"Tell me my fortune! Tell me my fortune!" They all picked it up and chanted it over and over, while Sam Kostecki played an imaginary violin and rolled his eyes. Phyllis stood up, shaking.

"I'm not a Gypsy! I've never even seen a Gypsy! I'm not going to do it!"

"Phyllis!" Miss Kirsch shouted. "Sit down." But Phyllis remained standing, hugging her shoulders. "It's fine for you to look so proud, Phyllis Marx. You can stand there. You have your two feet under you. But what about the children our fair is for? The children *you're* not willing to help? They can't stand at all because they're crippled."

Phyllis sank down behind her desk. "All right," she murmured, "I'll help." In the silent room it sounded like an exclamation. Miss Kirsch turned her back to the class and began to write in the lower left hand corner of the blackboard, which was already filled with names: P. Marx, Madame Lola.

What am I going to do? thought Phyllis. What am I going to do? Piled up in the corner of the bedroom was her costume, a black scarf, a dime-store necklace, a pair of green, pointed shoes. She didn't even know how to put it on. Was she supposed to stretch the scarf over her face like a Turkish woman? But then how could she talk through it? And what would she say? *You're going on a trip, you'll meet a handsome man, the next few days will be of crucial importance for you.* She wished she could sleep and not have to think about tomorrow. If only she knew what to do. If only she didn't have to do it!

Then, suddenly, Phyllis realized that she *had* seen a fortune-teller. She remembered the Gypsy's chipped hand. It had happened long ago. Her father was carrying her. When was it? Where was it? She had to think! The Gypsy's hand was chipped, it was her left hand; all the fingers were cut off at the first joint, leaving little circles of pink plaster. It was a plaster fortune-teller! Not a real one! What else about the hand? It moved. Slowly. Up and down. Rather, the whole arm moved and the four hurt fingers chopped the air, then stopped, stuck there until . . . until her father did something to make them move again. Then the left hand went up and down and the cupped palm of the right hand came forward, toward her, holding something, came closer and closer until it also stopped. "Again! Do it again!" she cried and her father put another quarter in and she remembered everything. They were at Ocean Park, in the arcade filled with mechanical games, the claw that pulled watchbands from a mountain of nuts, the bear that pawed the air and roared, hockey players whirling with metal sticks, and at the center, in the largest glass case of all, the wooden Gypsy who held out a handful of hearts, clubs, diamonds, and spades.

Off to their right a boy not much older than Phyllis was firing into the wings of a fat bomber that circled the sky on the end of a rigid wire. Behind him, an elderly man was vibrating his feet. "Again, Daddy!" Phyllis cried. "Make it move!" The Gypsy had no scarf over her face, which was lighter than Phyllis's, touched with red on the cheeks and with parted, painted lips. She wore her hair in a round black bun, in which pins were sticking. A tattered shawl covered her body, which sank at the waist, like a mermaid's, into the pile of tea leaves and playing cards scattered over the bottom of the chamber. The stars of various constellations were painted on the glass walls, and the front pane had, in addition, an occult figure: a narrow ellipse at whose center a triangle was inscribed, like the pupil of an unwinking eye. *Tacktacktacktack* went the artillerymen, ringing up a fabulous score. Phyllis squealed with delight as the light in the crystal ball came on and the torso of the Gypsy began to expand with life.

Up and down went the broken left hand, while the right inched forward almost to where, clinging to her father's neck, Phyllis bravely planted her own hand upon the glass. The wooden head twisted in its socket, the chest thumped outward, as if struck from within by a fist, and the single loop of gold in the Gypsy's ear gleamed in the amber light. There was a click, a scratching sound, and Phyllis heard a high-pitched voice ask her a question. "Good day! You have come to ask your fortune? Good day! You wish to know your fate?" There was a pause, and the scratching went on and on, until Phyllis let out her breath in a rush. "Yes!"

"Ha! Ha! Ha!" laughed the metallic voice, and the burning

ring of gold hung at the very center of the dark triangle, dazzling Phyllis's eyes. "Alaleia knows all! Alaleia tells all! Listen to Alaleia!"

"Tell! Tell!" Phyllis cried, but nothing happened. The raw scratching noise continued. The earring shimmered. The breast went on jerking in and out convulsively. "Please!" Phyllis wailed. In response, there was another click from deep within the machine.

"Good day! You have come to ask your fortune? Good day! You wish to know your fate?"

"It's broken," her father said, and his own voice, so near to her face, seemed to break the spell. The light in the crystal ball went out.

Phyllis lifted her head from the pillow and the memory of the amusement pier faded as rapidly as the damp impression of her palm upon the panel of glass. She turned on the light and checked her watch: a breathtaking quarter to two. She slid off the bed and stepped carefully out of the little pool of her pajama bottoms. She yanked off the top. She put on her plastic glasses. A bathrobe hung on a hook by the door, but she walked naked into the cool hallway. For the first time that night, for the first time in weeks, she was not shivering.

Mary had fallen asleep with the radio on. Phyllis knew it was an old-fashioned console, as tall, nearly, as she, but all she could see of it in the darkened room was an arc of yellow light. The spirituals were still playing. "It's real, it's real," the song went. "It's really, really real." She pinched her nose and tiptoed into the room, heading for the closet. Her father told her that the peculiar smell on the room — like split-pea soup — came from the gas heater; but the heater wasn't on and Phyllis knew the smell was Mary. That's why she wore "Persian Lilac" and took so many baths. Negroes smelled that way.

In the closet Phyllis, groping, found what she wanted and folded it across her imperceptible breasts. It itched but it was perfect. She had always thought there was something magical about the old purple shawl, about the way it stretched into hundreds of tiny rectangles when you pulled it, about the way your body lost its shape beneath it and could be anyone's, anything. Phyllis glided to Mary's bed. Only the black band of the fat maid's neck, and her black face, were visible above the cotton blanket. The knuckles of one hand touched the floor. The girl stepped closer. In a trick of the light she thought she saw Mary lying on her back with her hands clasped on her chest. In her mind's eye there were flowers around her. Slowly, with her heart pounding, Phyllis raised her arms beneath the shawl to tell the old woman she soon would be dead.

"Hummmmmph," said Mary, and blew air from her cheek like a horse. The blanket rose up, horribly high, as Mary turned onto her side. "You are going to meet a *dark* handsome stranger!" Phyllis declared, and that seemed so funny she buried her face in her hands and ran out of the room, giggling, tee-heeing, the long string tassels at the corner of the shawl tickling her knees.

It was a long way from where Phyllis and Mary lived to the bedroom of her parents. Phyllis slowed at the midway point, where the two wings of the house met over an elaborate spiral staircase. She halted. Elbows propped on the banister, her fingertips securing the rims of her glasses, she leaned dangerously out into space and dropped a pear-shaped glob of spittle down the shaft toward the copper umbrella stand in the shadows below. It struck with a satisfying clang. Thanks to the magic shawl, thought Phyllis, wrapping it more tightly about her and continuing down the hallway; for even under the best of conditions, in broad daylight, she was no crack shot.

She went quickly through the master bedroom, keeping her eyes upon the twin canopies that hovered calmly over her parents' empty beds, and into the bathroom, where the moon glanced off dozens of mirrors. From the open window she could see the grey cork tree in the center of the circular drive, and her bicycle leaning, as if asleep, against it. The garden was full of black flowers and formal hedges. Her mother's dressing table was covered with bottles whose stoppers were of glazed, milky opaque glass in a lozenge design. A few had silver tops, and still others had round gold atomizers which, even in this light, gleamed like rows of precious chessmen. There were jars and boxes of all sorts, filled with creams and jellies and powders, with pins and tiny brushes, and there was a tall cylindrical box, the size of a coffee can, to which Phyllis had glued the velvet herself a year ago in school, and which was empty.

Phyllis seated herself at the dressing table and pulled the two side pieces of the mirror forward, so that she could see most of herself at once. Her hair was in the way of everything. She gathered it together at the back of her head and secured it in an improvised bun with a handful of pins from a silver tray. She carefully worked the top off a box of powder, dipped her finger into it, and blazed a white line diagonally across her olive forehead. Then she rubbed the powder in, first on her forehead, then her cheeks and chin, even over her throat and neck, lightening everywhere the color of her skin. She used mascara on her eyes, patiently going over all her lashes, which was difficult in the darkness, with her glasses off. She drew a line of black through her brows. She looked through four or five lipstick cases before she found a shade she thought was bright enough. She applied it carefully, without smears, and blotted it on a tissue that rose like steam from a box. She added a round red dot of rouge to her cheeks. There were too many bottles of perfume to sample them all, so, resisting the plump plum of an atomizer, she chose the prettiest one, with a stopper blown in the shape of a stag. She put a little behind her ears, on the back of her neck, and under her arms. She paused, turned her head to different angles, took off her glasses, put them on again. She pulled one of the mirrors close to her face, touched it to her temple, and pushed it away again, watching her face change from front view to profile, profile to front. Something was wrong. It wasn't right. She brought the panel close again and blew across her image, obliterating it, then watched her face materialize out of the shrinking mist. She had it! She knew how to make it perfect.

She opened the drawer of the dressing table and pulled out a wooden jewelry box inlaid with mother-of-pearl. Inside, all the pieces were tangled, strands of pearls winding among emerald-studded tortoises and tarnished silver rings. Phyllis fumbled among the jewelry until she found what she wanted, a simple earring made from a loop of gold.

She turned it about in her hand. There was no clasp, and her ears were not pierced. Still, she held it up to the lobe of her ear, just to see how it would go, and leaned into the walls of the mirror. Miraculously, it exploded with light. Phyllis stared trans-fixed at her triple image — her mouth open, her eyes wide and bulging, her hand, holding the gleaming gold, pressed to her ear — and then let out a wail of fear. The light passed off the mirrors and the Buick swung around the drive toward the garage. They were home! She had to run! Yet she remained at the dressing table, trying to see, with eyes dazzled by the headlights' reflected beams, the red cheeks, the tangerine mouth, and the white and creamy skin. What most terrified her, what caused her heart to clatter wildly in her chest and made it impossible for her to tear herself away from the mirror, was not that she feared being caught but that she realized she was beautiful.

Even in that far-off part of the house she could hear the garage door rumble shut. She jumped from the cushion and ran through the bedroom into the hallway. They were at the back door by the time she rounded the corner of the staircase. "Give me two wings," the radio sang. "Do me like you did the angels."

She picked up her pajamas off the floor, pulled them into bed with her, and raised the covers over her head. With the earring clutched in one hand and the corners of the shawl in the other, she curled up, she waited. But their timing was off. They came so slowly up the stairs. And once there, they turned the wrong way, toward their own bedroom, not to hers. This had happened a lot lately. Didn't they want to see her anymore? She wondered if her mother was sick. By the time, a half-hour later, that her father quietly opened her door and took a cautious step into the room, Phyllis was already asleep and dreaming of a long line of crippled children who crawled on their knees and waved their crutches in the air.

II

Over the weekend the school had been transformed. A small ferris wheel with blue seats stood motionless in the center of the playground. Wooden stalls and booths were scattered about, with signs for cotton candy, soft drinks, darts, roulette, home-baked food, an exhibition of art. There was a machine designed to whirl miniature spaceships in a horizontal circle and another, meant to represent a diving bell, that shook its occupants up and down in a tank of water. A Shetland pony was tethered to the oak tree. Green and red plastic pennants were strung haphazardly in the air and made chirping sounds when the wind caught them. Here and there men ran about placing speakers for the audio system or stooped to drive iron stakes into the soft asphalt. From the bus descending through the foothills toward the school, they looked like the crazy hockey players in the glass cases. In fact, the whole apparatus of the fair looked like so many toys in a penny arcade. Phyllis turned away from the window in disgust: it was all helter-skelter. There was no order. Why didn't they arrange things along the yellow lines? What a hodgepodge!

It was warm inside the school bus, and very quiet. Most of the children stared at their reflections in the window, or squinted for a glimpse of the whitecapped sea. An older girl in the seat ahead was following a line in her book with a jumping finger. Toward the back Sam Kostecki was stuffing orange peels into the crack in the seat. A fat boy was actually sleeping. Phyllis could not sit still. She wanted to whistle, to shout, to make everyone look. Why were they staring out of the window? It was almost as if they were afraid of her, of her power, as if they felt the aura of invulnerability that clung to her, fragile as the face powder she had slept in that night, flaking, but intact.

Phyllis squeezed the paper sack in her lap, felt the shawl inside it, and turned about. Directly across the aisle Davy Olds was hugging a large piece of Masonite to his chest, trying to keep it from banging into the seat in front of him or slamming into the side of the bus on curves. He had signed the back, David T. Olds, with the date. Phyllis suddenly broke into a tuneless singsong, "Davy thought that he could paint! But his painting made me faint!"

"Shut up," Davy said.

"Come again?" said Phyllis, like a grown-up.

"Shut up, you black Gypsy," Davy repeated, but not clearly: the top edge of the Masonite came up under his chin and he had trouble moving his jaw.

"Don't mumble! Enunciate! You know what Miss Kirsch says." She made up a new verse of her song. "Davy said that he could sketch! But his sketching made me retch! And besides, I'm not black, I'm white, as even a fool could see. Obviously you don't know what you're talking about." David's own face had turned deep red; but he had to clench his teeth.

"Let me see, what's the T? Oh dear me, what can it be?" Phyllis sang, her voice cracking with excitement. What fun! You could do anything if you were pretty! "Timothy, Teddy or Tad," she intoned, spreading her fingers before her eyes. "No, that's not it. Wait! It's coming! Here it comes! Tyro-o-o-o-ne! Ha! Ha! Ha!

Davy Tyro-o-o-o-ne Olds!" She blew the word out like a foghorn. "No it's not either! It's Thomas!" yelled Davy, hiking his chin above the frame. "And you're just a jealous Gypsy. That's only powder on your face; you can't hide what you are." Just then the bus took a sharp curve and the painting, unsupported, swung around. It was a watercolor entitled *Laugh Clown Laugh,* but what struck Phyllis — it was like a blow — was the way the face of the clown seemed to suggest her own. Two red spots on the cheeks bled into the chalk-white mask of his face. Watery black lines perpendicular to the eyes ran like her own mascara. And his mouth, turned down at the corners like a telephone on its cradle, was painted the same shade of tangerine. Worst of all, none of the colors held fast, the whole face was fuzzy and splotched, as if the clown, too, had spent the night in his makeup. Phyllis felt her courage drain away, her power dissolve. Much like the clown's polka-dot hat which, meant to stand erect, a perfect cone, was drooping into the general blur.

"What's the matter, Phyllis?" Davy asked, his voice scared and polite. "Don't you like it?"

"Oh, Davy," she wailed, "couldn't you let the colors set?"

"You see, it's called *Laugh Clown Laugh* because he's really sad but he has to smile."

"It's very good. You are a very good artist, David Thomas Olds," she said. But instead of looking at the clown she hiked herself up on the seat so that she could see out the window. The ocean was all unrolled, a flat, flawless inverted sky. A triumph of geometry! She stared down at it for as long as she could, until the bus swung left on Canyon Road for the final run down to the school. When she turned away her face was serene and she smiled to think she would guess no more wrong names that day.

James Wada, a husky Japanese, shook a large sheet of tin and averted his head from the thunder he made. Joel Berman suddenly appeared, dressed in what looked like a woman's nightgown. His crew cut was dusted with ordinary household flour, and he rolled his eyes tremendously. Again the tin produced a vicious roar, and Berman covered his ears. "Oh!" he cried. "Oh!" he repeated and moved three steps forward. "Nor Heaven nor Earth have been at peace tonight." It was true, Phyllis thought — in spite of the disconcerting sunlight that lit up the conspirators' swords as they waited off to the side for Act Three to begin. For the previous half-hour Cassius and Casca, Cicero and Cinna, and finally Brutus too, had whispered and knocked on imaginary doors, all the while casting up fearful eyes at the fire-dropping sky. It was this that Wada, in his T-shirt, his flat face impassive as a god's, realistically simulated. Impossible not to believe this turquoise day transformed into a stormy Roman night, "this dreadful night," as Cassius had called it, "Bloody, fiery, and most terrible."

"More excitement!" Miss Kirsch had hissed from her seat near the stage. "Quake with fear!" The plotters had responded by shivering grotesquely beneath their makeshift cloaks. They actually scratched their heads when they pondered the meaning of the slave with the burning hand, the lion padding through the streets of Rome, and the blood which drizzled on the Capitol. What dummies! thought Phyllis contemptuously. She had, of course, spent just such a night herself. She too had shivered uncontrollably. And just like that boy-Caesar, lurching about in his nightgown, she had been unable to sleep. You couldn't tell her about "unaccustomed terror"! She took off her glasses and huffed scornfully on the lenses. These Romans were just too simple. They understood so little. They could not read the stars. She held her glasses in her hand and watched Caesar's fuzzy gestures in the direction of his servant.

It had not been her intention to attend the play. She had a lot to do before noon, when the adults would start arriving and the fair would really get underway. But as she had hurried past the stage toward her own bare booth, Ivan Mair had stepped from a multitude of sheeted fourth graders and cried, "Caesar!" And then, "Beware the Ides of March!" Murder, Phyllis had thought.

She had never read the play but she sensed at once what the Soothsayer was saying: murder, murder everywhere. As the play progressed, she realized that it was filled with portents and alarms — "instruments of fear and warning," Cassius called them — but no one, least of all skinny Terry Pinter, knew how to figure out what they meant. She'd had to snort out loud when that same stupid Cassius had told Brutus that they were masters of their fate, that their destiny was not in the stars but in themselves. How dense could you get! The next moment, there they were, with those same stars shooting all around them, comets and meteors showering onto their heads, and they still could not see the point of the tempest: death to them all. It wasn't worth watching, really. It was too obvious.

At that moment, however, Caesar ordered his servant to ask his fortune of the Priests, and her interest revived. She put her glasses on in time to see Berman joined by Norma Jean Blase, who had painted her fingernails for the occasion and now raised them, even as she begged her husband not to step from the house, to her crisp new permanent wave. Perhaps there was some hope for Caesar after all. Phyllis could see that he knew something about the nature of the stars. "What can be avoided whose end is purposed by the mighty gods?" he asked, and fell once more to his knees. The servant, red-haired and freckle-faced, returned, and Phyllis's heart skipped a beat when she heard his master ask, "What say the augurers?" The answer came:

> *They would not have you to stir forth today.*
> *Plucking the entrails of an offering forth,*
> *They could not find a heart within the breast.*

Phyllis was afraid she would faint. She shivered violently. She was imagining her own hands tipped red as Norma Jean's with the blood of some chicken, some lamb. It was a tradition that she was a part of. When, a moment later, Caesar let himself be tricked into a false interpretation of the augury, and hence into

an appearance before the Senate, she felt as if she, herself, had
been betrayed. "Don't be so proud," she whispered. Miss Kirsch
turned around and glared at her fiercely. It didn't make any
difference. She was immune. "Caesar!" she cried out loud. "Don't
be so proud!"

Too late. The crowd moved into the center of the stage. The
six assassins were head and shoulders above the others. "The Ides
of March are come," Berman declared, haughtily pulling his
robe — beneath which the nightgown peeked — over his shoulders.

"Aye, Caesar, but not gone," said Ivan Mair. As the petition-
ers began to fawn at the ruler's feet, Wada drummed his fingers
lightly over the slack sheet of tin, an echo of the storm. Listen to
it, Phyllis urged. She was silently moving her lips. Listen to the
Soothsayer, to the blood and the storm and the stars. But when
Caesar started to speak it was obvious he had not heard. Phyllis
got up off the bench and walked away. Thus she did not see
Casca's hand close around the hilt of his wooden sword. But she
did hear Caesar, in his ignorance, say:

I am constant as the Northern Star,
Of whose true-fixed and resting quality
There is no fellow in the firmament.
The skies are painted with unnumbered sparks,
They are all fire, and every one doth shine,
But there's but one in all doth hold his place.

The Gypsy arrived at her booth, whose four canvas sides were
nailed to tall poles. Above it, against the sky, a blue ferris wheel
seat swung back and forth, creaking slightly. She secured the
front flap and pushed one of the two chairs against the somewhat
drooping rear wall. She climbed up on it, clutching her pencil
box. After wetting the tip of a pencil with her tongue, and by
stretching as far as she could, she drew the outline, and then filled

in, a purple Northern Star. Without pausing, she began to cover
the walls with a series of constellations, drawing first the line
between Alpha Librae and Beta Librae of the pentagon of Libra,
symbol of balance; then she ranged far beyond the zodiac to
include just those configurations which were simplest and most
perfect, the triangles and Hydrus and Triangulum, the trapeziums
of Corvus and Crater, graceful Sculptor and lovely Antlia. While
she was doing this Caesar shrieked and died. She heard the
muffled cheering of the mob.

There were no stars on the back of the entrance flap. Here
Phyllis drew the narrow ellipse she had seen on the Gypsy's glass
case. At the spot where the pupil-like triangle had been inscribed,
she taped a small pocket mirror, and above the whole figure she
printed MADAME LOLA TELLS ALL. She fumbled in her paper sack
and took out a small glass ball that contained a winter scene,
several miniature skaters gliding across a frozen lake, at the bottom of a bubble of water. Phyllis turned the ball upside down and
the skaters, their arms clasped behind their backs as if nothing
were happening, disappeared in a blizzard. She set the stormy
ball in the middle of the table.

More than enough sunlight streamed into the booth for her to
arrange herself in the mirror. She touched up the smudges on her
cheeks and the mascara that had crumbled at the corners of her
eyes. She unbuttoned the front of her blouse and thrust her hand
under her armpits, then brought her fingers to her nose. They
smelled, still, of the expensive perfume. From the sack she took a
roll of cotton wadding and began to stuff it into the opening in
her blouse until she had built up two imposing though irregular
breasts. She buttoned the blouse and stretched the dark shawl
over her shoulders. Now it was still. There were no sounds from
the drama. The walls of the booth flapped a little, like sails in a
calm. Over her head the blue seat hung motionless, without passengers, and the pony snorted and struck its foot against the tar.
All the stars were harmonious. Phyllis took out one of the pins
that held her hair in a bun and drove it through the lobe of her
ear. Then she worked the clasp of the earring through the punc-

ture and watched as a drop of ruby blood hung trembling from the loop of gold. The crystal ball before her was mad with snow.

Forty-five minutes later the Gypsy received her first visitor. Phyllis thought she had seen her before with Marjorie Tenner. It was strange to think that this tiny dark-haired woman with a little beak of a nose, who fluttered about the booth as if looking for a way out, might be the mother of a girl so beautiful that she sold kisses and who had gold hair, like a halo, upon her arms.

"What a lovely job you've done here, Phyllis. You must have worked so hard to draw all these stars. And I know what *that* is, that's your crystal ball! Miss Kirsch must be so proud."

"My name is Madame Lola," Phyllis said, noticing the way the woman — she was sure that it was Marjorie's mother — avoided the mirror as she looked around the booth.

"*Madame Lola Tells All*. That's a very realistic touch. It's true to life. I know because I went to a Gypsy fortune-teller when I was a young girl, just sixteen years old, and you know what she said? She said that my lucky day was Wednesday. I always remembered that. Do you know what else she said? She said, 'You are going to marry very young.' That didn't turn out to be true because I was over thirty when I met my husband and we didn't get married for years after that. She said I was going to live a long time, too, over a hundred, but that won't be true either, I suppose. I can't think of anything lucky that happened on Wednesday. It's funny, isn't it, how we remember such things? I was frightened by her white whiskers. You ought to get yourself some of those! When it was over she gave me a wallet-sized card with a list of dates and signs and flowers and birthstones on the back — chrysanthemum and topaz were mine, I never forgot that either — and on the front it said something like DID YOU KNOW? and told the story of this man, I've forgotten his name but he was a famous Danish astronomer, who had a golden nose attached to his face with cement, because he lost his own in a duel. I kept that card for over ten years. Well, Madame Lola, what do you think? Will I live to be a hundred?"

"Say, 'Tell me my fortune,' " Phyllis said.

"That's what I'm here for," Mrs. Tenner said brightly.

"You must say exactly, in just these words, 'Tell me my fortune,' " Phyllis repeated. Mrs. Tenner stopped moving a moment. She looked at the Gypsy.

"Tell me my fortune," she said.

"Sit there," Phyllis commanded, indicating the seat opposite herself. The subject did so, with her back to the exit flap. "Put your hands on the table. Do not take your eyes from the sphere. Do not move." Mrs. Tenner focused on the crystal ball, but saw nothing but toy skaters on a plaster lake.

"Tell me my fortune," she said again.

"Remain silent," Phyllis declared, though with less authority than she had issued her other commands. The fact was, she saw nothing in the ball either, and could think of nothing to say. The ferris wheel had finally gone into operation, and its seats hove up out of the top of the booth like buckets taking jagged bites out of the sky. The woman's hands kept moving on the tabletop. In the handmirror taped to the canvas, Phyllis could see the back of her visitor's head and her own whitened face. Her earring flashed with light.

"You are really sad but you have to smile," Phyllis said. "All your life you have worn an iron mask. Sometimes your face hurts from having to smile, but you do not dare to show your own true feelings. No one understands this. You even forget yourself what you are going through. Now you are reminded. Now you wish to cry. How do you feel? You feel like years ago when you saw a dead person, with flowers, in a coffin. That is how you are feeling now."

"That's not true!" Mrs. Tenner exclaimed.

"This man had his hands clasped on his chest and was wearing a black suit and a white collar. That was when you wanted to cry."

"You mean my father!"

"That was the last time you had this feeling so strongly. From then until now it has been laugh clown laugh clown laugh clown laugh."

"But how did you know this? Who told you? Are you a friend of Marjorie's? Did she tell you?"

"Remain silent," Phyllis demanded, as she tipped the crystal sphere. "I spoke of your past. I speak of your future." She stared at the flakes descending onto the skaters' heads, their shoulders, onto the heel of each jaunty raised foot. Then she peered into the center of the dense blank blizzard. "The Gypsy you visited was true and she was false."

"You mean that I married late but I'm going to live long?"

"Beware! The Gypsy saw truly into the future, but she saw too far. Your *daughter* will marry early. Your *daughter* will live to be over a hundred. But you will die before you reach the age of your father, and from the same cause" — she heard her subject gasp, and saw, in the crystal ball, how the exhausted snow lay in pale white heaps and piles — "leukemia."

Mrs. Tenner stood abruptly; the chair clattered backward. "I'm late for an appointment. I have to go. That was a very good performance, Phyllis. It couldn't have been more realistic. Here," she said, holding out a dollar bill, "this is for the crippled children."

"I haven't got any change," Phyllis said, but Mrs. Tenner threw down the money and ducked out the flap. What the Gypsy did was hold her sides, she held them for all she was worth; then she broke into a tremendous guffaw.

"Hello!" said the next subject as she came through the flap. Phyllis was determined to waste no time on chatter; she waved the woman to her seat and told her to put her hands on the table.

"Madame Lola tells all," she announced, and looked at the newcomer for the first time. *This* could have been Marjorie Tenner's mother, or even her sister: her hair was swept upward, curl upon curl, into a golden cloud from which rays broke, like sunbeams, riding the few stray hairs that sprang from the nape of her neck. Phyllis was stunned. How did such a thing, this hive of gleaming honey, stay on top of the woman's head? The subject herself kept glancing upward, as if she were deliberately balancing the glittering mass.

"Go ahead," she said. "Tell me."

"No. Say 'Tell me my fortune.' "

"Tell me my fortune."

This time Phyllis knew right away what to say. Her heart beat steadily beneath her clumps of cotton. In the little mirror Phyllis saw her own face perched like a puppet on the woman's shoulder. She was a dummy, whispering into the ventriloquist's ear about a tall and dark and handsome man.

"Well, who could this person be?" asked the woman.

"This is the man of your dreams."

"I am married, you know."

"Madame Lola sees you together. You have been in his arms."

"I do not have any idea who you mean. Honestly."

"Now it becomes clearer. You and this man, a he-man, he crushes you in an embrace. You are turning in circles. Close together. This is passion. The floor is shining. Why are there balloons? Madame Lola sees red and blue balloons!"

"Wait! How did you do it? That's the Avalon Ballroom! That's where we were dancing! Who told you? How do you know?"

"Listen. This man is your true lover. He is your fixed Northern Star. All your dreams will come true."

The woman stared a moment, the mound of her hair tilting a bit to one side. "We better not say any more."

"Madame Lola tells all. She sees what she sees. Ah! Ah! His lips are like fire! They are dangerous kisses. His fingers burn. They burn right through you. You are melting. You are swooning. This is bliss. It is ecstasy!"

"I don't know what to say, Madame Lola! Can I believe you? This is a terrible time for me. I am speaking frankly. I am admitting I knew who you meant when I heard your first words. His name is Charles! We've only danced. We haven't been intimate. We haven't dared. And now you say that you see it! You put it into words!"

"Bliss," Madame Lola repeated, and covered her mouth with her hand.

"Oh! I wish I could make up my mind!"

"It has been fated. What must be must be."

"But my husband! He has such a temper! He bangs his fist on the table! You don't know how he hits me! I wish I were fearless. I wish I could say, 'Come what may!' "

"Now Madame Lola speaks of the future."

Strands of loose hair were spilling across the visitor's face. "All right," she said. "I'm ready."

Phyllis turned the crystal ball over and gazed into the snowfall. "It will be as it has been before. There is the shining floor. There is your lover. This Charles. Turning you in his arms. Colored balloons. Colored lights. Your whole head is shining." The Gypsy paused. She squinted into the crystal. "What is this? Is this danger?"

"Tell me! Don't spare me!" The woman was breathless.

"Beware!"

At the edge of the lake, apart from the skaters, a lone figure appeared to be stepping onto the ice. He was an amateur skater, not sure of himself, and he thrust out an arm for balance. A black scowl was slashed on his simplified face. "O, terrible! O, horrible!" Phyllis shrieked. It was like the unfolding of the play. "O night of terror!"

"No! No!"

"Fire drops from the teehee sky! Comets fall bloody and fiery and teeheehee, teeheehee —" Phyllis broke off and tried to smother her laughter with her hands.

"What? Oh, God! Is it him?"

"At midnight a man steps into the spotlight. The music stops. The dancing stops. Crash! He has a gun! A gunshot! Crash! It sounds like thunder. Your true love falls to the floor. The blood is spreading. It spreads further and further. Ohhh! The red balloons! Madame Lola has told all!"

"But that can't be all! There must be something else!" The subject's hair had come undone. It spewed over her shoulders. Her eyes shot out tears. She rose unsteadily and groped in her pocket-book. "Here," she said, holding out ten dollars. "Can't you tell me something else?"

"Say 'For the crippled children,' " Phyllis answered stonily.

"For the crippled children."

"There is nothing else."

The woman stumbled backward. She left the booth. Chortling like a miser, Phyllis arranged the brand-new ten-dollar bill beside the one-dollar note. She noticed that on the latter, at the top of a pyramid, there was an all-seeing eye.

"Next!" she announced. She said it with a serious face.

And in they came, one person after another. Phyllis worked quickly and efficiently, her task made easier by the fact that word of her rules soon spread through the fair and all of her subjects knew what they had to do. They did it like automatons: stepping through the flap, saying, *tell me my fortune,* sitting down with their hands on top of the table. They had heard that the Gypsy possessed supernatural powers and were surprised to see only a schoolgirl. How could this child make grown people weep? What did she know of the past or the future? Each of them thought, *I'll leave, I'll get up, I'll go.* But nobody moved. The girl's eyes were magnified and glossy and seemed to stare at some spot behind them. The ring in her ear glittered and gleamed. When she started to speak, slowly, mechanically, the sound seemed to come through her, as if the voice was someone else's, not her own. The miracle was, whatever she said was true.

But all of that only bored Phyllis. It was like a trick to her, like remembering something. The person was this, he was that. He had done something or other. She passed the information on. She didn't have any interest in her subjects' lives. What she looked forward to was when she could stop talking. Sometimes she did it in the middle of a sentence. All that she said then was, "Beware!" It was when the future began.

Immediately the subjects became stiff in their chairs. They watched as the fortune-teller stretched out her hand and stirred the toy whirlwind in the sphere. After that, the same thing always happened. No matter how the snowflakes blew, whether they rode a current in the liquid air, or smashed against the hill in the landscape, whether they came to rest in disorganized swirls or in unnaturally tidy celluloid drifts, the money saved for an important event turned into a crushing debt, the handsome stranger became a carrier of some dread disease, and the long journey ended in shipwreck. Ha! Ha! Ha! laughed Phyllis into the faces of her classmates' parents. Ha! Ha! Ha! at the unexpected twist, the ruptured hopes, the comical denouement. Then, throwing back her head so that she saw the California sky, which never froze, she laughed Ha! Ha! Ha! at her own immense success.

Even then the subjects were unmoved. They accepted the reversal of fortune without a complaint. No one grew angry. No one started to shout. When it was over they stood rigid, erect, like soldiers almost, and they held out handfuls of bills. "For the crippled children," they had learned to say. Madame Lola did not have to dismiss them. They went on their own. They were her collaborators.

As soon as each subject left, Phyllis quickly sorted the bills according to denomination. There wasn't time to count it all. Neat piles of fives and tens and even twenties rose higher and higher, and a row of one-dollar bills ran perpendicularly down each end of the table. She giggled, feeling silly. What a wonderful game of solitaire! *Next!* she called. Every moment she was growing more light-headed and drunk with power. Amazing! Terrifying! Defying Belief! She was unassailable now, the center of everything. *Next! Next! Next!* Still they came in, they went out. The piles of money spread across the tabletop and surrounded the crystal ball. And in that little world the snow continued to fall, like the pale dregs of an exotic tea, in patterns of disaster. "Next!" she called once more and looked up astonished to see her mother's lovely face.

"You have certainly made a spectacle of yourself, young lady. No one's talking about anything but you." Her mother sat down opposite her. A wave of perfume passed over Phyllis, and she simultaneously smelled the reek of her own stale perfume and sweat. Her mother looked angry. The little V lines stood out between her eyebrows. She wore a hat with a fluffy feather. She took it off with one quick motion.

"Madame Lola tells all," Phyllis said, as lightly as she could. But her mother did not return her smile.

"You may start by telling me how you dared to sneak into my jewelry box without asking permission. I thought I'd bought you a perfectly good costume. It's lying in your room this minute. Why on earth would you prefer Mary's filthy shawl? And look what you've done to your chest! Is that a joke? Is it meant to be funny? Phyllis, I wish you could see yourself in a mirror. You have paint all over you, a ring in your ear, and you even smell bad. I've never seen anything so grotesque." She turned her eyes away.

For the first time the wound in Phyllis's earlobe began to ache. Her chest heaved as she struggled for breath. She wished her mother would say the right words. Then everything would be all right. It had to be done according to the plan. This way, she was going to ruin everything. "Momma! You've come to ask your fortune? You have to say, 'Tell me my fortune' first. Please, Momma! Then Madame Lola tells all."

"I brought you into the world, Phyllis Marx. I know every detail of your life. Why should I go to you to learn anything? What could you tell me?"

"I can tell you lots of things. Did you know, did you know that you have a wonderful future? Yes! The most wonderful of all. Madame Lola sees a great surprise. A wonderful gift awaits you. Something you can love with all your heart."

"Phyllis, you're making a fool of yourself."

"Don't you understand that you're beautiful!" Phyllis exclaimed. "I mean *really* beautiful. That's why your future is beautiful and good. Because you're beautiful and good. Whatever comes to you will make you happy. Oh, Momma, I can tell you so many lovely lovely things. I can see it! I know what's true!"

"What is it you see? The future?"

"Oh yes! Just ask me! Ask me! Oh, it's glorious, Momma! Your future is glorious! Ask me!"

"Well, what is it? What's my fortune?"

"A blessed event," Phyllis shot back. Her mother gasped and tried to penetrate the gleaming discs in front of her daughter's eyes.

"How did you know, Phyllis?"

"Madame Lola," said the fortune-teller, her voice like ice.

"Can you tell me anything more? I'd like to know something else."

"Madame Lola tells all."

"What sex will the baby be?"

"I must look more deeply into the future," Phyllis said, reaching stiffly for the crystal ball.

"I don't know how you found this out," her mother said. "Probably from your father. But now that you've done it, let's see if you can predict whether it will be a boy or a girl. We'll write it down. *That* will prove whether you're a Gypsy."

Phyllis sat with the sphere in her outstretched hands, afraid to turn it over. What could she say? What should she do? She couldn't think of anything. A minute passed. Her pulse beat terrifically and made her ear ache. She closed her eyes and tipped the crystal ball. When she opened them the snow was spiraling about in all directions. There was no meaning to it. It didn't make sense. Her head simply swam.

"You have come to ask your fortune?" she asked stupidly. "You wish to know your fate?"

"What's the matter with you, Phyllis?" her mother said.

Phyllis tightened her grip on the base of the globe and shook it violently, back and forth. Then she righted it, set it back on the table, and waited for the storm to descend upon the huddled skaters.

"What are you doing?" her mother asked. "Why don't you answer me?"

Phyllis did not even hear her. For the first time she was listening to the sounds of the fair. It was odd how everything was going around. She heard the Shetland pony clopping about at the end of its rope; rocket ships circled with a sizzling noise; the ferris wheel spiraled over her head, rumbling and creaking, the foreshortened faces of its passengers openmouthed and seeming to cry. In the distance, Octavius's troops were marching in an endless circle upon the plains of Philippi. It was the assassins' reckoning.

Oh, how her own head was spinning! The stars of the constellations had broken loose from their moorings and whirled dizzily about her. The sides of the booth flapped as if caught in a wind. The world was in upheaval! Chaos was coming! She turned back to the crystal ball. One of the tiny figures had broken off at the ankle and lay face down on the ice. The last of the snow was funneling down the center of a cyclone, building up a mound over his body, a large white pillow whose underside was tinted green by the money spread out below.

"You have come to ask your fortune? Good day! You wish to know your fate?" She repeated this mechanically. Only the foot of the skater protruded from the snow. The storm had run out. The atmosphere within the ball was perfectly clear. She saw her own reflection bent back on the convex glass.

"Phyllis! I beg you! Don't frighten me!" her mother screamed.

She wanted to cry out, *Beware!* She wanted to say that the baby was stillborn, strangled, smothered by pillows or by the cord around its neck. But instead of that, from far away, in a different voice, she heard herself saying, "Madame Lola knows all, Madame Lola tells all, listen to Madame Lola."

She raised her arms straight out before her and slowly, by inches, extended her left hand, while at the same time her torso twisted from left to right, from right to left, as if by those calculated motions she could restore the collapsing universe and lift up the sky which had fallen onto her head.

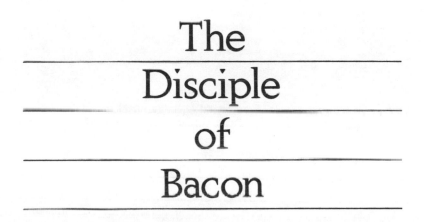

The
Disciple
of
Bacon

I

Hochbrucker, the scholar, was climbing the dark stairwell to his room. He couldn't see anything, but he could smell cantaloupes and pears and, on the third floor landing, dates from California. He lived, as it happened, on top of a warehouse for fruit. Light vegetables, too. A produce truck bumped against the loading ramp and the whole staircase shuddered. The banister crackled under his hand. Hochbrucker paused. What was that sharp, unusual smell? Radishes, he decided, bringers of luck. Then he tramped briskly upward. At the top of the stairs he reached for the light cord, grazed it, caught it, and the light came on. There he was, upon his toes, wearing sharkskin, with a green woolen cap on his head, and two large volumes slipping awkwardly from between his elbow and hip. He opened the door to his apartment, which smelled a little of figs.

It wasn't a proper apartment, it was only a room, an exact uncluttered square. In one corner there was a sofa and in another, diagonally opposite, an upright gramophone player. Along the other axis, a deep, enameled sink sat catercorner from a wooden chest of drawers. A fan hung down from the center of the ceiling, directly over a pedestaled table and chair. And that was all, no paintings on the whitewashed walls, no rugs on the unfinished floor, not even a lamp — nothing but a long file of books that marched in alphabetical order along the base of the walls, starting out from under the sofa and ending there too, head to tail, Adlgasser's great work on counterpoint pressed tightly against Zuchovsky's green-covered *Pieśni Ukochych*, "A Lover's Songs." It was, in Hochbrucker's words, "a perfect scholar's room."

Hochbrucker himself, as soon as he shut the door, went straight to the uncurtained window. He threw it open and leaned eastward out of the frame. Across the airshaft, behind smoking pipes, a round red sun hung quivering on a pane of glass. "No, no — how could it be?" Hochbrucker moaned; yet even as he watched, the sun began to bulge over the framing and onto the panel of glass below. The problem was that Hochbrucker had no money for such things as bulbs and candles. He worked by sunshine alone. How much was left? Three hours? Two hours? And such a lot to do! Was so little light worth so much effort? Half in and half out the window, the corners of the leather volumes pressing into his groin, he wavered, watching the New York afternoon spill away. It was a moment of despair. But a chance gust of uncrated dill struck him like smelling salts and brought him from his trance. "All the parsleys are propitious," he murmured, and banged the window to.

There was no time to dawdle now. Hochbrucker quickly set the two books in the center of the table, between a glass of water and a glass of pencils. Then, standing on the sturdily boxed set of Adalbert Gyrowetz's *Harmonija i Seksualnasa,* he pulled down his pants, shot a thin white stream of urine over the lip of the sink, and ran some water from the iron tap onto his hands. He crossed the room and took from the top drawer of the dresser a brown waxed-paper bag, which he shook vigorously back and forth. After this he removed a loaf of rye bread and carelessly dropped it back in the drawer. But from the sack itself Hochbrucker made a kind of a funnel; by tapping lightly on the bottom he managed to coax a steady fall of caraway seeds into a little glass dish. The next thing he did was take his horn-rimmed glasses out of their case and shine them on a single argyle sock. Then he took off his woolly cap and placed the glasses over his striking bald crown. This part of his head consisted of a long, bone-filled ridge with a slight depression in back, a scallop filled with baby's down. He was ready. He walked back to the table. He turned on the fan. He disliked seeing the cushion on the chair, it had such an unscholarly look; but aged seventy-four, with a gross of piles, he nonetheless sat down.

Time passed. The sun snaked over the sashes, the air in the shaftway cooled, smells from blueberries rose to great heights. On Horatio Street the trucks, coming and going, blew low, ship-like horns. But inside the room everything was still. No odor penetrated the vibrating blades of the fan, no sound overcame its powerful motor. The scholar sat with his chin on the backs of his bony wrists, his face blank and white. The row of books sagged listlessly. On the table a sheet of ruled paper rose at the corner and fell. In contrast, the caraway seeds jumped in their dish like a hill of ants. Now and then the old man's hand would fall among them; he would pinch two or three between finger and thumb, dip them in the glass of water, and force them between his teeth. All the while the light was draining imperceptibly off the walls.

Hochbrucker's mind was someplace else. The nearer his life's work came to completion, the more often he thought of the Cincinnyati, a radical nightspot where, in the winter of 1915, it had begun. His first memory of the back hall — of course no All-Bucharest Son of the Enlightenment was allowed in the front, that's where actual Rumanians drank yellowish drinks, pounding the tables, that's where Sophia Parados, the admired alto, sang songs — in fact, the first memory he possessed of anything, was of the water tumblers lined up on the Directors' table. This was approximately 1901. In front of the table there was a little raised platform, and on top of that was the Speaker's lectern. The rest of the room was divided left and right into benches, with an aisle down the center and a doorway in the back leading to the night-club area. A second door at the side led directly outdoors. From his seat at one of the rear benches, sitting on an intellectual cousin's knee, Hochbrucker watched the half-filled glasses winking and shining through the thick clouds of smoke. It was the fashion for Jews at the turn of the century to smoke cigars.

He remembered, even more clearly, how a few years later he had studied the glittering glass-beaded curtain that hung like icicles between Sleezing's lecture on dirigibles (or Saffron's on Neptune, the farthermost planet, or Dimshits's on Japan) and the clear, sunny flight of the following song:

> Vedrai carino
> Se sei buonino,
> Che bel rimedio,
> Ti voglio dar.

Sometimes this curtain would part and Sophia would lean against the jamb, clutching the elbow of one downcast arm, while Posner, the Speaker, described the reasons that fish always went upstream to spawn. She was near enough for Hochbrucker, on that knobby knee, to touch, close enough for him to make out the color, such a dark brown, of her deep-set eyes. Tiny ladders of black hair climbed up her temples and reappeared at the corners of her mouth. If she moved at all strands of light ran up and down her body. White teeth showed up in her mouth.

Every Son of the Enlightenment knew she was there (Hochbrucker's cousin pivoted his boot back and forth, as if grinding a stub out), though none dared turn around. She simply remained among the dazzling beads, her mouth falling slowly open, sometimes with a finger by her long, serious nose, until the pounding in the front room grew louder and, with a faint tinkle of the little bells she wore at her ears, she slipped away. Bernhardt, manufacturer of magnesium pastilles, owner of a French-made auto-car, put all of his fingers together and kissed them. "Look at that! She wants to listen!" he kept exclaiming. "Even a woman can learn!" Hochbrucker turned his already slightly pointed head and caught the light rippling across the glass curtain. He was growing older.

Nothing new in Manhattan. The scholar fumbled in the last of the caraways. He was staring through the window, not even blinking, as if he could see over the ocean, and the Carpathian Mountains, past even the curve of the earth, to where as a youngster he had been sitting. Yes, the Directors' tumblers! How they used to flash with light! He could remember each face behind the gleaming rims. Bearded, elegant Saffron, the Chairman himself. He had once visited Zagreb and seen the famous planetarium there. The Vice Chairmanship was a rotating position, and was once held by Popovitz, whom people called "the despotic Aaron." This was a reference to the Semitic tyrant, a sixteenth-century figure, who had exiled his own race from Rumanian soil. After him came Bernhardt, who was in turn replaced (owing to the immobilization of his auto in 1914, when there was an embargo on parts) by Mister Linting, who wore his hair slicked down in a part. One of his brothers, B. Linting, lived in America; L. Linting, his other brother, knew firsthand Traianu Kolotescu, a one-third owner of the Cincinnyati itself. Kelpman and Karp, by coincidence both from Tergu Frumas, alternated in the Treasurer's post. It was a regular rivalry between them. Kelpman said Karp was guilty of harboring Zionist feelings and that, moreover, he had held a secret Bar Mitzvah for his son. Karp suggested that Kelpman had been, in their native town, a rabbinical student, if not an actual rabbi, or even a Hasid, and that he only pretended to be an All-Bucharester. There was only one Secretary-Recorder, and he had held that office since the Sons of the Enlightenment began. This was old Smolenskin, in his own words "a revolutionary fighter," who had "carried the banner in '48." And even in Hochbrucker's time, when a world war was raging, he would read out the opening statement in a proud, defiant voice: "We meet according to our rights under Article XLIV of the Treaty of Berlin, and in the spirit of Disraeli, who secured them." Yes, Disraeli! Let the Rumanians pound!

That left, Hochbrucker knew, two unaccounted-for glasses. The face behind one was not present at the table, for it belonged to the legendary Moses Levai, the Emeritus. He was one of only eighty Jewish citizens of Rumania and hence, unlike the "protectees," entitled to sit in the front of the cafe, or anywhere else that he wanted. Later on, this was the rumor, he personally saved Sophia Parados from the general deportations during the Greco-Rumanian Disputes, 1920–24.

The last Director was Posner, holder of the Scholar's Chair. It used to be that that spot at the table belonged to the particular Speaker of the evening; but by agreement it came to be increasingly, and then exclusively, held by the brilliant academician who spoke so movingly about the lives of simple creatures. The Sons of the Enlightenment, who in their whole lives had never seen an actual animal except for a cat or a dog, would openly weep at the idea of a little mouse being eaten by an enormous green snake. Think of an Arctic tern, in a snowstorm, beating, beating its wings! Even Sophia would press her long wet lashes against her cheeks. Posner it was who stood on the podium that cold, windy evening in 1915 when, against all the rules, young Hochbrucker strode down the aisle and announced in a loud voice that W. A. Mozart was a Jew.

The silence that fell was complete. You could hear the wind gasp, as if in astonishment, out of doors. People sat up in the audience, for instance the Zuckerman twins, and asked each other what was going on. Old Smolenskin's mouth hung open; he couldn't shut it again. And at the lectern Posner froze, holding a tank full of newts. His spectacles had gone suddenly blank. Even the Rumanians seemed to be keeping unusually still. To Hochbrucker the whole world was hushed as, clearing his throat, he prepared to stitch up this gap in history.

Suddenly Popovitz stabbed a finger at the boy. "Out of order!" he shouted.

At once the current Vice Chairman, Mister Linting, jumped to his feet. "Be quiet! *You* are out of order!"

Bernhardt, who had held the post between them, calmly unwrapped a pastille. "Don't get excited, gentlemen," he said.

"The subject is salamanders," Popovitz piped. He stood up and read off the printed agenda: " 'Third piece of business — Lecture, *The Urodelan Amphibian and the Struggle for Life*. Full Professor N. Posner.' Unless Mozart had a tail," concluded the despotic Aaron, with a flash of that wit under which so many Sons had smarted, "the young man is out of order."

From the benches on both sides of the aisle came demands for recognition. "Mister Chairman," an old gentleman called, and threw his cap into the air. A knot of people began to shout at each other; it was a dispute of some kind. They all waved their index fingers like metronomes. A man wearing suspenders over a sweater began playing the clarinet. It was K. 564. In the next room the Rumanians pounded, and whistled for something. In short, it was tumult. In the middle of it all ungainly Karp dove for the Chairman's gavel and began to strike it so strenuously on the table that he knocked a glass of water into open-mouthed Smolenskin's lap.

"I differ with former Vice Chairman Popovitz upon the parliamentary question," he shouted. "Article twenty-two of our Constitution provides that in certain extraordinary circumstances, and at the discretion of the Chairman, the usual rules of order may be suspended."

"And what, I would like to know, is so extraordinary about W. A. Mozart or his religion?" shot back Kelpman from his chair. "Two decades ago, during a meeting of the Tergu Frumas Council of Citizens and Jews, we disposed of precisely this question, a question which, I might add" — and here, amazingly, a toothpick appeared in his mouth — "is typical of the Zealot mentality. Who is a Jew or who isn't a Jew is of no matter. We are all human beings here."

"Just a moment. Just a moment," said Karp, still swinging the gavel. "I am a rationalist. I want to speak. That question was not 'disposed,' to use our colleague's word for it, but was only suspended until such time as the report that W. A. Mozart named his son for a Jew could be proved. But perhaps you were too busy, my dear Kelpman, performing your mystical dances."

"The point, Karp," said Kelpman, "is that the rumor was *not* verified. Its foolishness should be obvious to anyone but a wishful thinker. I suggest, I make a motion, that we resume our proceedings where they were interrupted without further displays of Zionist enthnocentrism."

"I believe we were discussing the gills of the newly hatched newt," Popovitz interjected between the present and the former Treasurer.

"Why are my pants all wet?" asked the Secretary-Recorder, at that moment blinking his eyes.

Mister Linting cupped his hand over the old man's ear. "It's because W. A. Mozart named his son for a Jew!"

"His firstborn son," Smolenskin matter-of-factly responded. "Everyone knew that in the fifties."

"This," snickered Kelpman, "is a maneuver typical of Herzl and his crowd." But his warning went unnoticed as everyone began to argue with everyone else, it was the assimilationist left against the ethnic right, and the whole meeting fell into chaos — just as Popovitz, his arms crossed now in a caustic X, had predicted.

It was obvious that Chairman Saffron had to do something. Who was that pale young man with the handful of papers? What did he want? He ran his fingers through the yellow half of his beard, and then took the gavel away from Karp. Quite sternly, he started to speak: "Listen, young man, this is a learned society, it's not a marketplace. You are talking to savants here. We permit only scholarship, sound scholarship. Everything must be based upon the methods of the Enlightenment, in other words, upon the inductive technique originated by Diderot and Bacon and perfected by the Vilner Gaon and Voltaire. There is simply no room in Bucharest for rumor, innuendo, and appeals to emotion."

Hochbrucker did not hear a word. As the dealer in a game of

Klob will collapse the deck just before asking for the final wagers, so the spindly lad suddenly folded his notepapers together and with a deep breath began:

"Chairman Saffron, honored Directors, and" — here he swung about, the little frail fellow, and faced the roomful of people — "All-Bucharesters. W. A. Mozart's son, his first son, was born 17 June 1783 and was named — the word 'christened' is not appropriate — Raimund Leopold, after Baron Raimund Wetzlar von Plankenstern, son of Karl Abraham Wetzlar von Plankenstern, wholesale merchant, banker, Baron of the Realm. This Raimund Wetzlar von Plankenstern, whom da Ponte (whose real name, as I need hardly tell you, was not Lorenzo but Emmanuele, son of Geremia) called W. A. Mozart's 'great advisor and friend,' this Plankenstern was not only the infant Raimund's namesake, he was — how significant this is! — his godfather as well. The details of the ceremony are on record still at the Church am Hof in Vienna. I submit this fact, not to your emotions, but to your faculty of reason, and ask that I may be allowed to elucidate further the inherent logic of my research."

"Go on! Go on! Let him speak!" Everyone shouted this out.

"Of course we are going to let him speak," stammered Saffron. He beamed at the boy. "Please continue."

There was no need for Hochbrucker to spread out his notes again. The years of surreptitious study were arranged in an orderly file in his head. He was amazed how he could remember not only the location of a passage on the page, but the color of the binding, the typeface, even the smell of the dust that blew across his shaking fingers. (Thus Goethe's "I can remember the little fellow with his wig and his sword" was printed by Eckermann toward the top of the right-hand page dealing with February 3, 1830, a page that ran a crease down its center, ironically cutting the sword, *Degen*, in two. Why a wig? it occurred to Hochbrucker all of a sudden. To cover up Hebraic ringlets and curls? The Helbling portrait of 1767 was infuriatingly obscure precisely at the eleven-year-old's ears. Was this deliberate chiaroscuro? An example of Christian tact?) These thoughts darted through his mind even as he spun his thread of facts and logic about the hardly breathing Sons.

"On 19 August, 1783, R. L. Mozart, just two months old, died of an intestinal cramp, the German *Gedärmfrass*. What more may we say of the infant's godfather? That he was W. A. Mozart's admirer and friend we have already established. That he was his co-religionist too must be deductively pried from the few facts history has vouchsafed us. In December of 1782 the composer and his wife moved to a new apartment in Vienna, on the Hohe Brücke, number forty-two, third floor, the so-called Little Herberstein House. There were two rooms, an anteroom and kitchen. The landlord: Raimund Wetzlar, Baron Plankenstern. A month later a private ball was held for Mozart there, sponsored by the Baron. A month after that, February, 1783, our subject moved out, and again the expenses were undertaken by the good Wetzlar. We know, alas, little else, save that the Baron was named godfather in June, gave a quartet evening in early April, subscribed to all of Mozart's concerts and publications (a subscription list that included, by the way, Regine Josepha Aichelburg, née Wetzlar, old Karl Abraham himself, one Nathan Adam von Arnstein, and various Binnenfelds, Jacobis, Levanaus, and Schwabs — Schwab, Philip, and Schwab, Ignaz, wholesale merchants), and that the two friends at times dined together.

"These facts by themselves reveal little. It is in the juxtaposition of details, the addition of two of this and of that, that we shall reach the four of historical truth. Thus, when, *precisely,* did the two old comrades dine? The only date that has come down to us is the twenty-seventh of March, 1785, when W. A. Mozart supped at the home of the Baron. And why is that date significant? Because, in the first place, it is a Sunday, and in the second place it is Easter Sunday. Father and godfather quietly breaking bread on such a day, altogether apart from the celebrations in the rest of the world — just the gesture of sarcastic bravado we would expect from the creator of the fantastical Don — who also, we might add, was given to symbolic dinner invitations.

"Furthermore, we must ask precisely *where* did Mozart at last

settle down with the help of his devoted follower and friend?
Fortunately, we know the answer. On the twenty-fourth of April,
1783, W. A. Mozart moved to a first-floor apartment in the Inner
City, and to be yet more rigorous, more meticulous, more *exact*"
— and here Hochbrucker allowed himself a triumphant glance at
the podium, where Posner, to whose porcupines and sleeping
bears he had been forced to attend for week after week, year
after year, all the while his own idea swelling in his head like a
melon, remained paralyzed with shock, his eyes peering sense-
lessly through dead spectacle lenses — "to be more scientific in
every way, W. A. Mozart's address was number two-forty-four,
number two-forty-four *Judenplatz!*"

There was no calming the waters now. Each faction united in
crying "Up front! Up front!" Hochbrucker shouldered his way
through the pandemonious crowd. A group of men had overturned a number of benches and were performing a kind of handkerchief dance. Dimshits, the expert on Japan, had apparently
fainted. People were slapping his face. It must be said that irre-
spective of the spirit of Disraeli, quite a few All-Bucharesters
were rocking backward and forward and saying their prayers.
Meanwhile, above it all, the old gentleman's cap flew like an
albatross, an omen, thought Hochbrucker, as he approached the
Directors' table, of imminent success.

Mister Linting greeted him, shook his hand in both of his own,
offered him "in my capacity as Vice Chairman" the floor. An
excited Karp slapped him on the back and yelled into his ear,
"Mozart, Mendelssohn, Meyerbeer, the three M's, eh, my dear
fellow? What an achievement!" Even Saffron was standing and
holding out his hand. The boy refused to take it. What right had
that personage, with his odd two-color beard, to lecture him,
from the beginning a disciple of Bacon, about the inductive
method? What they had heard so far was nothing! Just facts! He
would show them what real scholarship was! Thus Hochbrucker
turned his back on the Chairman and walked straight for the
lectern, where Posner still stood.

What was the great piece of learning Hochbrucker had ready?

It had nothing to do with such vulgar commonplaces as comparing the Masonic ritual of *Die Zauberflöte* with the secrets of the Zohar. Nor did it depend upon his own discovery that the Greek setting of *Idomeneo* was merely a clever disguise for the Old Testament story of Jephtha. No! He meant to plunge his audience directly into his interpretation of K. 118, W. A. Mozart's oratorio based on Metastasio's *Betulia Liberata*. This opera — Hochbrucker was mentally going over his dissertation — far from being the usual celebration of the beleaguered Jews or the traditional depiction of Judith's heroism in freeing them from Holofernes' grasp, concentrates instead on Achion, an Ammonite prince who is won over to the Hebrew cause and eventually to their religion. Why, we must ask, this focus upon a hero who, when living among the gentiles is described as a prisoner (*"prigioner"*) trapped in horrid night (*"orrori"*), and who, arriving safely in the Jewish camp, is said to receive the splendor (*"lo splendor"*) of daylight (*"i lumi a'rai del giorno"*), unless the composer was in fact transposing into harmonic terms his own isolation within a society of night, trapped in the *"orrori"* of silence and dissembling, unable to express his thoughts save to himself, to declare himself — except in his art, in his music? Thus the conversion of Achion —

> *Giuditta, Ozia, Popoli, Amici, io credo.*
> *Vinto sonnio. Prende un novello aspetto*
> *Ogni cosa per me. Tutto son pieno,*
> *Tutto del Vostro Dio. Grande, infinito,*
> *Unico lo confesso. . . .*

must be understood as W. A. Mozart's only recorded testament of faith:

> *Judith, Ozia, People, Friends, I believe.*
> *I am convinced. Behold, everything*
> *Takes on a new aspect for me. I am full,*
> *Full of your God. Great, infinite,*
> *One, I acknowledge him.*

Hochbrucker arrived at the lectern. This was no time to be magnanimous. The crowd was saying, *Shhh! Shhh!* "There has been a change in the agenda," he announced, knowing full well that the substitution was permanent, that the reign of the Full Professor upon the Scholar's Chair had come to an end. But Posner, the shock victim, yet refused to move. Why wouldn't he go? Even the newts seemed to be stricken, with their little arms against the glass.

"Am I dreaming, or what?" Posner asked.

Hochbrucker puffed up his body. The overhead light picked out the white of his scalp beneath his soft, black, close-cropped hair. There was a large brown mole on the bridge of his nose. "It is not a dream," said the boy. "The old must give way to the new."

Some spring seemed to give way in Posner's back. His head slumped down. His knees struck each other. "You have the key to knowledge," he told the fifteen-year-old, and wearily, like one of his aged turtles, the natural scientist dragged himself away.

Briskly, the prodigy took his place. "Friends!" he said. He looked out into the audience, who had politely put their cigars out. They were rapt. A movement of light caught his eye. "Friends!" he said once again, and halted. There was a ringing sound in his ears, like little bells. He raised his eyes a little and saw, perfectly clearly, Sophia, glistening like a mermaid among the beads. Sophia! She had come to hear him! She was interested in what he had to say! A warm, tingling feeling rushed through his entire body, and all of his notes fell on the floor. No matter! He knew each word by heart! His narrow chest kept swelling and swelling. "Distinguished Sons!" he started to say.

Then he saw something awful. There, next to Sophia, with his hand on her neck and his white thumb against her throat's swarthy hollow, stood Moses Levai. Hochbrucker took in all at once how her breasts heaved, how a shiver ran down her body in a sparkle of light, and how she cast toward him, the Speaker, a look of anguish, yearning, and despair. The faithful crowd did not suspect that a drama was taking place. But he understood.

She wanted him to save her, to free her from the Emeritus's grasp, to help her to learn. He staggered somewhat. Was he equal to the task? The answer came to him: yes! Had he not conquered Mind, that is to say Posner, and driven him from the field? He would triumph over Body as well, over Levai, who so easily, so familiarly, laid his fingers like a strand of plump pearls upon Sophia's neck. He would shatter his hold! He imagined the fat flesh withering, crinkling like ash before the bright flame of his revelation!

"The Zohar speaks of the marriage of day and night, light and dark," he began. No, not *Die Zauberflöte,* the Masonic parallel had already been dealt with by Hernski's publications. "It is no accident, Distinguished Members, that *Idomeneo* was W. A. Mozart's favorite among all his works." This wasn't correct! He wanted to speak of something else! What was it? Metastasio! "*Betulia Liberata,* far from being the usual celebration of the beleaguered Jews . . ." His voice trailed away. When, over the years, he had seen Sophia, it had been from his seat on the bench, from below, the slight projection of upper lip over lower, the round, thoughtful tip of her nose, the edge of her brows, the brilliant black crown of hair only partly deflecting the bundles of light on her earrings. She sighed now and her breasts pressed against the stiff sequined front of her dress and then fell away, so that it was possible to follow them downward into endless shadow. Once more, desperately, he tried to pierce the thunderous silence with the words of the Ammonite prince, but once more Sophia breathed deeply, taking his own breath away as her breasts threatened to hurl themselves over the rim of her dress and then fell back, at once exposed and obscured, like the hot springs he had seen in the Transylvanian alps: one moment bubbling over their craters and the next withdrawing to the center of the earth. His tongue stuck to the roof of his mouth.

At that moment Smolenskin, whose crotch had been dampened, either sneezed or yawned, you couldn't tell which, and that seemed to break the trance of the spellbound Sons. The whole room, all together, seemed to sigh. It was as if someone had taken the lid from a pan of frying food, and released the smell of fraud in the air. The All-Bucharesters muttered and shrugged and wrapped long, disenchanted mufflers around their throats. No one looked at the adolescent on the podium. Sophia and Levai had disappeared, leaving only a plash of excited light on the curtain's beads. Icy wind swept through the open door like a broom.

Hochbrucker did not feel it. Nor was he aware that his audience had all gone away. He was insulated from everything by the moment, which he knew to be the most crucial of his life. For it was at this moment that the ripple of light around her body, the darkness between her breasts, the regret in her eyes, became inextricably and forever part of his being, the source of all his future power, the sustainer of his life's work, his illuminator, destroyer, upholder, inspirer. He had lost the Scholar's Chair. He had gained a Muse.

Former Treasurer Kelpman was the only Son who stopped at the doorway to look back, and this only for an instant, just long enough to turn his toothpick with his tongue. The boy remained at the lectern, stock still, as if made of stone; at his feet the scholarly notes rustled and blew, like scraps about the base of an heroic statue.

II

The sun fell off the bottom pane of the distant glass, and the fifth-floor room became impossibly dark. You could hardly see the white square of paper. Two bloated seeds lay under an inch of water, whose surface was barely ruffled by the whirling fan. The two leather volumes, *Nifluot Maharal,* "Miracles of the Maharal," and Giovanni Bertati's *Il Convitato di Pietra,* "The Stone Guest," remained at the center of the table, unopened. Hochbrucker groaned in the dismal light. This was the day dedicated to the relationship between the Commendatore theme of *Don Giovanni* and the Golem myth. And he had yet to write a word! He plucked a pencil from the glass, pulled the lower edge of the notebook against his chest; but before his eyes the swatch of paper faded further, like a TV screen going out.

The scholar pushed himself from the table and pulled the cord that stopped the fan. Heavy trucks were idling in the streets. Inside the building someone was shouting, feet rang on the metal edges of the staircase, and at the end of the hall the toilet began to cascade. Hochbrucker felt his way to the gramophone player, which he opened outward, like the doors of an ark. It was an old-fashioned Capehart which held a thick pile of records in the crook of a black mechanical arm. These were 78's, and the machine knew how to turn each completed disk upside down and play, in just the right order, the other side. It could go through, without an error, a four-act opera, and then automatically stop.

The uppermost record label showed clouds shooting sunrays over the names of the most illustrious Central European artists of the 1920's, Hanna Hrušková and Jiri Čermak, while in addition two angels aimed bows at the manufacturer's name: PRAHA. Hochbrucker engaged the changing mechanism and returned to the table; as he was sitting down again, the Commendatore knocked seven times at the door — just as Isaac ben Shimshon circled the homunculus of the Maharal seven times in order to make its clay eyes glow with the fire of life.

"*Apri, apri dico,*" Giovanni ordered his dumbstruck servant, and the music swelled with what was meant to be terror, but was now the shrill laboring of a toy-sounding band. Nevertheless, the Commendatore entered on two magnificent chords which retained something of their original ominousness, the very notes, Hochbrucker maintained, that Rabbi Yehuda Loew blew upon the shofar when he created the famous Golem of Prague. "You have invited me to dinner," the stone guest announced, "*e son venuto.*" The Don ordered his servant to set another place at table, but the Commendatore stopped him with the words "*Non si pasce di cibo mortale.*"

"Exactly! Exactly!" the excited Hochbrucker, in Rumanian, shouted. The best way to unmask a suspected demon is to offer it food, which, lacking an alimentary canal, it will be forced to reject.

"*Chi si pasce di cibo celeste,*" the statue continued, in what could only be a reference to the tetragrammaton, the "celestial food" of God's Ineffable Name. Yes! The Shem ha-Meforash!

After thus getting around Don Giovanni's offer, the Commendatore explained that he had more important ("*più gravi*") matters to discuss. The Don asked him what it was, then, he wished ("*Che chiedi? Che vuoi?*"). The Commendatore's voice dropped an octave as he asked his host to listen with care since he — like the Golem, whose span on earth is circumscribed — had little time left to speak.

"*Parla, parla,*" Giovanni replied bravely, and when the Commendatore failed to answer he said it, with some impatience, once again: "Speak, speak, I am listening to you."

At which point the record ran out and there was nothing but a nervous, scratching sound. Hochbrucker glanced into the open Capehart, which, in the gloom, appeared to be an enormous black beetle contorting itself over the spindle shaft. When at last a new side dropped down, instead of the Commendatore's return invitation to Don Giovanni, "will you come to dine with me?" there was for some reason a woman's voice. What was this? A mistake? The sequence of play had gone wrong. This was not the end of the opera, it was Zerlina's remedy for her lover's wounds, which closed Act Two, scene one.

> *Vedrai carino*
> *Se sei buonino,*
> *Che bel rimedio,*
> *Ti voglio dar.*

Although sung in this case by a soprano, and by an artist undoubtedly dead, Hochbrucker knew the tune. Decades burst around him, the shining curtain began to part. This was Sophia's lullaby, the Muse's song, the salve for all his afflictions. For it was he, not Masetto, who had been beaten, had suffered shame, scorn, humiliation, the laughter of the academies, the musicologists' neglect, and, the deepest wound of all, the disgrace of self-doubt. Thus it was to him that Hrušková offered her wondrous balm ("*un certo balsamo*"), the ministration no druggist knows but which every woman, in a secret place, possesses:

> *Dare tel posso*
> *S'il vuoi provar!*
> *Saper vorresti?*
> *Dove mi stà?*

"If you want to try it, I can give it to you. Do you want to know where it is?" sang the siren, inspirer, uplifter, coquette. Hochbrucker squirmed in his seat. Zerlina took Masetto's hand, as Hrušková took an unknown basso's, as Sophia took now her scholarly admirer's, and placed it beneath her dress and over her heart.

> *Sentilo battere,*
> *Toccami quà!*

"Hear it beating, touch me here — " here at the shadow's end, at the source of the hidden spring. Without warning, beneath the shiny sharkskin, his Jewish member began to stir. The soprano had repeated her closing phrase four times and Leporello was already figuring out a way of escaping Donna Elvira by the time Hochbrucker, his cap pulled down over his ears, stood in the street, pineapples all around him.

The warehouse over which Hochbrucker lived was an island of vegetarianism in a sea of meat. Only four steps east were the packinghouses of Friend and Monahan, as well as W. 11th Street Poultry, Inc. He passed them at a near trot, dodged the water that always dripped from the railway bridge, turned left on Washington Street and lost sight of the looming funnels of the hawsered ships. He was accompanied, as always, from Gansevort, past Little West Twelfth Street, by a stretch of wall whose stenciled signs he had never mastered, a list of organs — top rounds and bottom rounds, fillets and knuckle faces, livers, kidneys, and tongue — he could not recite or read. *Gooseneck Liverwurst*, the sign said, *from Seiler's Phila. Scrapple.*

He was forced to slow down at the corner of Fourteenth Street and pick his way through the wet, stained sawdust, the wrapping paper, the ubiquitous abandoned gloves. Even at this hour the central packing area was crowded. Barrels with fat in them blocked his path. There were pools of blood at the bottom of plastic sacks. Meat-eating pigeons flopped over his shoes. Like the Don, he had been plunged into an awful inferno! Trucks, like mammals, mounted the curbs and forced the old man into the street. Here there were medieval-looking hooks, and belts, and scales, all stamped: Cincinnati Butchers' Supply Co., 98 Forsyth St. Despite the misspelling, he knew that word. He kept his eyes on writing he could not decipher, "eviscerated turkeys," for instance, or on those, *Meichman, Seligman, Hoffman* and *Mayer,* it seemed safer to read.

At last Hochbrucker reached Ninth Avenue and turned into residential Chelsea. A few blocks ahead, past the boys playing ball with a hoop, on the other side of the seminary students who were carrying a rug, was a colored girl who flicked a pink ribbon at him and asked, "Where you headin', Daddy?" whenever he went by. He always walked quickly past and turned at Twenty-third Street, without explaining that he was going for a bath at the Y. This time, however, he simply stood and stared at her while she rolled her ribbon back up on her finger; when she opened her coat to him he stepped without hesitation into her arms.

No one paid any attention. The men in the tavern across the streets kept on drinking, women skirted them with shopping carts, and two policemen in a parked car continued their conversation. Hochbrucker, lost in the folds of her coat, smelled the brilliantine of her hair, saw the dark skin, and the darker creases, of her neck. "Like a harem beauty in *Die Entführung,*" he thought to himself and leaned against her, catching his breath when he felt her lean back. He thought, in his horrid English, of what to call her. Constanze, Dorabella, Zaïde, the Queen of the Night; "Vot's de name, honey?" he blurted at last, but a merciful bus drowned him out. They remained on the sidewalk embracing, gold lettering of the Wm. Gong Laundry over her shoulder, a tricolored barber pole spiraling from the top of his head.

Hochbrucker heard her say, "We gonna fiddle 'round here all night, or are you gonna come upstairs with me?" The streetlights snapped on. Blinded by the incandescent arc, he reeled back from her and fumbled across the intersection. Outside the bar he found two empty liquor bottles and a gallon jug once filled with wine.

Scooping them up, he headed downtown, but stopped soon in front of an antique store, where he discovered half of a discarded chandelier. From a wire trash basket he plucked the pane from a broken picture frame. At a novelty shop on Fourteenth Street he bought three dollars' worth of beads, bottles, trinkets, and mirrors. With his pockets overflowing, gathering into his loaded arms all the stray light from shopfronts, from headlight beams, he retraced his steps, running. And as he ran, past the nearly deserted packing center, past the arcane writing on the walls, and up the scented stairwell, the crystal lozenges of the chandelier struck each other, tinkling like bells. In his pitch-black room, with three free fingers, he managed to pick up from the table the two glasses and the little dish. He crossed to the window and nudged it up with his shoulder and hurled out his armfuls of glass. Then he groped his way to the sofa and lay down, his shoes on, spent. The fan was motionless. The books lay collapsed around the room. The edge of the notebook paper rose once, like a pale flag of surrender. *Shhhh!* went the needle, over the black, grooveless center of the record. From the faint luminescence that moved on the walls, Hochbrucker knew that high above him, embedded in the sky like an auspicious birthmark, the moon shone down on the mountain of shards.

Memory

I

"Herman, pardon me, but did you take a bath lately?"

"What's the matter, Sam, is one missing?"

Both men in brown suits, entering from opposite sides of the stage. Regina remembered how one man, Sam, wrinkled his nose.

Herman, indignantly: "I want you to know I have a bath three times a year, whether I need one or not!"

A series of violinists, with white handkerchiefs under their chins. Eyes shut. Every note memorized.

The Family, a play. The right part of the stage, as you faced it, was Russia. America on the left. While a man and woman and their daughters were wondering if a character were alive or dead, why they had not received a letter, you could actually see this person opposite — behind bars, or through a sweatshop window, or on a box making a speech. At the turn of the century this had been a sensational technique; when Regina had seen it, in the thirties, it was already old hat. And most of the seats were empty.

In 1934, it must have been, Zilbayarsky came out of retirement. What a lot of people! As many standing as sitting. "How sharper than a serpent's tooth it is," the actor cried, striking his chest, the *thump-thump-thump* awful to hear, "To have a thankless child." He said he would not weep. "No, I'll not weep"; but the spotlight lit up the tears that came out of his eyes. In the storm his back broke, he used a stick, fed cheese to a mouse. At the end he pointed to his daughter. "Look there, look there." But nothing happened. Then he died.

Endless jokes. For example, a Jew gets on a train at Krakow, on his way to Lodz. After a while a clever peasant spreads out his lunch, a half chicken, thick salamis, peaches, three smoked trout. Opposite, the Jew unwraps the head of a carp. Thinks the Pole to himself, well, how come these Yids are so smart? Maybe it's what they eat. *A police car, or ambulance, or fire truck, raced down Second Avenue.* Three hours later they come into the station. All the bones are by the feet of the Jew. *Another followed, drowning everything out.*

Regina, with a notepad on her knee, nervously twittered a pencil between two fingers. She could, after forty years, remember the punch line — "See? Already you're smarter!" — but not what made it funny. The comedian had a long head, a long face, and blue thin lips.

The sound of the sirens died away. On the stage teen-age girls were chanting prayers and shaking bells. Sweat shone on their faces, their breasts. The incense they burned smelled like overripe fruit. Soon, she thought, people would take off their clothes. It was hot, airless. She glanced quickly at Charles, but could not make out his expression. Looking up, around, she tried to remember how much of the theater remained from her childhood. The seats, with their plywood backs, wooden armrests, the red plush worn through to pink threads, were original fixtures, as were the wall lamps, once fitted for gas. But the masks above and to either side of the proscenium, grinning and grimacing, looked new — installed, probably, to mark the return of the theater to drama, instead of the films that had played there for years. Boxes hung over the orchestra, and the gilded figures on each —

mermaids and centaurs and little Pans — were broken and chipped, so the white plaster showed through. A large chandelier dropped down from the vault of the ceiling, and this she remembered, a circle of bulbs on curved metal necks, every one of them lit. The dim glow was touching, like Englishmen in English novels, Kipling's or Conrad's, dressed for dinner, their shoes shined in the jungle.

"Jesus," said Charles to her. "Look at that."

A small lamb was at the front of the stage. The girls sat in a semicircle around it, while it simply stood, its head stretched downward, as if to graze, its hindquarters shaking.

"What's going on here? What are they going to do with it?"

"I don't know," Regina told him.

Someone in the audience began to sing, "We're little black sheep that have gone astray!" The sound of a flute, played by a cross-legged girl, her face hidden by dark hair, cut across his voice. Others joined in: "Baa! Baa! Baa!" But a drum was playing, and the lamb raised its white head.

Charles leaned toward her. "I've got a terrible feeling."

"Don't worry." Regina said this with a laugh, her teeth showing sharply against the shade of her skin. He nodded, and turned to the stage. She looked at him, carefully enough to make out the long lashes, black and incongruous in what was otherwise a strong, square, masculine — almost an athlete's — face. He wore his hair long and ruffled up, wreathlike (is this why she thought of him as athletic? She didn't think, actually, he was), over a bald, tan patch. She was glad he hadn't changed his tie, which she thought very beautiful. He had been wearing it that afternoon, in the office elevator, and on an impulse she had asked him if he could use her extra ticket to the theater.

He answered, because of the elevator, staring ahead. "What is it? Off-Broadway?"

"It's an old movie theater, on Second Avenue."

"I don't go to the theater much any more. I don't go at all. It embarrasses me."

"What does?"

"The flesh-and-blood. The actors. To me it's just guys walking around, talking, waving their arms, whatever."

"You can't forget they're actors?"

"Yeah. Right. I want to protect them. To screen them off. Poor suckers. I'm ashamed for them."

"Well," she had said, "do you want to risk it?" The colors of his tie were red and green, bled together, with here and there a yellow parrot, upside down.

"Sure. But I'd prefer a movie. I'm crazy for them."

They dropped thirty stories. Regina worried. Was she going to ask men to take her out?

Charles was right, really. People said the theater was boring — but that wasn't it. It was embarrassing, mortifying. And movies *were* different. She used to say — had written a waspish article — in a plastic age, celluloid is the natural medium, like spun soybeans. She knew herself it was a shabby explanation. Light passing through a film; that was more the shape and manner of the brain itself. A beam projected from behind; in front, the screen, an expanded retina — the whole drama, the vague, shifting ideas, inside of one's head. Regina always looked at the crowds. In the movies the faces were tilted up, row on row, pebblestones, moons. Here — she threw an elbow over the back of her seat — people were yawning, grinning, looking away. Their faces seemed red to her, as if they were humiliated, the way Charles had said, by the actors' flesh and blood. It occurred to her that the imagination, like any other part of the body, could become diseased. Was this (smiling a little, against the line of her mouth) the illness of their time? Still, she doubted that things were ever different. All the Jews standing in these aisles, craning over each other for a glimpse not of Lear, not the King, but Zilbayarksy, Zilbayarsky with his cancer, how he wept, hobbled, pounded his chest, although a dying man. "Look there, look there," and they looked, squinted, said to each other, *What's going on? What's he talking about?* But from the balcony Regina, age four, or age five, had followed the line from his finger and saw something, like a small animal, a white pet, moving on his dead daughter's lips. She knew it was Cordelia's soul.

This audience now made an O with their mouths, and gasped. She turned back toward the stage. The girls huddled together, the light glancing off their backs. A black thick liquid rippled under their heels, staining them.

"All right," Regina told Charles. "It's not real."

But he had hold of the back of a seat, and was leaning forward. To the flute and the drum the girls drew apart. The lamb lay on its back, its heart still pumping blood. People lifted their heads, smelling it. No one said anything. The girls came into the aisles and picked out a boy, blond, with a blond girl friend, and made him stand. He was wearing a light college jacket in blue and white. Yale. He stepped into the aisle. The blond put her hands over her open mouth. He went onto the stage. He was taller than any of the girls, and very thin. They took off his clothes. He turned away. They brought him back. He crossed his hands before him. They raised his arms. His penis was small, retracted, his testicles drawn high with anxiety. Regina stood up.

"I want to go," she told Charles.

He stared at her. He didn't know her.

"Excuse me," she said, and stepped over his planted feet.

He followed her out. "Look," he said, at the door.

On the stage the boy was standing, all bony, with a spot of blood on his eyebrows, and on his right hand and his right foot's great toe.

The avenue was as hot as it had been during the day. The street lamps were on. Blocks down a group of red trucks, with red lights, had gathered, but there was no smoke, no fire. A lot of people were in the streets, moving in front of lighted windows. Regina took hold of Charles's arm. "I'm sorry," she said.

"What for?"

"I didn't know it would be like that. How rotten you had to see it."

"I enjoyed it. I guess I wish I didn't, it sounds so lousy, but my heart was pounding like hell. My heart never pounds. I can control it. When they killed that lamb, when I knew they really killed it, my hair stood, I sweated. A lamb is a big animal, it's not like killing a fly."

"Then I'm sorry I made you leave." Regina smiled a little, which again contradicted the downward lines of her small, flat face. She put a cigarette in her mouth. He lit it.

"Are you all right, Regina?"

"Yes. I am. I was fine until I felt this confusion. It was as if all the air had gone out of the room. But instead of not being able to breathe, I couldn't think. My brain stopped."

He laughed. "No one will believe it!"

So did she. "It's started again."

He asked her if she had eaten. He knew a place nearby where they had baked stuffed artichoke. They could split one, with wine.

She hesitated, unsettled that it should be so hot — at night, and still only May. She would go home, bathe, allow herself three cigarettes. But she was surprised to feel hungry. "How do you stuff an artichoke?"

A boy, white, Italian-looking, with damp curls on his forehead, stepped from behind a car and said, "Give me a quarter."

Automatically Regina snapped open her bag. Charles pushed her behind him. "What?" he said to the boy.

"I want some change."

"What?"

"You got ears."

The boy was wearing a white undershirt, the straps over his bare shoulders. "I could waste you easy," he told Charles, and took a step back. His hands were in the pockets of his jeans.

"Say it again, okay?"

Regina saw a cab and waved her arm. "I want to go home."

"Riverside and a hundred and second," Charles told the driver. He got in beside her. The boy put his head in the open window.

"Watch out for me, Jack."

The cab went west a block, then moved skillfully in and out of the cars on Third Avenue. The driver's name was Griminoux — Haitian, Regina guessed, staring at the thin black face, the compressed lips, in the photo. Charles put his arm on her shoulder.

"You take out the heart," he said.

She edged toward the corner. He stayed with her. What was he talking about? Oh! Artichokes! Breadcrumbs! She let him try to kiss her cheek. His leg trembled alongside hers. She realized the performance, the killing, the backs and breasts of the girls, even the Yale boy, a teen-ager only, had excited him. What if he thought she had been aroused? That that was why she wanted to leave? To take him home? It would be a misunderstanding. She thought of many things she could say; but what she said was, "You were married once, weren't you?"

He started to tell her about his wives, the poetess, the novelist. He said he liked lady writers. "We're still amicable."

Regina looked out the window, at the cross streets, and Charles kissed the lobe of her ear.

"Lady writers!" Regina said. "Is it a species?"

"There are characteristics. They neglect their teeth."

"I don't know you well enough to kiss you. I don't know if you have any children."

"Look, I think I know what's bothering you. That kid was giving orders. He wasn't asking. Do you think I care about a lousy quarter? It's got nothing to do with the principle of the thing. I give away a lot of money on the street."

"Well what were you trying to do, make him say please?"

The driver turned around to ask where they wanted to go through the park. He was heavy, with an American drawl. It disturbed Regina that the man and the photo did not match.

"Okay, forget it." He took her hand, in a conciliatory way, but Regina let it lie there, knowing that would be maddening.

What breeze there was that evening came from the west, and carried with it the pale sour smoke from the factory, or refinery

— Regina did not know what it was, only that it ran night and day, Sundays included, turning out a large pile of white ash, Jews' bones, she thought in her wildest moments — on the other side of the river. There were nights, winter nights, all the city's furnaces burning number 6 fuel under flat clouds, the sulfur spreading to where she lay on her bed, when she felt herself to be just that: a Jewess in a giant oven. The smell was in the lobby, and inside the lobby door, on which someone was banging. She looked back. Charles pressed to the glass.

"You should have kept the cab," she told him.

"I want to walk you upstairs."

"There's an elevator."

But he followed her across the black and white tiles.

They rode up silently; then he walked behind her down the narrow hall. She took the door key out of her bag, and turned about. He asked her if she would be at the magazine the next day. She said she would stay home to write her review. He said he would like to see what she had to say. She would, too, she said, again with a laugh. He put his left hand on her waist and bent near her. She pulled back and put her key to the lock. It was upside down.

"I like your hair," he was saying. "I like your mouth. I like your neck. I like your ears. Smile, I like your smile."

The key went in. The cylinder turned. Double locked.

"You smiled three times tonight."

The cylinder went over again.

"You have the kind of face that belongs on a statue, a lasting face. You look as if you were seeing ruins."

"Is that from the novelist? Or the poetess?"

"You think that I'm mocking you?"

"No."

"I like the way you smell."

"Don't say that. Any of that. There's no reason to mention my hair."

Her hair was black, parted in the center, with a few long white wiry strands in it. He scooped it up, squeezed it. She gasped. It was as if he held a handful of nerves.

"Goodnight, Charles," she said.

"Okay."

He went down the hall. She waited, gave the key a half-turn, and pushed. There was a chain across the door. Foolishly she closed it, hoping the chain would drop away. It held. Though she had left a light on, there was only a black crack on the other side of the door.

Regina went back to the elevator and called Charles's name. A pile of weights sank into the shaft. The box rose, like something approaching in space. The cage arrived, empty. Then she heard someone skipping stairs. Charles was running. She saw his bald spot, saw the hair slipping from it.

"Regina, what's wrong?"

"I'm locked out. There's a chain across the door."

He led the way to the apartment and pushed the door as far as it would go. "Have you got a key for this?"

"There is none. It slips off from the inside."

"Well how did you get it on?"

"I didn't. I locked the door, but I didn't put on the chain."

"Then someone's inside. Who?"

"Benjamin. Francis. But they wouldn't throw the chain. Francis can barely reach it. Ben never did this before. He knew I was coming back late. He knew I had to get in."

"Maybe he put it on and meant to take it off. Only forgot. Wait a second." Charles worked his right hand through and pulled at the links. His body shook. He clamped his lower lip.

"Are you going to snap it?"

"No! Christ!" He pulled his hand out. The fingers were white, pinched. "You'll have to call your boys."

She did, loudly, and rang the bell. There was no response.

"Try it again."

"They can't hear me. They must be asleep."

"What about the back door? Isn't there a service door to the landing?"

"Yes. But it's locked."

"Well, do you have a key? Does the super have a key? It's not that late —"

"No, I mean, it's bolted. It doesn't work with a key."

"Okay. Then I'll telephone. I guess they'll hear that. I'll tell them you're out here. There's a booth on West End; if it's working I'll use it."

"You hurt your hand."

"That's a strong chain, Regina."

"I am sorry. It's so stupid."

"I've counted the times you said I'm sorry. Four times."

"My God, what don't you count! I don't like it. What are you trying to find out about me?"

"I just want to know one thing. What did they do to that boy? What happened after we walked out of the theater?"

Instead of replying, she wrote out her number and gave it to him. He walked down the stairs.

Regina counted, too. Cigarettes. She lit another and leaned against the wall. She saw herself, as she sometimes did, from above and outside, with an elbow cupped in her hand, the posture of a bored woman, a prostitute, an usherette. But she was not bored. It occurred to her that she was looking at herself with Charles's eyes. He thought she would sleep with him. He thought she would show him the theater. *What did they do to that boy?* She remained, with one foot against the wall.

All right, what *did* they do to him? She would face it. She recalled his thin stick legs, the points of his pelvis, his hands crossed before him — that's what doomed him, that gesture. It was from another world. Whiffenpoofs. And she had stood up. Run away. Why? Why hadn't she stayed? She had been panting like a fish out of water, no air reaching her brain. "See? Already you're smarter!" *Ziehst? Du bist shoyn klieger!* But why was everyone laughing? Because the Jew got the Pole's food and the Pole got the Jew's. What was funny about that? Then she realized that the Pole had sacrificed everything for intelligence and had ended with the head of a carp. At the same time, and here was the twist, the wry Yiddish joke: he got his money's worth; he had learned. Such snorting! She had made a bad mistake about the comedian. The long face, the wide dark lips were her father's, the way her father looked now. Mentally, she added the white wisps of hair that fell uncombed over his collar. He used to have shelves of fragile things. He used to blow animals for her out of glass. Warm tears came into her eyes. She thought of Zilbayarsky saying, *Didst thou give all to thy daughters? And art thou come to this?* Oh, how could she turn her father, the old gentleman, into a gagman, some Herman, some Sam? But she suffered too, gave everything to her children, and what did they do? They locked her out! She stamped her foot in irritation.

The hallway was dim, and pink-painted. "Eight," said Regina, lighting one cigarette from the hot tip of another. The door was open a crack. She shut it. She thought it perfectly possible that the boys were wide awake and that the door was locked as part of a game. For a moment she was certain of that. She could almost hear them giggling, holding their sides, pounding a pillow. Some joke! Practical jokers! Francis liked to hide behind doors and shout, *Boo!* Once she had heard Benjamin warn him it would turn her hair grey. Ben liked disaster. Burned with fever; gagged on a bone; always smelled smoke in the hallway. She told him about the boy who cried wolf until no one believed him when the wolf really came. He thought about this and said, a few days later, "There are no wolves in the city." Regina looked at him, at the round forehead, the still round baby's eyes: "Yes there are." "Grey ones?" he wanted to know. She nodded. "With yellow eyes?" She nodded again. "Teeth?" "Teeth." That was how they frightened each other.

The elevator whirred and the door opened and Mrs. Berenson, the honey-blond, came out with a plump man that Regina had not seen before. They turned away from her, down the hall. He had her elbow in his hand. "You're hurting me," Mrs. Berenson said. "You're hurting me, Jonathan." She was taller than he was and he had to reach up to put his hand on her neck. "Ouch!

Ouch! Don't treat me like that!" The man's suit was too small for him. Didn't he speak? Silent Jonathan! At the door they both turned and saw Regina, shrinking against the wall. "It's okay," said Mrs. Berenson. "She's a neighbor." They went inside, and she heard them laughing, a high laugh and a low laugh, through the door.

Well, thought Regina, a boy might be frightened hearing things in the hallway. Of course the chain had been thrown before Mrs. Berenson arrived. Maybe they heard Charles talking to her. He said he liked her smell. Could he smell her? Were his senses sharpened because he was aroused? What did he mean, she was gazing on ruins? That she was timeless? That she was old? She was sure she was older than he was; he was probably forty. Or forty-one. Did he think she neglected her teeth? She did not need a mirror to see her face. The skin was naturally dark, darker than olive, the lips turned downward, there were deep lines on either side of her mouth. Davy used to call her an Inca, though he probably meant a Mayan, an impassive Mayan, with broad flat cheekbones and black hair low on her brow. When they were first married he used to take hundreds of photos, the light dramatically behind her, looking for, finding — Davy was a good photographer — just that: the abiding Indian. So her face *would* be preserved, would gaze, from all angles, on the ruins.

Here was another possibility. What if Davy had come around? She had warned him not to. Yes, that was it. The boys had locked the door on him, not on her. He would have called and discovered she wasn't at home. He got indignant when she left the boys alone. Not that she did. Not often. She had been to one party since he had moved out. Still, he had sensed it, and when she got home he had been there, holding Francis, rocking him, crooning over him. "He was scared silly," he had said, and smiled. He always smiled. He would stand in public and discuss the most serious matters, and his lips would pull back. What did you call it? A shit-eating grin. She hated it! He would point a camera at her, all she saw of him was the smile. The wink and the smile. It didn't come from high spirits, but just the opposite

— from a knowledge of chaos. That's where she'd seen it. On the face of Oswald. On Bremer. On Sirhan Sirhan. It was the smirk of an assassin. She thought of what he did with his camera: load it, aim it, shoot it, as if it were a gun.

The phone rang inside the apartment. Regina tensed against the wall, hugging herself. The silence after the sound lasted so long she was sure one of the boys had picked up the receiver, was sleepily rubbing his eyes, saying, who, what did he want, who was it talking? But the phone rang again, and continued ringing, many times, jeering, then stopped altogether. Regina discovered that her body, which seemed stock still against the wall, was in fact tensing and relaxing, bunching itself, at the intervals of a telephone's bell. She calmed herself. She blew smoke in a stream. But when, after a time, the phone sounded again, her whole body rose, as if she were leaping a hurdle. As the ringing continued she saw something, not in an imaginary way, not as a dim hallucination, but realistically, as if the door to the apartment did not exist. What she saw was a figure, in shadows, hovering over the receiver. It seemed to her a man. He put his hand out, reaching hesitantly, but after the ring withdrew it. She understood then that this was the explanation, really the simplest, of the chain thrown over the door. A man had got into the flat. Perhaps through the skylight. Perhaps by tricking the boys. A thief. A junkie. When he heard her on the outside he locked himself in. But it was a trap. She in the hall. The skylight too high. The phone incessantly ringing. What would he do? What if he took hold of Francis? At that instant she thought of the boy on the stage, the blood daubed on him. She ran forward. The telephone stopped. Before she could pound on it, the door opened wide. Impossibly, it was Charles. In his shirtsleeves. Without a word she slipped by him and went inside.

Benjamin and Francis slept together in a room that overlooked 102nd. The window was shut. The air smelled of socks. Regina turned on a small lamp above a chest of drawers. A blade of light fell directly onto Francis's face and his wet brown hair. First he smiled, then he grimaced, then he smiled: after many difficulties, a happy ending. His eyes opened and he looked directly at his mother. "Don't look under the tablecloth," he said. "It's extremely dark there." Then he turned on his side and put a hand like a little paw under his chin.

Above Ben's bed an air battle was taking place. Planes were suspended on thin wires, dipping and diving. Behind one, a large bomber, red cellophane simulated flames. The Germans were losing. Their swastikas and crosses plunged toward the ground. Benjamin himself was nearly invisible, three fingers clutching a blanket over his head, and a brown ankle. Regina wanted to see him. He looked to her, especially sleeping, like a poet, like Shelley, with Shelley's curved eyelids and brow. But it was impossible to lean close to the bed. The slightly shining wires sprang over him like a cartoonist's drawing of a man's thoughts. She wanted to sweep the whole network aside, as she might take a broom to a cobweb. There was a rule in the house against playing with guns. Wasn't this a violation? It was warfare. Murderous. More murderous for its grace and charm. She had never forgotten how Mussolini's son said his bomb blasts were flowers. That was the essence of fascism, the way they tried to make death a drama, a flower, a show of lights. She put her hand out to rip the wires away, but stopped at the sight of a tiny parachutist, underneath an orange and white parachute. With a finger she touched him. At once he spiraled down to the bedpost, and the little parachute folded like a beach umbrella. She pushed the airman up his wire, and released him. He wobbled down slowly, past the dogfight, the bomber in flames, the Messerschmitt with the crippled wing. Regina lifted him again. For a moment she did not think of anything else. She was watching him tumble and glide, a dark plastic inch of a man.

"Your boys?" It was Charles. He was in the room, his coat on, holding a drink in each hand.

"Yes. Don't talk so loud."

He walked over to Francis, then to Ben. "I made you a drink. Scotch and water. No ice."

"Can't you lower your voice?" she asked, but she realized he Davy, the smiler, to scream. *Relax,* was what he always told her. couldn't, that it wasn't in him, any more than it was possible for She took the drink.

"A moment ago we were trying to wake them up."

Regina shut off the light and walked out to the living room. He came after her and circled the room, picking up ashtrays, fingering lampshades, turning the covers of books. Prowling.

"Sit down," he said to Regina, like the owner of the place.

"Thanks," she said, confused, and sat on the sofa.

"Nice room. Nice rug. Good pictures. Especially that." He gestured toward a Victorian painting, done on glass, of a group on a lawn. They were about to go up in a balloon.

"Yes. Look at the dog. He's not going into that basket. Not for anything!"

"Oh yeah. Yeah." He looked about, distracted. "Regina, why did your kids lock you out?"

"How did you get in here, Charles? You went to telephone. You frightened me when you opened the door."

"I came through the window. I counted the floors from the street. On your floor there was a window with a curtain blowing out. I did start to phone, from the booth on West End. I got my dime in okay. But it was like a urinal in there. I looked down and I was standing in a puddle of urine. There are a lot of animals in the city."

"What do you mean? Do you mean people?"

"What do *you* call someone who pisses in the public streets? If you can't wait ten minutes you don't belong in society. Society is ten minutes' worth of restraint. The sphincter is a voluntary muscle."

"We're not talking about defecation."

"I've seen that, too."

"Look, this is crazy. There aren't public toilets, that's all."

"That's not my opinion. The way I see it, anything goes. Everybody does what he feels like doing. Period. What was that case in Brooklyn? A guy goes into a delicatessen and asks for a cheese danish, and the poor sucker behind the counter says no cheese danish, we've got prune danish, and the cat pulls a gun and kills him. It might have been cigarettes. It might have been a stick of gum. Maybe someone steps on your shoe. The other day a man told another man that's no way to treat a dog. Dead. Slashed. Jugular. The threshold of frustration is zero."

"I really think you are trying to scare me. I think that's the whole purpose of that speech."

"I don't have to. You were already frightened when the door opened, because for all you knew it was a black man there, a black rapist, instead of me. That put your heart in your mouth."

"Why a *black* man? Why rape? I didn't think anything like it, and I resent your suggesting I did."

"You're kidding yourself on a lot of scores. Look, I was standing in that booth, in a piss-puddle — an animal can't wait ten minutes; for an animal, ten minutes is the same as eternity — and I realize that the night is dark, the streetlight is out, burnt out or knocked out and no will to repair it, and that the booth is glass, it's lit up, the only light in the street. What am I? A target. There's a war on, lady, in case you forgot."

"A deer will wait six hours before she walks into a meadow to drink. Spiders sit day after day next to their webs." Regina said this softly, holding herself still, afraid to tip the tears that, to her dismay, had come into her eyes. But he saw them.

"Now why are you crying?"

"Don't call me *lady!*"

"It's an expression. Look, let's drop it. We aren't getting through to each other."

"Yes we are. This isn't a failure of communication. It's a disagreement."

"Don't leave your windows open, Regina. Not the ones by the fire escape."

"You *are* dropping it, and I have more to say!"

But he wasn't looking at her, he was looking at the old painting, with its crimson balloon. Regina had a moment's confusion,
in which she thought the issue between them was whether he was
mistaking animals, with their patience, for men. Charles turned
then, and said, almost as if he had been reading her mind:

"Animals don't kill their own species, except, I hear, for rats.
And as far as I know they don't rape either. I guess the female
shows the male when she's ready. Ruffles her feathers or exposes
her rear. I don't want to defame them with comparisons to
human beings."

This remark, which ought to have deepened her confusion,
which almost seemed calculated to do so, in fact clarified what
she wanted to say. The trouble with animals was their simplicity
— by that she meant their simplemindedness. They could not
suffer, or love, because suffering and love were always complex.
It was the same with rape. "A rapist is diseased," she told
Charles, "because he has to deny the part of his mind that knows
the woman is real, is the same as himself. He has to deal with a
thing, a toy, she might as well be rubber, or dead. The disease is
simplemindedness. And the first symptom is calling her *lady*."

"If you want a disease to explain things, I'll tell you what it is.
It's that all over this town kids wake up in the morning, kids in
their teens, and they go over to their mirrors, and they look in the
mirrors — at those lips and those noses and that kinky stuff on
their skulls — and they get an idea, it's like getting the flu, just
one idea. It dawns on them: *Man, why not?*"

"You call people animals, black people, people who threaten
you, who you think threaten you, because *you're* simpleminded.
The disease isn't even racism — and I think you're a racist, obviously you're a racist — it's this refusal to bear anything compli-
cated at all. What softheadedness! In reality everything is mixed
up and ironical and difficult, and our minds just give way, as they
never have before, just collapse into black and white, including
the black and white races, and good and bad, and light and dark,
and cut and dry, oh, and the rest of it. We have to kill everything
that gives us an argument, beginning with ourselves, like a self-

lobotomy, and then everything around us, until the world is still and simple and clear. Like ice."

Regina held on to her glass, wondering what would happen. She wanted a cigarette, but didn't dare move. She even thought he might hit her. But he only finished his own drink and set it on the table. Then he took out his wallet.

"This is a picture of my daughter. It's about a year old. She's fourteen now. She lives with the novelist. She plays the piano, the violin, and reed instruments. Clarinet. Oboe. Sax. And she's got a hell of a ravishing voice."

Regina took the snapshot. The girl was not pretty, particularly, but fresh-faced, light-eyed, clear-eyed, with freckles and, over her shoulders, braids. She looked like the child of settlers in old photographs. There was the same gingham dress.

"What's her name?" she asked.

"Sarah. The same as her mother's mother."

Regina handed the photo back. She wondered why he showed it to her. She said, "She has a wonderful smile. A sunny smile."

"I went to hear her six weeks ago. As a matter of fact, it's the last time I saw her. She's in the orchestra at Music and Art. Eighty-five kids, and she's about the youngest one in it. Leonard Bernstein was conducting. He was modest. He was serious. He didn't give a fuck about us, Regina. He wasn't there for us. They were doing *Israel in Egypt* by Handel. I got there a minute before they started and saw Sarah right away, in the line of singers, in a dark blue dress, a white collar, at least a head and six inches shorter than anyone else. She didn't see me. She couldn't know I'd be there. I saw the ad in the paper that morning, in fact. I didn't know if she'd be on oboe, or violin, or what. It turned out she was singing. Okay. I know something about music. I've got a good enough ear to tune a piano. I tell you this was remarkable. The most remarkable oratorio I ever heard. It was what Handel had in his head. The audience was old people, grandparents, great-grandparents from Vienna, from Prague, from Berlin. They knew. So did Bernstein. You could tell from his back. Remarkable. Kids wearing glasses and the kettle drum said 'Property of the Board of Education of the City of New York,' but there was no such place, not after a while, there was Moses, there was Pharaoh, and the plagues. Locusts, lice, flies. Hailstones and fire. Wheat withering. Cattle dying. And the sky coming down in a great storm of dust. Sarah started to sing. All alone. An air. 'Thou didst blow with the wind, Thou didst blow —' She wasn't looking at the score. She was looking at me. She must have seen me come in. 'Thou didst blow, blow, bl-ow, bl-ow, bl-ow-ow-ow, ow! ow! ow!' "

He stood in the center of the room, his hands at his sides, and he snapped his head back and forth.

"Please stop," Regina said.

He stopped, picked up his drink, saw that it was empty. "I could be wrong. Maybe she wasn't singing to me. Maybe she was looking over my head."

"No. It was to you."

She watched as he came to her and put his hands on her shoulders. His weight pushed her into the sofa. She trembled, feeling something cold passing from him to her, from his arms and hands into her shoulders, like cold electricity. It was almost as if he were transferring to her a part of himself, something awful, through his hands. She wasn't dumb. She got the point. The point was she now had to kiss him. Kiss him? She would have to sleep with him, too. She did not want to, would forbid it, would tell him no, and don't touch me, and please go home; but all the time she felt the chill of his loneliness running into her, and did not resist.

He covered her mouth with his mouth, and set one of his knees between her legs. There were black cloth buttons on her green blouse. He undid them. He put his face onto her breasts. She could feel the temperature of her body falling, her blood sluggish and thick. Her teeth chattered once. She looked for Charles and saw him down by her feet. What was he doing? Unrolling her stockings. Kissing her toes. He rose and touched the top of her vagina; it made her feel brittle, breakable, like glass. She ripped with a nervous laugh, then put her arms around herself to keep warm. Her blouse, her pants, her white underthings were drifted around her. Poor man, she thought: rubbing, rubbing, rubbing sticks.

"What's the matter?" he asked.

She unstuck her lips. "I'm cold."

"Scared?"

"Cold."

"I'll lie on top of you."

Her feet had been on the floor. He lifted them and put them over the edge of the couch. He lay next to her, his clothes loosened. Then he rolled above her. It was worse. She felt as if she had been blocked from the sun. In that shadow she hung on him, threw her legs over his, moved her hands through the hair on his back, until her fingers came to metal that was colder than ice: absolute zero.

"What's that? What's that on your back?"

He made a slight space between them, but she held on to the metal part of the gun, stuck to it like the tongue of a child on a freezing gatepost.

"I'm no Jew in a delicatessen. I'm not going to die like a dog."

He said that, lowered himself, and forced his way in her. Regina, aghast, felt she would shatter, break into shards. Again, she wanted to laugh, and thought of a joke to explain it. A pane of glass. Get it? The pain of glass.

"Like a dog," he repeated, and was done.

They lay briefly without moving or speaking. Then he surprised her. He rose on his elbows, leaned forward, and kissed the place above her eyebrows, midway between them. He soon lifted his head, but the warmth remained, spreading from the spot, which almost seemed to be glowing. The chill drew slowly off her. Her hands opened. Regina felt like an Oriental, like an Indian woman, with a jewel in her forehead.

But when she woke some hours later, she was cold, as cold as before. The room was dark, except for city light that was reflected off the low clouds, through her window. She got off the sofa and, in her bedroom, wrapped a housecoat around her. She returned to where Charles was sleeping, his face in the cushions, the knuckles of his hand on the floor. She could make out the strap on his back, and the dim shine of the metal. She knelt and quickly removed the gun. It was immensely heavy. She held it in both hands, turning it over, the handle, the barrel, the trigger. She knew that it made her cold. She carried it, like something alive, across the room and placed it, really slid it off her hands, onto a shelf. There was a faint rattling sound at the window, which stopped at once, then began again. A shift in the wind. The white smoke, invisible at night, was dropping its ash on the window-panes, on the sash, in a fine black layer across the sill. She listened. One of the boys cried out, and was quiet. Laughter boom-boomed from the next apartment. A few streets away a car sounded its horn. She went back to the sofa and sat next to Charles. He did not stir. She ran a hand through her hair. She was thinking about the city. She thought it was like Pompeii.

II

By mid-morning Regina was at work on her review. Ordinarily she wrote with ease, not thinking about style, putting down the words more or less as she would speak them. There were times — they were coming more frequently — when she completed an article at a sitting, without crossing out or adding a word. People praised her language; her own pride was that she met her deadlines. She was, however, about to miss one now. After hours of work she had only half a sheet in the typewriter, which she ripped out and threw on the floor. She had begun work drowsily, and as she pushed herself through a description of the evening — the hot blank faces of the dancing girls, the fixed smiles, the wide eyes — she became stupid as well. Her ideas struck her as silly; her memory failed at each detail. Then she began to worry about her writing. Wasn't that a flat-footed phrase? Hadn't she used the same word before? What a dumb metaphor!

In the middle of this, Ben and Francis came home from school. She made them a sandwich and sent them off to a movie on Broadway. But when she attempted to resume her work, she found herself growing short of breath. The more she concentrated on the drama, the closer she got to the moment when the lamb had appeared on the stage, the greater her sense of suffocation grew. She opened a window. No good. She was reexperiencing the same feeling she had had the evening before. The skinny boy. His shyness. The flute. She stood up from the typewriter. I can't think in here, she told herself. She looked around the room. She wanted to go. She didn't. I can't think *in here,* she repeated, and this time she knew she meant inside her skull.

She sat down slowly. She understood now that the play had succeeded. Its purpose was to make it impossible to think. The conflict was not on the stage, between this character and that; it was between the entire ritual and the ordinary man or woman in the theater, the separate person, the individual. The many would be made one. Consciousness was the enemy. Overwhelm it. She thought of a line from a Greek play. "Oblivion is best." Sophocles. No wonder there had been wisecracks in the crowd, those songs, the mockery: they were attempts to ward off the spell, to keep oneself whole. *Lord have mercy on such as we.* She remembered that when the lamb was killed there had been a gasp. Air rushing into sudden vacuums. They were being drawn out of themselves. She, too. Her mind's membrane was touching that of the group. It wasn't suffocation. It was ecstasy.

This was not drama as she believed drama to be. There was no tragic movement, no catharsis, no attempt to free the soul — that's what the Greeks had called it — from the grip of unknowing instinct. The drama was civilizing. It lightens the mind, Aristotle said. It delights it. But this — ? She thought of the wild Bacchantes roaming the hills of Thrace. These girls, with their loosened breasts, the streaming hair, were no different. The followers of Dionysus danced past exhaustion, they dressed in the skins of foxes, kissed and touched one another. And when the sacred goat was brought into the circle they fell upon it and ripped it apart and in their intoxication devoured it raw. She understood that. It was a way of being part of things, of becoming wind, or grass, or the beast that feeds on grass, the blood in

its veins, that god that lies along the sinew. Wonderful is forget-
fulness!

But even then, in a primitive time, the city came up from the
South, from Attica. Regina had long ago worked out that it is in
such periods, when an expanding civilization demands a new
order of renunciation, that the drama is most needed and most
flourishes. The Greeks set everywhere their gates and palaces. In
Shakespeare's time colonies stretched into the Americas. She
knew that it was the mind that was a palace, that the Elizabe-
thans had sailed into the far hemisphere of the brain. But she
couldn't find words for that. You had to use images, like the
wonderful one of Freud's, Dutchmen reclaiming land, the Zuider
Zee drained by inches. And then you said, Where Id was there
shall Ego be. She thrilled at that, at the language, at the idea. To
Regina, a patient herself, psychoanalysis and tragedy were similar ways of regarding the mind. That new world! Still, at the back
of her mind, something was nagging, something violent, pas-
sionate, dreadful. Oedipus, for instance. His eyes. You had to
explain the horror.

She concentrated on the moment the tyrant gouged out his
eyes. How did he do it? She didn't know. How could she? All
right. With a brooch. A gold-chased brooch. Whose brooch was
it? Jocasta's. It held her robe together. So that when he took it
from her, the garment fell open. In an instant he sees the naked
body of his mother and puts the pin in his eyes. For that —
because the final stripping is only a reenactment of the original
violation — the witness is banished. He can't see, but that is only
another way of saying he cannot be seen, he's untouchable, pol-
luted, not for men's eyes. The crowd does not eat him. They
don't want to become one with him. He has been part of them
too long already. The whole tragedy is one of separation. Let him
go. Let him wander. But not in the city. Somewhere else. In
wilderness. Then Regina remembered that the scene of blinding
took place offstage, inside the palace. All that the audience sees is
a mask with missing eyes.

In *Lear* (again *Lear!*) there are no niceties. *Out vile jelly!* On

Cornwall's thumbs. She recalled a phrase: *bleeding rings.* Had she seen that in Zilbayarsky's production? She did not think so. She could not remember Gloucester at all. Perhaps they had cut him, like the battles, the Fool. Time was short. Money scarce. More likely they had performed the act in the shadows, or screened it with the back of the Duke. There were children in the audience. Of course she had seen it elsewhere, had had to tell herself, all right, calm down, it's grapes they're using. Poor Gloucester! As they said in the movies, he'd seen too much. Afterward, they let him go. A servant brought flax and eggs for his eyes.

Oh! Regina lurched for the telephone. She wanted to call Charles. She had the answer to his question. She actually dialed a digit, two digits, then forced the receiver down. The boy on the stage. They were going to take out his eyes. Not literally. Only symbolically. He stood for everyone who would not go along. Who kept apart. Who put his hands in front of his body. And why not literally? They would *do* it. If not this time, the next. If not the next, soon. We've all seen too much. A person was larger than a lamb. She was thinking of Charles's remark. A sense of irony overcame her. Here was Charles — what would you call him? You had to call him a law and order man. He's the one who had said you can't let people do what they want: and he had been excited, his hair stood on end. But Regina, who had wanted to ask, why not, what *would* happen if people did what they wanted? had been horrified. Then this feeling of irony, which grated her, passed off, and left her determined. She would draw a line, like a magic circle, around the idea of sanity.

These, more or less, were the ideas that underlay Regina's review. It was long, longer than the others, but it came now as quickly as they, at a sitting. She heard the boys come in, shortly before she had finished. When she had done she went straight to the kitchen. She mixed raw egg and onion in patties of meat, and put them under the broiler. The children were shouting at the back of the house. She called them, but they did not hear. She went down the hall to their room. There, Francis revolved on one knee, so as to face, always, his brother. Benjamin rode around him, striking his legs with his hands, war-whooping, releasing arrow after arrow into the chest and head and curly hair of the defender. How their eyes gleamed!

Regina had always received a fair amount of mail concerning her work, and she spent some time each week responding to it. She enjoyed the task. She pretty much knew what to expect: a few letters of praise; a few more pointing out that she had missed this detail or got another one wrong; philosophical or political interpretation of a scene or a plot; never a note from a press agent, nothing from actors or actresses or their irate fans. All serious stuff. Over the years she had come to know some of her correspondents well, and wrote back to them by their first names. These, especially, turned on her in the days following the publication of her long review. Regina understood why they felt betrayed. They had thought they knew what to expect from her as well. Charles said he would divert the letters; he thought they must depress her. She said no, she would read them, she had let too many things go. But she no longer replied, not to ten letters a day, and some of them were ugly. She was a bitch, a cunt, a whore, by which it was meant to say she was changeable as a woman. But even women wrote her that way.

It was while going through a weekend's accumulation of this mail that Regina came across a letter from the National Foundation for the Arts and Humanities. It contained an invitation, embossed on a cream-colored card, to "An Afternoon of Entertainment for the President." This was to be held in the White House garden, weather permitting, in six days' time. There was a short note, too.

> Your critical article, OBLIVION, has come to the attention of the President, who has asked me to convey to you how very much he enjoyed reading it, both from an artistic point of view and for the very important mes-

sage it contains. Indeed, the President feels very strongly
that the time has come for us, as a society, to "draw
the line," as you put it, unless we are to sink beneath
the waves of chaos and immorality. He is pleased that
intelligent and influential writers and artists, such as
yourself, are now beginning to speak out on these matters which have concerned him for many years. The
President has asked that your name be added to the
guest list for our occasion, which includes many of
America's best known stars, so that he might be able to
tell you himself of his admiration for your work. If I
may add a personal note, I would like to say that I have
read your article in its entirety and found it beautifully
written and mentally stimulating. I sincerely hope you
will be able to join us on the fifteenth of June.

It was signed Sylvia de Kruiff, for the National Foundation.
There was a postscript, handwritten:

Because of the late date, I would appreciate it if you
would respond to the enclosed by calling me collect in
Washington.

The number followed.

What a gag, thought Regina. Someone she knew, perhaps one
of her old correspondents, was telling her what he thought of her
piece. It was a way of shouting, Look who your friends are now!
She ran through the note again. It was really quite funny. The
tone was perfect. That *artistic point of view!* That *mentally stimulating!* She had never minded being the butt of a joke. She
returned to her stack of mail. A man called her a witch. Another
man, a professor of law, asked if she had left her senses. Well,
she knew who her friends had been. And if the invitation was
genuine? How could it be? She had established her position —
never a Communist, but even these days well to the left — over a

period of twenty-five years. That had to count for something. The idea of sitting in the White House garden was morally grotesque. Her perception of the President was that he was empty, empty the way a ship was without ballast, and as vulnerable. She suspected he knew this as well as anyone, and was always trying to fill himself, to weigh himself down. Other people's contempt served him as stones. She spread out the letter once more and reread the sentence about the waves. It was laughable! Her head seemed to float off her shoulders. It was true! Charles came up behind her and put his hands on her. It helped to control her.

"Lunch?" he asked.

But she silently folded the letter.

"What's that?"

"It's a scream."

Regina had lunch by herself and went out into the street. It was an odd, dry day, under a white sky, with tight little whirlwinds, full of dust, spinning on the sidewalk. She had a job to do, taking notes mostly, and started downtown. About six months before, she and Davy had started a book together, whose premise was that the geography of the City was a projection of the individual psyche. Like Freud's *Anatomy of the Mental Personality*. Photos by husband, text by wife. They had finished one chapter, on the Superego, before Davy moved out. It was set on the East Side, with its doormen, its cleanliness, its poodles in collars. Charles had printed it, without the pictures. On her own, she'd done the chapter on the Ego: Central Park, a sliver of green space, some breathing room. She'd put in, against her better judgment, Greenwich Village: the relief from straight lines and right angles. She imagined a taxi lost on Waverly Place: Wa-a-a-averly! Now she was on the track of the Id. At the light she crossed Forty-sixth Street. Then Forty-fifth. Forty-fourth. This was the center, the bullseye, the raw Hypothalamus. She thought of the Id in Freud's figures of speech: the boiling cauldron, a horse running off with its rider. On the next corner, facing Broadway, at a spot where she imagined the hairlines of a sight on the city must meet, was a small magic and souvenir shop called A MILLION LAFFS.This sign was painted in peeling red over green woodwork, and again in red on the door. There was a crowd of boys in front of the window. Regina watched them, how they stood with their arms over each other's shoulders, and leaned their foreheads against the glass. Then she stepped forward and saw through the window row upon row of pearl-handled and steel-handled knives.

The shop itself was small, square, and lit only by the sunlight that broke on the windowpane. The back wall was covered by female parts, breasts with magenta nipples, thighs and pieces of thighs, spongy buttocks, lips, feet, hair — all floating and disassembled as if on a large votive screen. In the center were three life-size women, two blonds, a brunette. Someone had blown them up and hung them on hooks. She supposed you put your arms around them if you were a man. Well, it was neat, sex and knives — the instincts she wanted. The only trouble was that it was difficult to take them seriously, since they kept veering off into jangly, jumpy tricks. She picked up a gun, pulled the trigger, and it stuck out a tongue. A little wooden man had a corkscrew for a penis. A cockscrew, she laughed. When you looked at the dancing girl drawn on the outside of a cardboard tube, you got a black eye. She saw that what the shop sold mostly — they were spread out on tables, in hundreds of little grey cellophane packets — were practical jokes. Here was a bar of soap that glued your fingers together. Next to it a lump of brown plastic feces: "place it in a corner and watch the results." (Regina snorted to think that someone had played this on Charles.) There was a packet of gum, it looked like Wrigley's, but from the illustration, a line drawing of a face with rays of pain coming out of the profile, it was obvious that when you drew a stick a spring like a mousetrap snapped on your finger. For a quarter you could buy two glasses of wine: one filled with crême de menthe, a lovely green, that would not pour; the other dribbled whatever you put in it across your chin. An exploding cigar! It was true, the Id had no sense of time. She remembered putting one of these devices into the end of her father's panatela, it must have been thirty-five, thirty-eight years ago! It went off, banging a little, and she screamed from surprise. He only said that that was a good one.

"Are you feeling okay?"

Regina spun around. A little man, bald and gnomish, with an oblong mole on his cheek, was sitting behind a high counter near the door. He wore a lapel button with the name Jake on it. "I asked if you was feeling out of sorts?"

"Yes. No. I'm fine."

But she wasn't. She was finding it, once again, hard to breathe. She leaned against a table. A whoopee pad — you were meant to hide them under cushions — made it sound as if she were breaking wind. Jake laughed, *hee, hee-hee*. "I thought you was feverish your face is so red."

Involuntarily she felt her cheek. It was burning. She felt drastically ill.

"Whatsa matter, lady?"

That was what, fighting past quick waves of nausea, she had to work out. She knew it had to do with the packets, spread out like grey matter around her. The point of them, what bound them together, was the creation of a precise instant of shock, the moment at which some ordinary human expectation was overturned, like the teacup that stuck to the table. It left you stunned, it made you an object, mortified. Regina felt now as if she were close to something true, as if she had strayed into a deep part of the psyche, past sex, past violence, and what she found at the center was a buzzer that stung the hand offered to you in friendship; or a box of matches that would not light; or hot gumdrops, false dandruff, itching powder; rubber ham and rubber eggs; this little devil of a man, this Jake on a stool, going *hee, hee-hee-hee*. She took out the letter and showed it to him.

"I have been humiliated," she said.

He stared down at her. She wanted him to see that the paper was like filth in her hand. It made her ugly. It turned her to stone.

Not in her life, she told him — and he smiled, grinned, bounced as if sitting on springs — had she been so ashamed.

A long block east she caught the number 5 bus home. Just inside the door of the flat her gorge rose, and the vomit flew at her feet. She made her way to the toilet and hung over the bowl. Her stomach went through spasm after spasm, as if it meant to wring her out. The ends of her hair trailed in the stuff. When she was done she called Dr. Geneva in Connecticut, but got her husband instead. He told her the Doctor was on vacation; but then the Doctor came on.

"I did not want to call you at home, Dr. Geneva, not on your vacation, but I think I have to see you, as soon as I can. Tomorrow. I could be there in the morning."

"I never see patients at home."

"I know, I only said that because —"

"I could refer you to someone else if it is urgent."

"Dr. Geneva, I guess this is what is called the cry for help. Help! Ha, ha. Like someone who's drowning."

"Who is this speaking?"

"Regina."

"Oh, Regina, I just realized it was you. Is there something seriously the matter?"

"My God, I almost said no. I almost said automatically that I was fine. I'm sick. It is my stomach but really my head. In there I've made up my mind. I've made a resolution. I've got to break it but I can't by myself."

"What is it? What have you decided?"

"It's very strong. It's the end of me. The trouble is I'm in love with the idea. Do you know what I mean, Dr. Geneva? I mean that in about a minute I am going to regret making this call. I know that's because you could save me. In about half a minute I am going to start telling myself you are not necessary. I want you out of my way."

"I cannot see you here, Regina. You understood that when

you called. But I am coming to New York in three days. That is, on Thursday. I could see you then, at three-forty-five."

It would be too late, Regina knew, though she said it would be fine. She ended on apologies. A pleasantry. But as soon as she replaced the receiver she was sick again. It went on for a long time and produced only black and green, then colorless, bile. At last she pushed herself up. Both boys were standing silently in the doorway. Francis was biting his lip. Benjamin said, "Regina, are you going to die?"

She got them to bed and sat the rest of the night by the open window. She watched the white curtain rise, slip to the side of the incoming air, and fall. At exactly nine in the morning she called Sylvia de Kruiff at the National Foundation for the Humanities. The woman on the other end said how delighted she was that Regina could accept her invitation.

Charles took her to dinner the next night, and afterward they walked uptown, over thirty blocks, to his apartment. He played a lot of music for her, old 78s that dropped down hard on each other and went very fast. What surprised her — she must have known, but had forgotten — was the quality of the sound, better than long-playing records. There was an upright piano, and he whimsically played that as well. They went to his bedroom to make love, and though she embraced him, she could not help pushing his hand aside whenever he touched her vagina. She was afraid of a laughing jag. This time he kissed her sooner, and she felt him go into her only after the dark light had spread in circles from the spot on her forehead. They were like broadcasting beams. "Where are you hiding?" It was Charles, hunting her. She said nothing. He searched a little longer, but she felt him grow halfhearted, and then spend himself. She knew that he knew she was lost.

After an hour she dressed. Charles was asleep and did not know where he was when she woke him. He sat up. Regina asked him if he would lend her his gun. He looked at her, but he did not ask her what she wanted it for. "For a few days," she said.

He got out of bed and after a moment brought it to her. "You stole it from me. When I wasn't looking. If anyone asks."

She nodded and took it, already used to its coldness, its weight.

"You know how to use it? This is the safety. Leave it on until you want to fire the weapon, then push it forward. There isn't any hammer. It's automatic. To aim you line up this with this, and this with the target. Try to squeeze the trigger. Don't jerk it. It's got a hell of a kick. It makes a hell of a noise. It's not a gun for a lady."

She took some things from her handbag and put the gun in their place. She went to the door. "Regina, ask me. I'll do it for you."

There was no way to answer. Then he caught her, collared her, and put his large bare body against her small one, with its green clothes. She allowed it. Then she went out.

Regina worked as usual for the next two days, and carried the gun with her in the bottom of her bag. She did not touch it, or see it, but both nights it was in her dreams. The gun was the one in the magic shop, and when she reached for it, it spat flames, tongues of flame. The first night it scorched her; the dream ended with her looking at the fused fingers of her hand. But on the second night she pointed the weapon and Jake (though his baldness might represent Charles) caught fire and burned.

"What about this magic-gun?" asked Dr. Geneva, when Regina had told her both dreams.

"At least there's progress. First I'm hurt. Then someone else is. I'm turning my anger outward. I suppose if that's an omen it's a good one."

"And the flames?"

"I don't know. Not so good. You get burned when your plans *don't* work out. Oh. The electric chair. Do they use that any more? I think what's being shown is the act and the consequence of the act. Crime and punishment. Of course I've thought about escaping. There will be a lot of confusion. But I know realistically I haven't a chance. I know I'm going to — going to fry."

There was a pause, and Regina looked where she always did,

at the cunning painting, anyway cunningly hung, that seemed to be sometimes barnyard animals and sometimes a wedding dress. Dr. Geneva went on inexorably:

"Spitting flames? Tongues of flame?"

"You aren't interested in the reality of what I tell you. You don't hear that part of what I say. For God's sake, spitting, tongue, I know it's oral. But I'm not going to speak against the President. I'm going to shoot him."

"Is it possible your dream is suggesting that you *should* speak against him? Or write against him? Perhaps the dream says the pen is mightier than the sword."

"It's not, Dr. Geneva."

"Perhaps in one way it is — is as mighty as a gun. I am thinking of how a pen spits, too. Ink. Angry fluids."

"I don't want to pursue this. We don't have the time."

"I remember, not long ago, when the President said the people were like children, and must be treated like children, you were upset."

"I was infuriated."

"Yes, infuriated."

"But it was not as a child, or a girl, or some neurotic. It was as a citizen. Don't you believe in citizenship? In righteous anger? We are supposed to overthrow tyrants. It's in the Declaration of Independence. Does that mean that Jefferson and Madison and Adams had an unresolved Oedipal conflict? That the King, King George, was their father? And what if it does? That's the real question: does it matter? Is it as important as their democratic feelings?"

"I would like to discover, Regina, who the tyrant is you wish to overthrow, and whom you wish to declare your independence from."

"The President."

"The President. Who is that?"

"Nobody. Nothing. Emptiness. There is something missing in him. I think it's conscience."

"I would have said that the President has a conscience. A terrible one that makes him suffer."

"I believe he is a criminal. A war criminal. I know he deliberately postponed the settlement for his own purposes. For *years*. That means that hundreds of thousands of people died — and horribly, bombed, napalmed — so that he could be reelected. He called it pulling the issue from under his opponents. Like a magician with a tablecloth."

"How exactly does that work? The napalm?"

"You don't know — ?"

"This is the gasoline bomb?"

"In the form of jelly. Anyone, anything it touches it consumes, it burns."

"Again, death by fire —"

"Dr. Geneva, I have to reject what you are doing. I am speaking to you of torture and misery, of intolerable crimes, and you respond only to the quirks of my nature. They exist. Obviously. But what is the point of the years we have spent together if we can't get past orality and penis envy and discuss what is real?"

"The answer to that is your wish to kill the President is not real. It is a fantasy."

"No," was all Regina could say. The painting was white geese, white chickens, white ducks. What was clear to her, clear as print, was what she would do. Why she was lying here, and what the point of this conversation was, only confused her. Like a bird on her shoulder, the voice of her analyst replied:

"Then I do not know why you are here. It confuses me. If you *are* serious, then you must want me to stop you, either in our conversation or by calling the authorities, the Federal Secret Service police. What other purpose could there be in our appointment? Are you hoping, Regina, that I, I think your oldest ally, will betray you?"

Regina considered this. But Dr. Geneva, always plausible, did not wait. "If so, we must ask: who am I? Which terrible traitor? Where have you felt these feelings before? In what old scene are we acting? In other words, it is still a fantasy, or a memory, or a dream, that we are discussing."

"I am almost in tears, it's so vexing. What do you want, what would I have to do, to make you believe I am in earnest?"

"Oh, earnestness!"

"All right. That I am responding appropriately. That I am *sane*. My God, Dr. Geneva, to adjust to some things is mad. Were Germans sane when Hitler came to power? Or were they dangerously repressed? Would you or someone like you, a Berlin disciple, have said to me, my dear excitable young lady? Even while Freud himself was being driven away? I'm raising my voice. I know we have been through this before. But I won't put my head in the sand! I won't be used! I remember what Freud said when they made him write out a statement that he had been well treated. After ransacking his home! *I can heartily recommend the Gestapo to anyone.* I love the sanity and cleverness of that. I have been thinking of Freud, of things he said. I feel moved now. It's because I've heard you speak like him so often. I do not think you'd betray me."

It was as if Dr. Geneva had not heard her. "I would accept your seriousness more readily if I thought you were respecting your own intelligence. Instead, don't you abuse it? In elementary ways? How are you going to carry out your plans? I recognize the President is a cautious man. A highly suspicious man. You will be searched. I am certain there are detectors for metal, the same as at the airport gates."

"I know the mentality of these people. They would search me if I were a man. I'm not. I'll get in on a smile, a pretty smile, like any daffy woman."

"You mentioned Thomas Jefferson and James Madison and their democratic instincts. I am not a political scientist. Politics and government are not as real to me as you would like them to be. It may be I am a bad citizen. Even so, I am able to see one thing clearly, which is that the system of popular feeling you wish to protect cannot survive another assassination. There is a limit to fear, to distrustfulness. When you cross such a limit the army moves in. If you were thinking, Regina, you would know this also. Isn't that so? What do you say? Perhaps we can return now to the quirks."

Regina's handbag was on the floor beside the couch. She went into it and took out the gun. "This is not rubber, not a magic penis, and not a Marx Brothers prop. It doesn't spit flames. I am going to get it as close as I can to the President's head or the President's heart, and then I swear I'll pull the trigger."

"But at this moment you are aiming it at me. Please don't. I do not like it, whether it is or is not a toy."

Regina realized that she was holding the weapon at arm's length, stiffly, and that it was pointed at her analyst. As a rule, she did not see Dr. Geneva in her armchair for more than a few seconds at a time. She saw her now, sitting with her legs crossed, with a cigarette in the corner of her mouth. She wore clear plastic glasses that magnified her eyes. Regina put back the gun and lit, herself, a cigarette.

"I have asked myself already," Dr. Geneva was saying, "whether your real target was me. I do not mean to shoot me, though sometimes, rarely, this happens. But to put me in an impossible position. Or, should an impulse carry you into attempting this assassination, to shame me, or jeopardize my practice, since of course it would quickly come out that you were one of my patients." The doctor said this with a smile. It so touched Regina with its whackiness — that she should go way roundabout, kill a President in order to embarrass her analyst — that for a time she could not think of herself as a patient: they were, the two of them, middle-aged women talking together, smiling and smoking.

Then Regina lay back and the other woman, with her pop eyes, said, "The Marx Brothers. These are the film comedians?"

"Yes. Movie stars. I used to watch them when I was a child." Regina broke off, full of feeling for the questioner. Lord, how lovable! What doggedness! It was actually quaint. "Especially Harpo. I mean I especially liked him. I thought he was an Angel. The harp. The hair. I hated my own hair. I wanted to dye it, with gasoline, somebody told me, but I never dared. I used to dream about an Angel. When I was a child. Did I ever tell you? The Angel had blond hair and would lean over and throw it down to my bed, like a ladder. When I woke up the Angel was saying things. Not with words. The language was winking and smiling and making birds out of fingers. That was like Harpo, too. What the Angel said was the world was burning. On fire. Warn the people. And I would get out of bed and run through the apartment and shake my father. I'm embarrassed. It sounds like Chicken Little. The sky is falling. Only I thought I was Joan of Arc. A martyr, a saint. I even used to go into the streets. Into other people's houses. It was a Jewish neighborhood and they were shocked by such craziness. They used to carry me home and put me to bed — it was the middle of the night — and a little later, in a day or two, I would feel ends of hair on my face, it was the Angel's hair, and it felt like flames."

"How old were you then?"

"Seven. Eight. Then I gave it up. Everyone thought I was a serious person. But in 1945 — my periods had just started, I remember — they set off the atomic bomb, and I got into bed for days, waiting for everything to end. I knew that, that fireball, was what the dream, in dumbshow, was saying."

"Why do you remember your menstruation? Are you afraid that your periods will soon stop? Is that why you tell me now this fantasy?"

"Dr. Geneva, what that Angel said to me was no different, was as *real*, as what occurred to Oppenheimer in the desert. His certainty that the light there would be the last thing the last man would see. There is a long tradition of visions in the desert."

"Nevertheless, in the unconscious there is little to distinguish blood and fire. I think I am able to interpret what the end of everything means. Does it not mean the end of your life as a woman?"

"No. The end of the world."

There was a brief silence. The content of the painting was a wedding dress. Then both women rose and walked to the door together. "I shall be in the city next week," the analyst said, around the cold cigarette in her mouth. "We shall meet then." But at the same time she held out her hand, which meant she knew their work together was over.

Regina passed through the waiting room, where a man in an open shirt and a sportcoat sat wringing his hands. It was Berenson's, her neighbor's, plump lover. He stared at his shoes, at the space between them, and the skin wrinkled far up his scalp. He did not look up, but if he had done so, he would have noticed the departing patient, and especially her wide sunny smile.

That smile stuck to her face. She got a glimpse of it in a bakery window and again in the glass of a darkened doorway. *I like your smile. Smile.* Charles did not mean this silly grin. So sweet. Like Billie Burke or Gracie Allen: the empty-headed woman. Was it practice for the White House guards? *See? Don't mind me!* Waiting for a light, she took out her compact. Still there, though she could not feel it, or help it. She knew she ought to come to some conclusion about the way she had led her life; or anyway, like the drowning man, go over her childhood. What came to her was how she had knocked over the display in her father's store, six shelves of glassware, all crystal, not a loud noise, just popping and pinging; but both her legs bled under the knees, as if scratched by a cat. Her father lifted her dress and put his square handkerchief over the cuts, while she screamed not to, no don't, it was white, he would ruin it! *Walk*, in green: Regina crossed. She was glad that green meant go and red, the color of danger, of blood, warned her to stop. That was intelligent. The bench in the middle of Broadway was freshly painted, in yellow and blue sections, and a woman sat on it, sleeping, and a man sat on it, jiggling his knee. She felt toward them, and their bench, as she had toward her analyst. They were rather lovable, and in spite of the serious time, her smile stretched even wider.

Wearing this dotty expression she floated home, drifted from armchair to armchair, and let days go by. She worked, ate in restaurants, and slept, with her hands joined at the base of her skull. The heads of people, Benjamin and Francis, Charles, flowed past, and she nodded to them, and to others she saw, as if she were on the bank of a river. She avoided mirrors, however. The sight of her fixed smile disturbed her. It made her think of a comic's impression — the lipsticked teeth, the frozen features — of the President's wife. She walked out of doors, where there were white clouds in the blue sky. That was how she saw things, wide-eyed, freshly, but in two dimensions. The streets and sidewalks, for instance, took on the flat surface of a child's painting. People had black shadows behind them. Teardrop shapes of smoke hung motionless, connected at the bottom to chimneys. A stiff dog barked. How naive! How quaint! Yellow taxis, blue buses. A black man in a striped sweater was shining shoes. The last light lay on everyone's shoulders. A hot-dog umbrella. A barbershop pole.

Then the sun dropped down a side street and the moon rose overhead. Regina walked on, past a policeman, past a bicycle that leaned in the shadows, past a man smoking a cigarette. On a corner a bright lamp shone through the small green leaves of a tree. One window, beneath the level of the street, was lit. There was a Chinese ideogram above it. And *First Class Laundry,* in English. Through the glass she saw three men. One worked an iron, one worked a press. The third man was folding shirts. Regina stood for a long time. It was dark except for the lamplight and windowlight. The men worked without a break, not looking at each other, not speaking. She watched the iron, she watched the arms of the shirts, one arm folded over the other, she watched the press descending and rising, and then she felt her smile fall apart. "Fools!" she said. Her lips curled. "Fools!"

She went home at once, afraid of everything. When she opened the door of the flat a light burst, blinding her, circling everything with a red rim. Quickly, it went off again. She stared through it. "Davy," she said.

"That's fine, Reg. Hold it there." The strobe flashed once

more. Davy came out of the glare. He had three cameras strapped to his neck.

"You know I don't want you here. We have an agreement. It makes it very hard for me to have you in the apartment."

"Well, I'm not going to be much longer. A few more rooms." He walked down the hallway. Regina saw that, thin as he was, he had put on weight around his hips. "Regina, will you look at this!" He swept his arm around the square kitchen. She knew what was there, but it surprised her to see it. Dishes, cups, glassware piled in the sink and on the counters; a pan, a scorched pot on the stove. The garbage bag lay on its side. And everywhere were broken, burnt-out cylinders of ash. The house was full of them, like slugs. "Look at those roaches. Cockroaches! We never had cockroaches before." He dropped to one knee and began to fiddle with his lenses. She saw the roaches, casually ranging back and forth on the floor and the wall. "It's like an insect *Grande Jatte*. Little dots as far back as the eye can see." He got the picture.

"Davy, what are you doing here?"

"Taking pictures."

"Do you know that it is after midnight? That it is almost one in the morning?"

"Is that when you usually come home? I called last night. Ben answered. You were out. *Just out*, he said."

She hesitated. The last three days had broken, like a fever. She wondered if there were some way she had caught her smile from Davy. He was smiling now. "There isn't room here for you and me. I know it's a line from a Western, but I feel it's true. I feel you filling up the place. Why are you taking these pictures?"

"For evidence."

"Evidence of what?"

"The condition of the apartment. The filth. The deterioration. The way that you live."

Regina looked at her husband closely. There were white patches under his light freckled skin. He had Francis's hair, short, overlapping curls, hardly thinning, and a boy's face, boy-ish, in spite of its hundreds of lines. Narrow shoulders. An aging boy.

"I am not going to let you keep the children, Reg."

She spun around and ran to the boys' room. It was empty. A shambles. Toys, jeans, twisted underclothes were strung everywhere. Books lay spine-up on the floor. Davy came in behind her. "See? It smells in here."

"Where are they?"

"At my apartment. They have their own room and their own beds, captain's beds, with brass fittings and drawers for their things. Ben brought his planes. As soon as they got there they took a bath and went to bed.

"Francis won't take a bath. He won't take off his clothes, except in the shower; even in the shower he wears underwear."

"It's very neurotic, I would say, if he is afraid to take off his clothes in front of you."

"Don't tell me he went naked in front of *you*."

"In front of Ruth. She gave them their bath. I only came in at the end."

"Ruth is the woman you live with?"

"Yes. She is. The water was black."

Regina picked up a pair of Levi's and began to pull the legs right side out. She did not know Ruth, but she imagined her, for some reason large, heavy, on her knees by the bath. Sit down, stand up, she thought of her telling the children, passing her hands over their bodies, and she turned her face, which was burning, to the cuff of the pants. "You're a shit, Davy. You come here and whine about the dirt in the apartment, the Goddamned *mess*, and you bring the children to stay with a strange woman, to where you are living in sin."

"I wish you could see your face when you shout. I wish I had a mirror. It's distorted. It's disfigured."

"Oh, Lord, Davy, you are just the same. I knew you would find someone to live with. I knew it would be soon. But I thought, I had the feeling that — there was so much talk about self-discovery, and wasted years, and how conventional our lives were, wasn't there? — that I thought that the person you lived with might be a man."

"You must be eaten by jealousy to say something as vicious as that."

"Eaten by it. Yes. It is like that. Everything is like what people say. What's the color of jealousy? Green. It is making me the color green. But, Davy, it is not sexual envy. That's not why I said what I did. I am jealous of Ruth. I can't bear to think of her wrapping Francis into a towel."

"I hope you're not thinking of using Ruth to fight this, because I know about your sex life, too, about your affair with the editor, fucking on the couch when the boys are sleeping, and leaving them to fuck in his flat, every night fucking, last night, tonight, and then you lecture *me* about living in sin? You use that kind of language, when I look at you and there is dirt on your shoes, and your dress is crumpled and, Regina, when did you wash your hair? Or comb it? You look like *The Absinthe Drinker,* it's like a picture of a fallen woman."

Regina thought of where she had been that night, and the other nights, walking in a cardboard village, the cutout moon, the pasted five-pointed stars, and silent Chinamen; and she threw back her head and laughed.

"Nothing is funny."

"Go away, Davy. I'm going to bed." Regina took off her pearls and took off her shoes and carried them into the bathroom, where she ran water into the bath. Davy came after her, talking:

"Now listen. I did not come here tonight to spy on you, whatever you happen to think. I arranged with Ben over the phone to take him and Francis to the stadium. I have a field assignment for Black Star, and I promised them seats over the dugout. That's important for them. That's where you get autographs. When I got here tonight Francis was waiting, in a Mets hat and shinguards, the kind catchers wear. There he was, sitting in your cigarette butts and pounding his fist in the glove. All right. But no Ben. He wasn't there. I couldn't find him. Do you want to guess where he was?"

Regina had stepped out of her dress and unhooked her brassiere. Through habit she got on the scale. Steam from the tub came around her. She frowned down at her tan nipples and sat in the water. Davy looked over her head, at the tiles.

"I went through the closets. I got on my knees and looked under the beds. You have playful children. I went through every hallway in the building. Francis was crying. He was in tears, Regina. I did everything I could think of to get hold of you. I called this Charles, I called your shrink. And then at eleven o'clock, the super, the goddamned fucking *super* calls up and says that Ben is on the roof. So I ran up there, up the service stairs to the roof. There's a water tank in the middle. It's wood, Reggie, set way up on a steel scaffold I would say a hundred feet above the surface. Ben was on a ladder on the side of the tank. I could see his white shirt."

Regina soaped herself and rinsed off the soap with a hand attachment. She got a cigarette from a pack by the soap dish and lit it. She was listening.

"I called his name, I had to call it over and over before he came down. What was he doing up there, Regina? What is an eleven-year-old boy doing on the side of a water tank in the night?"

"Benjamin," said Regina, "is afraid of wolves."

"He won't be anymore. I took them both home on the spot."

"Not quite on the spot. Not quite. Not — tell me if I am wrong, Davy — not before taking a picture of Benjamin, not before you got him in his white shirt against the wood planks, and the wood planks against the black sky. Lord, I know you!"

"I had my camera. I was going to the game."

"Coincidence! Like those two new little beds!"

"Why don't you admit you have always despised my art?"

Regina was washing her hair now. She raised her chin and let her hair float away from her on the surface of the water. Then she sat up and began to squeeze it dry. "About your art, Davy. It's not true. I loved your pictures. I thought you were talented. But you know something that the rest of us don't, that we forget or repress, and it comes out in your work. How all things are futile, I mean. I used to rack my brains, Davy, trying to remember if you knew that when I first met you or if on the other hand you picked it up over the years. Did you always smile? Or did you learn that through a viewfinder?"

"I wish I had this on tape. You're going crazy, Reggie."

"Davy, I have seen the same thing on the faces of your friends, on the faces of all the professionals I know. I think that's why photographers used to put their heads under hoods. To hide the smile. And all the time they would be telling others, *smile, smile please, smile.*"

"They used those things for technical reasons, because with a focal-plane camera the light would expose the plate of the film!"

"No, I don't think so. I think they wore the hoods the way executioners wore shrouds. I don't despise what you do, Davy, but it frightens me. I am frightened this minute. Here I am standing in front of you, completely naked. I feel like a primitive woman. I have the same fear as a savage in the jungle, it's anguish, that you are going to snap my picture and steal my soul."

Regina stepped dripping from the tub and turned away from her husband. Her face, usually dark, had gone pale; her whole body was red from the bath. Then she took a towel, held it beneath her chin, and walked out. Before the mirror in the bedroom she dried and brushed her hair. She took the old sheets off the bed and put fresh linen on. She slipped a nightgown over her head. She set the clock. On the white sheet, watching the white curtain, she sank steadily toward sleep, not even half aware of the bright lights that still burst like suns.

III

In the morning, starting out to Washington, Regina made a bad mistake. She found a cab quickly on Broadway, and asked the driver to take her to LaGuardia. In less than twenty-five minutes, good time, she saw the tails of the jets high on her left, over the parkway, wavering in kerosene fumes. She would make the ten o'clock shuttle. It was only when she was inside the terminal, in line for the plane, that she realized they were bound to search her handbag, where the gun lay, under a wad of crumpled tissues. She looked ahead; a woman passed between two metal poles. The line moved forward. *Detectors at the airport gates:* she remembered her analyst's warning. But why did she forget? For a moment she stood rooted, mortified by the thought she might want to be captured, to be undone. The man behind her tapped her shoulder, and urged her to move; but Regina turned, tossing her head, and ran to the doorway. It slid smoothly open before her.

The ride back, which caught the end of the rush-hour traffic, took much longer. She thought of asking the driver to take her all

208

the way to the White House, but she knew he would refuse, might
laugh, even if she had the money. Instead, she got out at Penn
Station, and bought a ticket on the next Metroliner. "Round-trip
or single?" the man at the window demanded. Regina paused.
She was cautious. She remembered a kind of a riddle, in which a
man murders his wife on a Swiss skiing vacation. How was he
caught? the riddle ran. Because he bought one round-trip ticket
and one no-return. "Round-trip," Regina replied. She was determined that there be no more mental lapses. In an hour she got on
the silver car. She would be late, late for cocktails, for introduc-
tions; yet that suited her, since she did not want to meet anyone
she knew. She would not be too late. The train started with an
imperceptible motion, and then plunged under the ground, under
a river. They came up into watery sunlight, which glanced faintly
off factory towers and storage tanks and towns of bent metal.
Down in the dumps, thought Regina, and looked away for many
miles, until she saw, in a green field, a cow, a horse, and a second
cow, each one with its neck stretched to the ground.

The haze was thick, the wind at dead calm, in Washington.
Everything, the monuments, the people, had a brown tinge, like a
daguerreotype. Regina paid her cab at the front gate of the White
House. A guard stepped forward and took her invitation. He
went back to a little room, where she saw him speaking over a
phone. Then he beckoned her to him. She went through the gate,
past the black bars, half expecting alarm bells to ring. He showed
her her own picture, one that Davy had made years before. A
Mayan, serious, with braids. "Right, Miss. Just over to the limousine. They'll take you up. Have a *lovely* afternoon." The man
smiled, an even-toothed smile. He seemed to Regina, with that
smile and the crook of his finger, and the word *lovely* in *lovely
afternoon*, and come to think of it, the *right, Miss,* too, ineradi-
cably Irish, full of sly charm, and she worried at once whether
she would cost him his freedom, his job. A chauffeur opened the
door of a dark limousine. Regina got in, and as they started up
the curved drive she looked back, out of the absurd little loop of
a window, toward the gate, and the Irishman who kept it, but

could not see anything: so she swallowed, she renounced, any further remorse.

Instead of swinging around the side of the mansion, as Regina for some reason expected, the limousine stopped at the front door. A tall woman with light brown hair came down the steps and, as Regina got out of the car, seized her arm. It was Sylvia de Kruiff. Regina realized that they had met once, years before, she didn't know where. The woman herself did not seem to remember, only said how glad she was she had come, they were starting to worry, had it been a good trip, such sunny weather, and more, which Regina shut out. She noticed, though, that she wobbled on her high heels, and clutched her arm. Drunk, she assumed.

They went down a hall of the old house, through several rooms. The handbag, over Regina's left shoulder, was between them, pressing against both their arms. Regina wondered whether she was supposed to be sightseeing, and tried to listen, but the pressure of the weapon, which shifted, which pushed at her ribs, held her attention, and she hardly saw the woodwork, or the ceilings, the double bed with canopy, the pink-cheeked subjects of paintings, the Bible of President Taft. Her companion stumbled, and laughed at her own awkwardness; and it occurred to Regina, as she watched her grip the strap of her bag for support, that she wasn't drunk, wasn't clumsy at all, but was simply a decoy, a woman impervious to another woman's beauty or guile or charm.

Double doors opened, and they stepped outside. A deep green lawn, bounded by hedges, fell away before them toward a far-off depression, a natural bowl in the earth. Rows of folding chairs, orange-backed, had been placed there, facing away from the White House toward a raised platform stage. The stage, it looked like canvas stretched over planks, was set between two huge copper beeches, whose leaves and branches hung over the playing area like a proscenium, or theatrical wings. Men and women stood about in the aisles, holding drinks. Many were seated, with hats in their laps. A band was tuning. The air hung thick and unstirring.

Then a brilliant glow caught her eye, on a knoll above and to the right of the stage. A group of men were standing there, in front of a bank of flowers, operating floodlights. The roses on the rosebushes seemed to be burning. "We'll meet the President now," her hostess said, and took Regina down a slight slope of lawn and then up a ridge, where the lights were much brighter than day. From there, the President was no longer screened by the men and the cameras, and Regina saw him plain. He wore a blue suit and a blue and red tie. He was much tanner than his image in newsprint suggested, and his hair a little more white. He was talking to someone and stood clasping one wrist below his belt. Then he put his hands behind him. After a while he put his right hand forward and shook hands with somebody else. Regina was close now, at the end of a reception line. She saw the little metal flag he wore; he smiled and she saw the canines in his teeth. His hands kept doing the same thing, clasping protectively before him, disappearing behind. Sylvia de Kruiff let go of her arm, and went off to the side. There was no one behind her, and only a man and a young couple ahead. She saw the Secret Service agents scattered about, but their sunglasses made it hard for her to tell which way they were looking. There was a glare on her from the lamps. Still, she swung her handbag around in front and undid the snap. The man stepped forward. The President turned to meet him and she saw how, a little like Davy's, his hips flared, and how his shoulders were hunched. They talked for a moment, and then the couple went forward. There was a large red rose near the President's neck. Regina could smell it; all at once she smelled the hundreds of flowers and thought she must smother in the sweetness of the scent. What a curse, how like a woman, to faint!

"Oh, I know you. I want to talk to *you!*" It was the President. With one hand he waved the Head of the Humanities Foundation, who had started forward, away. Contemptuously. He was pointing at Regina with the other. A little king, she thought, and stepped resolutely into the hot light and the perfumed air. "I don't need an introduction," he said, smiling, and Regina smiled back. But she was thinking, from Shakespeare: "Now might I do it pat!" From *Lear?* she wondered, always *Lear?* With her right hand she groped under the open top of her bag. The President held out his hand to her, and without thinking, in a reflex, she held out her own. No. *Hamlet.* Procrastination. The President gripped her hand and did not let go.

She heard her own words coming back to her, accurately quoted, but she could not concentrate on what he was saying. The smell of the flowers acted like a drug; the bright lights heated her face. It was like being in an operating theater, hearing the voices of others (*the mind is a palace,* he said, *delighting the soul*) through a wall of fear, giddiness, ether. What was this? Flattery? She had thought of the man — it was a common assumption — as without a sexual life. He was the only President in twenty years who had not once shown up in her dreams. Why would he flatter her? Why did he grip, with a force she took to be longing, her hand? She looked at his eyes. The pupils were drawn down to pinpricks, so that you could not see through them to what — what soul, perhaps — lay behind. She thought of where the other Presidents, the ones she had dreamed of, came from. Texas. Boston. Abilene. But the eyes she saw came from nowhere, there was no place attached, only black dots responding to perpetual sunlight. California. He released her. The lamps shut down. He was saying what a rare pleasure it was to meet such an attractive and intelligent woman. She started to ask him, why rare? Were such women freaks? But down below the brass band was playing and he turned, still smiling — *a man can smile, and smile, and be a villain* — and did not hear what she had to say.

A white poodle in a blue hat with a blue feather in it walked on hind legs across the stage, and disappeared through the door of a miniature house. A few seconds later the same dog emerged, this time wearing a dress, also blue, and pushing an empty perambulator with its teeth and its paws. It went through a door in a second house on the other side of the stage. It reappeared. There was a patent leather purse around its neck, and in the perambulator, with a pink cap on its head and a milk bottle in its mouth, was another, much smaller, white dog. The audience laughed and clapped loudly. The dogs went into the first house, and when the applause continued the poodle came out, now wearing a pair of black leather shoes. It bowed. The purse dropped. It picked it up and bowed again, its brown eyes rolling. The President laughed loud enough for Regina, just two rows behind him, to hear.

A comedian stood with his hands in his pockets and made jokes about his wife. How stupid she was. How ugly. How bad in bed. He said he fell in love with her at first sight; but then he looked twice. She had her nose fixed, and her nose grew back. Actually, he said, it wasn't so bad, a mud pack helped a lot; except she kept taking it off. *Ha, Ha,* he laughed at himself. All through the audience women laughed, too. During the outburst Regina raised her handbag off her knees, so that it rested on the back of the seat before her. She took out her compact and held it against the open flap of the bag, as if she meant to powder her nose. But with her right hand she dug in the tissues and came to the gun. She got a grip on it and turned it around. The man in front of her was watching the show with his face cupped in his hands. That gave her a clear view of the side and back of the President's head.

The comedian was telling a story about three politicians, two Republicans and a Democrat, who were traveling together to meet with the people. They spend the night in a farmer's house, and the farmer has a blond, blue-eyed doll of a daughter. In the middle of the night the first Republican comes down the stairs and the floorboards creak and the farmer comes out with a gun. *Meow!* whines the Congressman. *Meow!* The farmer goes back to sleep and the Congressman enters his daughter's bedroom. Regina decided to aim directly through the side of the handbag. She knew it might be better to use the sights, but she did not see how, from four feet away, she could possibly miss. She pushed the safety off with her thumb. *Meow!* It was the second Republican, sprawled on the stairs. He spends an hour with the willing girl. Then it is the Democrat's turn. When the floorboards creak, the farmer comes out, demanding to know who is there. *The cat!*

the Democrat cries, and the farmer blows off his head with the gun. So. Now. But the man leaned back in his chair, applauding the grinning comedian with both his hands.

The cast of a musical show came onto the stage and sang a group of songs. Then the chorus started to dance. All the girls looked exactly alike, with loose caps over their hair. Their breasts were pushed up in sequined bodices and their buttocks showed when they turned around. Everything they did, they did as one person, all in a line. The President looked up at them, squinting. His mouth hung partway open. The girls kicked high, showing the ruffles and dark panties between their legs. There was a large smile in red paint on each of their faces. Regina drew her breath and fired the gun. Nothing happened. The band played very loudly. She pulled the trigger again. There was a hardly audible click. She shot at the President a third time, but the gun did not fire. Regina stood up and cried, loud enough for the President to hear, that the world would remember his crimes. The girls danced and dipped, in step, in time. Someone touched Regina's arm. She clutched the handbag and edged out to the aisle. Two men came after her. "I'm not feeling well," she told them. They stood, looking at each other, and let her go.

The sun went down on Regina's right, and the train swept north in darkness. She looked at her own reflection in the window glass. Once she thought of Charles: what a smart man, to give her an unloaded gun. One more trick. Another gag. *The sky is falling! The sky is falling!* What a comical chicken. So frantic. So mistaken in all of its fears. She had been, then, as Doctor Geneva insisted, performing or dreaming or acting a role in a play? The idea of that oppressed her. And so did this: that she had, for such an occasion, washed her hair. She put her seat back to doze. Unless, she wondered, there was to be something else.

When the conductor announced Trenton she stood up; and when they drew into the station she got off the train. She took a cab to the bus terminal, and a bus to Atlantic City. She walked the length of the boardwalk there, with the black, foaming sea on

her right side. Then she turned up a side street, up the three short
blocks to the building her father had owned for the last twenty-
five years. It was unlit, except for an occasional light falling over
a sill from within. A sheet hung by a corner from an upper
window. Regina went in, hearing a baby cry, and people shouting
upstairs. She turned the corners of the staircase until she came to
an open door. There were many women, and a few men, inside a
green apartment. The baby she had heard was in a crib by the
wall. Her own father was in the middle of the room, stooping
somewhat, holding a cigar. He was saying, "But missus. But
missus "

"But nothin'! We ain't got no hot water by tomorrow morning
I am going myself to the police!"

"The water is hot. The steam is not hot."

"You can say that again. I got to wake up and put my foot on
a cold floor. I ain't going to stand this kind of treatment from
nobody. You been gettin' away with this shabbiness for years!"

"The boiler is being repaired. Deliberately I waited until the
summer."

"That boiler is *always* being repaired. This is a Jew-boiler, you
askin' me. You ought to be ashamed what you don't do for
nickels and dimes."

"This is already June, missus. Outside it's hot. Look, the
window is open. Hot water you have, but you do not need now
more heat."

"I just hope you ain't trying to tell me when I want heat. I
hope you ain't trying that. The doctor said I'm cold-blooded, I
got to have the radiator any time that I want."

The other women crowded around him.

"What about last January? That boiler was busted!"

"That was the worst time I ever had! I could see my breath in
front of my mouth!"

"You remember I had that water in a water glass and in the
morning it was froze solid."

"But missus, this is why we must have now repairs. Otherwise,
the next January it will break down again. This is why I wait

until we have June. The men must work on the machine when it is shut down."

"I am tired of this argument, you understand! In the morning I am going to the police. And I ain't payin' one penny of rent until there is steam heat in this house!"

The woman put her finger to the chest of Regina's father. None of the tenants came up even to his shoulder. He stooped to be polite. The wisps of white hair on his head were uncombed and fell over his ears and his collar. There were deep, long lines on either side of his mouth. He had a mournful face, like Buster Keaton. He was speaking softly, reasonably, and nodding, trying to smoke his cigar. At the sight, some fierce tightness, like knots, which Regina had not been aware of, began to give way in the pit of her stomach. She thought of him as he once had been, blowing animals for her out of glass. She was not sure now whether this was a true memory, or something he had said he had done. It did not matter. For a while she stood, out of the light, listening; then she turned around and went down the stairs and out another door.